# Christmas Moon

# Christmas Moon

## Elizabeth Lane

OPEN ROAD
INTEGRATED MEDIA
NEW YORK

This edition published in 2014 by Open Road Integrated Media, Inc.
345 Hudson Street
New York, NY 10014
www.openroadmedia.com

# PROLOGUE

*- THE CHEYENNE DAILY LEADER -*

February 21, 1872

## FAMED LAWMAN MURDERED
## IN WYOMING SALOON

On the night of February 17 of this year, J.D. McNulty, once counted among Wyoming's greatest lawmen, was shot dead by a gambler in a quarrel over a card game.

The incident occurred at Glory Gulch, a played-out gold mining camp located in the Wind River Mountains above South Pass City. According to witnesses, McNulty was seated at a table in the Laughing Lady Saloon, playing poker with a gambler named Virgil Pomeroy, a traveling photographer named Asa Smith and two local miners. An hour into the game McNulty, who was unarmed at the time, accused Pomeroy of using a holdout. After an angry exchange of words, the gambler drew a derringer from his vest and fired two shots. The first bullet wounded McNulty in the shoulder. The second toppled him backward onto the floor where he expired in the arms of an unidentified saloon girl. He was 44 years old at the time of his death.

Pomeroy fled on a stolen horse after the shooting. His present whereabouts is unknown.

J.D. McNulty was appointed deputy sheriff of

Fremont County in 1868. Subsequently, he served as Marshal in Cheyenne and later in Laramie, where he single-handedly dispatched the murderous Cleary gang in Wyoming's most famous gunfight.

His body was taken by wagon to South Pass City for burial, there being no level ground for a cemetery in Glory Gulch.

Mr. Asa Smith, a witness to the shooting, photographed McNulty's body laid out in its coffin. For those wishing to pay their respects, the picture will be on display for the next 30 days in the front window of this newspaper office.

Cletis Morgan, Reporter

# CHAPTER ONE

E mma Carlyle was on the trail of a man.
  A man who'd been dead for more than a hundred years.

Here, in the old mining town where he was buried, lay her last hope of learning his secrets.

Emma's '95 Subaru wagon fishtailed as she swung into the icy parking lot and pulled up next to a gritty eight-foot mountain of plowed snow. Outside, the winter hills glittered in blinding sunlight. The sky was a clear cerulean blue. For a December day it was downright breathtaking. But Emma had lived in Wyoming long enough to know that when she opened the door, the air would be cold enough to sear her skin and freeze the moisture in her lungs.

Grunting with effort, she twisted toward the door and struggled to zip her goose down parka over her bulging belly. Beyond the barrier of snow piles she could see the half-buried entry booth and the large, painted red and white sign that welcomed summer visitors to South Pass City. December 24 was not the best time for a visit to a ghost town turned tourist attraction. But Emma had come on an errand of desperation.

She was trailing a man—a compelling, elusive and troubled man who'd captured her imagination and more than a little of her heart.

Jethro Darlington McNulty had stood six-three barefoot and towered another two inches in his boots. His eyes, set in a hauntingly chiseled face, had been as blue as an October sky. When he was out for a good time, those eyes could flash enough sexual magnetism to make women tumble into his bed. Lit by anger, their cold fury would have sent the likes of Eastwood and McQueen scurrying to Wardrobe for a change of underwear.

Legend and loner, J.D. had been an enigma to all who knew him—which made him an absolutely maddening subject for Emma's master's thesis. The man's penchant for secrecy would have driven a saint over the edge. And Emma was no saint. In conservative Lander, where she'd taught high school history for the past ten years, her burgeoning belly and lack of a wedding ring said it all.

The thesis had given her a good excuse to request a year off. By now, however, the whole town knew why she wasn't at school. As the locals put it, the very proper Miss Carlyle had gotten herself knocked up.

The baby, a girl, was kicking like a healthy little ninja. No cause for worry there, thank heaven. But the thesis was driving Emma toward an emotional meltdown.

She had promised her advisor at the University of Wyoming that she'd have the first draft mailed before her January 3 due date. But she'd made that promise five months ago, before she'd understood the juju that a solo pregnancy could work on a woman's mind and body. This morning, as she'd stood by the fridge in her flannel nightgown, wolfing down Pepperidge Farm Chocolate Chunk cookies and staring at the Vesuvius of paperwork that littered her kitchen table, Emma had broken down and bawled. It was no use. Her research on the legendary gunfighter had more holes in it than J.D.'s Peacemaker had blasted through the infamous Cleary Gang. She needed help, or maybe a confounded miracle.

An Internet search had brought up the name of an expert in local history, a woman who ran a little bookstore in South Pass City. After a quick phone call, Emma had struggled into clean black maternity slacks and a baggy red sweater, dabbed on a smidgen of lipstick and too much mascara, and slicked back her dark blond hair. That done, she'd stuffed her notes and manuscript into her canvas briefcase and shoveled a path to her car. South Pass City was less than an hour away on State Highway 28. The weather was decent, the road was clear, and just in case anything went wrong, she had her cell phone in her purse, fully charged.

Given a choice, Emma would have taken the graveled Loop Road through the mountains, to the place where an overgrown wagon trail wound up a side canyon toward Glory Gulch. She'd hiked that trail last fall, on a sunny day when crimson maple and bright gold aspen blazed across the slopes. Nothing had remained of the mining camp but a few tumbledown shacks and rock chimneys rising out of the bracken. A pimply-faced young ranger had shown her the ruined cabin where J.D. had spent his last winter, and the saloon where he'd died. A chill had passed through her fingers as she'd touched the faded brownish bloodstain on the floor.

Emma had tried to picture Glory Gulch in the dead of winter. But there'd be no going back to see it now. The mountain road was closed and wouldn't be passable again till spring.

So here she was, after a pleasant drive on a highway that wound upward between glistening walls of snow. She could only hope that her visit to Tilly's Book Nook would turn out to be worth the trip.

South Pass City was a restored historic site, a relic of the late 1860s gold rush. In winter the exhibits shut down, but a few hardy people lived there year round. Tilly Farson was one of them. She'd mentioned over the phone that since her shop was also her home, Emma would be welcome to drop by anytime.

Now Emma picked her way between the huge mounds of plowed snow, taking shallow breaths and shifting her weight to anchor the soles of her fleece-lined boots. Snowmobiles had packed a trail along the street, saving her from having to flounder through hip-high drifts; but a frigid wind had sprung up, blasting sheets of snow across her path. For someone who couldn't see her own feet, it was treacherous going. By the time she spotted the quaintly lettered sign on the bookstore, her face was a frozen mask.

Tilly's Book Nook was housed in a vintage barbershop with a squared false front. The windows had been shuttered against the cold but the front door swung open at Emma's knock.

The woman on the threshold was built like the Willendorf Venus—short and stocky, dressed in plum velveteen stretch pants and shearling boots. The buttons of a hand knit snowflake cardigan strained over her outsized bosom. Her silvery hair was cut in a plain Dutch bob with rimless bifocals jutting from beneath her bangs.

"Oh, you poor dear!" she crooned, sweeping Emma inside. "You must be half frozen! Here, don't worry about your wet boots. Just take off your coat and have a chair by the stove!"

The bookstore was a haven of cozy warmth. Floor to ceiling

shelves lined the walls, crammed with books on western history and used paperback novels. Tendrils of asparagus fern trailed from a hanging pot in one corner. Two tartan-covered wing chairs with a rosewood tea table between them were drawn up before a glowing potbellied stove.

Emma hadn't planned to unburden herself, but over homemade oatmeal cookies and steaming mugs of hot cocoa, the whole soap opera came pouring out—the man she'd thought of as her lifetime love until she'd answered that phone call from his wife; her surprise pregnancy and, finally, her wrenching decision to give the baby up for adoption.

"It won't be easy, but I know it's for the best." Emma laid a hand on her belly and felt the subtle stirring beneath her palm. "My own mother was unmarried. We lived in a trailer park, and she was so steeped in pills and alcohol that I practically raised myself. I..." Emma paused to swallow the tight lump in her throat. "I'm afraid I don't have the genes to be a good mother."

Tilly listened, punctuating Emma's words with sympathetic little clucks. "Does the father know?" she asked gently.

Emma nodded. "He offered to pay for an abortion. I told him to go to hell."

"Good for you! Men can be such jackasses!" Tilly sighed as she refilled Emma's mug from a blue enameled pot. "What a shame we women can't seem to get along without them. It would make life so much simpler, wouldn't it?"

Emma forced her mind back to her quest. "Right now the only man in my life is J.D. McNulty, and he's driving me crazy."

Tilly chuckled. "J.D. was known to have that effect on women. And you can see why. Just look at him!"

She inclined her head toward a framed poster that hung on the wall behind the antique brass cash register. Emma had seen the photograph before. Taken in Cheyenne, where J.D had been marshal for eighteen months, it showed a rangy man in his late thirties, dressed for work in a dark woolen shirt and knotted tie. His left hand rested lightly on the ivory grip of his Colt .45 Peacemaker, which hung in its holster from a heavy cartridge belt. The silver star of his office blazed on his cowhide vest. With his long square jaw, sharply chiseled face and melancholy eyes, he looked like a young Henry Fonda. Throw in one devilishly quirked eyebrow and a body that would do credit to Tarzan, and you were looking at Hollywood material.

"How could you not fall in love with *that*?" Tilly teased. "Confess now, haven't you at least developed a little crush on the man?"

"Does it show that much?" Emma's cheeks blazed as she recalled the erotic dreams she'd been having the past few nights. Good grief, she was pathetic! A woman in her ninth month, as big as a cow, with a raging case of the hots for a man who'd been dead since 1872!

"I thought so." Tilly flashed her a wink. "Now, how can I help you, dear?"

Emma reached for her briefcase. "For starters, since we're talking about men and their attributes, was J.D. ever known to be a jackass?"

Tilly's eyebrows crinkled above lenses the diameter and thickness of silver dollars. They reflected the light in the room, masking her eyes.

"Oh, J.D. had his moments. He was a man, after all, with a full set of male complications. But he was honest in his dealings and, as far as I know, he never raised his hand against a woman. That's more than you can say for some of our so-called western heroes. Take Wyatt Earp—now there was a real jackass for you, the way he treated his first wife. And Bill Hickock wasn't much better, especially in his later years."

"You almost sound as if you knew them."

"Look around you, dearie." Tilly's gesture encompassed the overflowing bookshelves. "What do you think I do here all winter, with nothing but a cranky old tomcat for company? I read. Histories, journals, letters, you name it. Some of those old boys are as real to me as you are—J.D. in particular, because he spent so much time in these parts. Why, it's likely he got his hair and whiskers barbered in this very room." She set her cup down and leaned closer. "Sometimes I imagine that when the barber was sweeping up, little bits of J.D.'s hair fell between the floorboards. They could still be there, right under our feet."

In the warm stillness, Emma could feel her baby kicking. She willed herself to unzip her briefcase and ease out the sheaf of papers she'd stuffed into a manila folder. A single page slipped loose and fluttered onto the braided rug. Tilly bent down, picked it up and handed it back to her.

It was a copy of the most widely published photograph ever taken of J.D. McNulty. He was laid out in his open casket, dressed in a suit and tie, his eyes closed, his long, elegant hands folded across his chest. He looked older here than in the picture on Tilly's wall. His dark hair was longer and lightly silvered at the temples. His weathered face sported a well-trimmed moustache. Even as a corpse, J.D. was beautiful. But Emma had never liked looking at the grisly portrait.

"I know that picture well." Tilly leaned back into her chair, gazing into the ruby glow behind the stove's mica panes. "J.D.'s grave isn't far from here. But nothing really dies, you know. The chemical elements, the energy particles that hold us together, they just get rearranged. Wood becomes heat and smoke and ash, and then maybe soil for a new tree. As for people..." Her voice trailed off for a moment. "Every place we go, every life we touch, we leave a little piece of ourselves behind. We're all connected, in the present, in the past, for all time. If that isn't immortality, I don't know what is."

The silence in the room was warm and deep. Emma felt herself growing drowsy. Blinking herself awake, she held out the sheaf of papers to Tilly.

"Here's what I've done so far. I've tagged my questions with these pink sticky notes. Maybe you can help me fill in some blanks."

Tilly was more than willing to lend her expertise. Most of Emma's questions were swiftly answered. But there were some puzzles that even Tilly couldn't resolve. One of them concerned the saloon girl who'd clasped the dying J.D. in her arms.

Emma dug into her briefcase and pulled out a file crammed with photocopied research. "I have the newspaper accounts here, and this later story, based on an interview with Asa Smith, the photographer who was there. He adds a few more details—like the piano playing "Beautiful Dreamer" in the background, right up until the first shot. But even he doesn't mention the name of the girl.

"I'm guessing no one knew her real identity. A lot of those girls would change their names to keep from shaming their families. The person who reported the shooting probably didn't think her name mattered."

"But she could have been important," Emma protested. "What if she was in love with J.D.? What if he was in love with her?"

Tilly's lips tightened in an enigmatic smile. "We'll never know, will we, dear? It's one of those mysteries that make the past so intriguing."

Emma shuffled through her pages. "Well, here's an even bigger mystery for you. Why did J.D. drop out of sight after that big gunfight in Laramie? What happened to him? How did he end up in a rundown mining camp like Glory Gulch?"

Tilly's fingers toyed with a loose pewter button on her sweater. "Only J.D. could've answered those questions, and he was the sort who played his cards close to his vest, as they say. But I can tell you one thing. J.D. McNulty was a man who carried a load of pain in his gut. It ate at him something awful. Made him do things that weren't in his best interest. Self-destruction—that would be the fancy term they use for it these days. In the end, I suspect that was what really killed him."

Emma waited, eager to hear more, but Tilly had fallen silent again. The only sound in the little shop was the slow crackle of burning sapwood in the stove.

From the next room, an unseen clock chimed four. Tilly rose from her chair, wincing as her legs straightened. "I've kept you too long, dear," she said. "This twinge in my left knee tells me there's a storm moving in. You'd best be heading back to Lander before the roads get bad."

Reluctantly, Emma stuffed the papers back into her briefcase. She had a world of questions for this woman who talked about J.D. as if he'd been a close friend. "I wish we had more time," she said. "But you've already been so much help. I can't thank you enough."

"It was my pleasure. Come back anytime." Tilly had begun clearing the tea table. "I'll bag some of these cookies for you to take along. You can nibble them while you work on your thesis."

Emma shrugged into her parka, picked up her purse and gratefully accepted the bagged cookies. "Will you be all right out there?" Tilly asked. "I'd be happy to walk you back to your car."

"Thanks, but I'll be fine." Emma moved toward the door but Tilly stopped her with a touch on her arm.

"Are you sure, dear? About giving up your baby, I mean. Forgive an old woman's meddling, but I sense such a deep sadness in you, such reluctance..."

Emma shook her head. "It's all arranged. The papers have been signed and the parents are waiting to take her home from the hospital. This little girl deserves a better life than I could ever give her."

Her vision blurred as she opened the door and stepped outside into the brittle sunlight. In the west, a bank of mud gray clouds drifted along the horizon. There was no other sign of the storm Tilly had predicted, but the air was so cold that every breath formed a frosty puff of vapor in front of Emma's face.

Minutes later she was in her car, teeth chattering as she waited for the heater to kick in. The frigid steering wheel stung her palms as she pulled out of the parking lot and headed back toward the paved highway.

She had every reason to feel elated, Emma told herself. Tilly had given her enough information to finish the thesis, maybe even on schedule if the baby wasn't in a hurry to get here.

But it was Christmas Eve and she'd be going home to an empty house. The thesis had drained so much of her energy that she hadn't even vacuumed, let alone put up a tree or hung a string of lights. All she wanted for Christmas this year was to get the miserable holiday behind her.

The baby was kicking hard. Emma stifled a yelp as the tiny feet delivered a volley of rapid-fire jabs to her bladder. The sensations that shot through her body would have made a nun swear.

She sighed as the kicks subsided. "None of this is your fault, kiddo," she murmured. "You can't help it if your mother was a silly old maid who thought she'd found love and your father was a jerk in disguise. But never mind that. You're going to have a life—a wonderful life with a mom and dad who'll read you bedtime stories and go to your soccer games and love you as much as if you'd been born to them. Maybe more."

*Maybe almost as much as I do.*

Lord, she was getting maudlin now. Desperate for a diversion,

Emma punched the radio button. A twangy country-western version of "Santa Claus is Coming to Town" blared out of the speakers. Turning up the volume, she began to sing along.

By the time she'd made it through "Silver Bells" and "Grandma Got Run Over by A Reindeer," Emma was actually feeling a glimmer of Christmas spirit. But the disk jockey at the radio station couldn't leave well enough alone. The next selection was Elvis Presley's "I'll Be Home For Christmas," a song that had always made her weepy.

This time The King's velvety tenor triggered a freshet of tears. They spilled out of her eyes, trailing black mascara down her cheeks. For Emma, home was no place at all. Her mother had long since died of drink and despair, and she had no other family. Soon her baby daughter would be gone, too. There'd be no little stocking by the fireplace in years to come, no cookies for Santa, no dolls under the tree.

Emma's fingers tightened on the steering wheel. "Oh, damn..." she muttered, biting back sobs. "Oh, damn, damn, damn!"

It was then, by chance, that she remembered her briefcase. She had left it at Tilly's, next to the chair.

Muttering, she swung the Subaru around and headed back toward South Pass City. The text of her thesis was on her computer, but her edits, her notes and her photocopied research were all in that briefcase. She couldn't afford to leave it behind.

The sun had vanished behind a pall of dishwater clouds, darkening the late afternoon sky. The music on the radio had degenerated into static. She caught the words, "severe storm warning." Then the station went dead.

Ahead of her now, black clouds were closing in. A drop of sleet splattered the windshield. The fast-moving storm was stampeding over the mountains and across the high desert plateau. Minutes from now it would swallow her in snow and wind. It was too late to turn around and make a run for Lander. Her best hope of shelter lay with Tilly.

She was watching for the turnoff to South Pass City when the full force of the storm struck head on. Going too fast, she hit the snow-slicked pavement and spun crazily. An eternity flashed past before the Subaru crunched to a stop on the shoulder of the road.

Dizzy but unhurt, Emma slumped over the wheel. Huge flakes of snow swarmed around her, piling up on the windows of the car.

Pulling herself together she punched the defroster buttons and switched the wagon to four-wheel drive. She'd be fine, she told herself, as long as she kept her head.

Turning on the lights and wipers, she pulled back onto the road. By now she was driving in total whiteout. She could only pray that she'd recognize the turnoff to South Pass City when she reached it.

Moments later she sensed the rising of the shoulder that marked a side road. Emma swung the wheel and felt the welcome crunch of gravel beneath the tires. She laughed with relief. Before long she'd be back at Tilly's, warm and safe.

Half an hour later she was still driving. Even more unsettling was the fact that the road seemed to wind upward through the blinding snow. Could she have lost her bearings and taken the wrong turnoff?

She was searching for a wide place to turn around when she felt a crumbling sensation beneath one wheel. The car lurched sideways, flinging her hard to the right before it came to rest at a slant, its weight on the front axle.

Sick with dread, Emma jammed on the emergency brake and clambered out the driver's side door. The Subaru's right front wheel hung over the edge of the road with nothing visible beyond it except swirling snow.

Now what? Emma willed herself to stay calm. If the wheel was in some sort of ditch, she might be able to jack it up and back onto the road again. But first she needed a closer look.

Blinded by flying flakes, she groped her way around to the passenger side. Her legs went watery as she saw the tire. It hung over empty space where the edge dropped off. There was no way she was going to get the vehicle back onto the road. In fact, it might not even be safe to get back inside the car.

Creeping closer, she strained to see the slope below. If it wasn't too steep, she might be all right. Otherwise—

Emma screamed as the snowy edge gave way under her boots. Down, down she plummeted through powdery white drifts. Then something struck her head and the world exploded in blackness.

* * *

When she opened her eyes the sky was dark. She was lying on her back, cradled by snow and cushioned by her down parka. Tiny crystals of ice drifted onto her face. Dazed and chilled, she began moving her fingers, then her arms and legs. Slowly the memory returned—the storm, the car, the fall...

*The baby!*

Emma sat bolt upright. Her lips moved in silent prayer as she clasped her belly. An eternity seemed to pass before she felt a tentative push, then a spunky little kick. Dizzy with relief, she staggered to her feet. She was sore and stiff, but aside from a tender lump on the back of her head, she didn't seem to be hurt.

A full moon shone through the clouds, flooding the landscape with light. Looking up, Emma could see the slope where she'd fallen. It was steep, but not so steep that she couldn't get back to the road. Jamming her boots into the snow, she began to climb.

"Don't worry, little one, we'll be fine," she murmured. "We'll just get into the car and call 911. Then we can keep warm and munch cookies while we wait for the Search and Rescue hunks to show up. How does that sound for a way to spend Christmas Eve? Just you and—"

Emma's words died in her throat as her eyes came level with the road. There was no sign of the car—not even tire tracks to show where it had been.

Shaking, she sank onto a snow-covered rock. She'd left the car keys in the ignition and her purse, with her cell phone inside, on the seat. Clearly, the temptation had been too much for some passer-by. Now she was in real trouble.

Her eyes scanned the moonlit terrain. From where she sat, the road seemed to disappear into a wooded canyon. Wherever it led, she had little choice except to follow it. It might be her only hope of finding shelter.

By the time she reached the mouth of the canyon it was snowing again. The wind had risen to a howl, blasting snowflakes into her face. Head down, Emma trudged through the stinging blizzard. Once, then again, she stumbled to her knees. Reeling with effort, she pushed on. She knew the danger. If she stopped to rest, she and her baby could freeze.

She had just fallen a third time when she saw the light. It was little more than a glimmer through the bare aspens, but even when Emma rubbed her eyes the light remained. She staggered toward it.

As the trees thinned out she saw a log cabin with a tall stone chimney. Soft amber lamplight glowed faintly through a tiny glass-paned window. Something about the place—the ramshackle slope of the roof, the off-kilter set of the door, looked familiar. Emma had the vague feeling she'd seen it before, but she was too exhausted to remember where or when.

On the wide, covered porch, she hesitated, working her hands out of her pockets. Just because she'd found the cabin, that didn't mean she was safe. Anybody could be on the other side of that door—maybe the very people who'd stolen her car. She could be taking a dangerous chance, but she'd run out of options. It was knock or freeze.

Her knuckles rapped feebly against the rough-sawn planking. There was no response from inside the cabin. Maybe no one had heard her, or maybe they didn't want to answer.

Her eyes fell on a pile of kindling next to the door. Choosing a long, stout stick she banged it on the door with all her strength. From inside the cabin she heard a crash and the sound of a male voice cursing. Heavy footsteps lumbered across the wooden floor. A bolt slid back and the door burst open, flooding the porch with lamplight.

Emma found herself staring up the barrel of a nasty-looking Colt revolver. But it wasn't the gun that made her gasp. It was the man holding it.

Dressed in nothing but faded red long johns and riding boots, he was tall and rawboned. An evil-looking black cheroot was jammed into one corner of his scowling mouth. The bloodshot eyes that glared down at Emma from beneath a mop of dark, silvered hair were as blue as an October sky.

"Who in holy hellfire are you, lady, and what in do you want?" he growled.

Heaven save her, he looked exactly like J.D. McNulty.

# CHAPTER TWO

The woman on J.D.'s porch looked as if she'd just staggered out of a nightmare. She was wild-eyed and tarnally spooked, gripping a stick of kindling as if she wanted to bash in his face. The fact that she was dressed like some kind of Chinaman, in sagging black trousers and an enormous, puffy green silk coat, only added to his befuddlement. What lunatic asylum had this female escaped from?

"Easy, now, lady." J.D. kept the Colt leveled at her collar bone, but mostly for show. "Put that stick down, and I'll take my itchy finger off this trigger."

Slowly and shakily she lowered her arm. He could see now that she was half-dead from cold and exhaustion. Her lips were the color of laundry bluing and her hair was plastered around her face in frozen strings. She was swaying on her feet like a drunkard.

J.D. cursed under his breath. He'd been looking forward to a peaceful night with his books, the old tomcat and a bottle of the finest rotgut whiskey in Glory Gulch. Maybe if he drank enough of the stuff, he might even forget it was Christmas Eve.

Now his plans were blown to hell. He wouldn't have minded female company of the soft and willing variety. But this woman didn't strike him as the sporting kind, and it appeared he was stuck with her. The devil himself wouldn't close the door and leave her outside to freeze.

Muttering words unfit for a lady's ears, he eased off the hammer and laid the Colt on the bookshelf. "Well don't just stand there. Come on inside. And don't expect any apologies for my state of undress. I wasn't expecting company."

The kindling stick clattered to the porch as she dragged herself across the threshold. She was tall for a woman, with a body that appeared too stout for her heart-shaped face. But maybe that was because of the coat. Her eyes, when she looked up at him, were the warm, translucent brown of sarsaparilla on a sunny day. They were staring at him as if she'd just seen Abraham Lincoln's ghost.

Her chilled lips worked in an effort to speak. "Where...am I?"

J.D. bolted the door behind her. "Glory Gulch, Wyoming. The upper edge of it, at least. Main part of town's further down the canyon."

"Glory Gulch?" Her eyes widened. "People are living here?"

"A few score, maybe, most of us down on our luck. Not like the old days before the gold played out." J.D. bit down hard on his cheroot as a new thought struck him. "Any other folks out there with you? Any of your family lost in the storm?" He didn't relish searching in a blizzard but if there were other travelers with the woman, he'd rather find them alive tonight than dead tomorrow.

Distrust flickered across her face, and he realized she'd misread him. "Oh, there'll be plenty of people looking for me by morning—police on snowmobiles, maybe even a helicopter or two. As long as they find me safe, there'll be no trouble for you."

J.D. shook his head. The woman was touched for sure. "You're talking gibberish, lady. Sit down and have a whiskey. Maybe it'll bring you around."

He turned toward the hearth, where he'd set the jug next to the cat's favorite warming spot. She stopped him with a touch on his arm. Her fingers were like icicles through his sleeve.

"Tell me one thing." She was staring up at him, her wild, scared doe's eyes searching his face. "Who are you? What's your name?"

"McNulty, for whatever it's worth to you. J.D. McNulty."

Her eyes widened for an instant. Then the pupils rolled back in her head and she swayed to one side. J.D. lunged, catching her as she went down in a dead faint.

She was heftier than he'd expected, and her belly, where it pressed his arm, felt as round and solid as a brood mare's. Only then did it dawn on J.D. that under her puffy coat, the lady had company. She was in a family way, and damned near ready to deliver.

A cold knot clenched in J.D.'s gut, jerking tight. Lord almighty, not that. Anything but that.

Lifting her by the shoulders, J.D. dragged her to his bed, which was partly screened from the rest of the cabin by one of his bookcases. As gently as he could, he laid her out on top of the quilt. The last thing he wanted was to handle her rough and start her labor.

As he eased her onto the pillow, his fingers brushed the lump on the back of her head. A nasty blow could account for her odd behavior. He'd keep an eye on her, make sure she didn't sleep too much. With luck she'd come around soon and start talking sense. Otherwise, what in Sam Hill was he going to do with a crazy woman in his cabin?

For a moment he stood gazing down at her. Even in her present condition, he could see that she wasn't bad looking. Her shoulder-length hair blended the streaky hues of molasses taffy. Her golden brown eyelashes lay wet and lush against her pallid cheeks. Her blue-tinged lips were full and sweetly shaped. A kiss or two might warm them up nicely, J.D. mused. But he wasn't about to risk getting his face slapped.

Despite her ungodly getup, she had the look of a lady about her. It crossed J.D.'s mind that he should put on some britches. But he'd washed both pairs that morning and they were still damp, and he'd be damned if he'd drag his black suit out of mothballs for modesty's sake. Anyhow, being great with child, she'd likely seen worse than a man in his underwear. He'd worry about that later. The important thing now was getting her warm.

Moving to the foot of the bed, he eased off her loose leather boots and damp woolen stockings. Her feet were on the verge of frostbite. He began a careful massage, working his fingers along the arches and cupping the toes in his work-roughened palms. There were flecks of red paint on her toenails. Another puzzle. Who the hell was this woman and where had she come from?

The tomcat jumped down from its perch on the mantel and padded over to investigate. Battle-scarred, bobtailed and one-eyed, it had wandered in from nowhere before the first winter blizzard. J.D. had let it stay, figuring it would move on when the time came. Like him, it wasn't a creature to be owned.

Jumping onto the bed, it thrust its scruffy yellow head against J.D.'s hand, demanding attention. J.D. scratched its ears briefly, then went back to working the woman's icy feet. By now the color was returning to her toes. Maybe it was time he saw to the rest of her.

The odd green coat was beaded with melting snow. On closer inspection, it appeared to be stuffed with feathers, like a quilt. It struck him as a dandy way to keep warm, especially since the outer fabric seemed to repel moisture like the feathers on a duck. But the device that fastened down the front was like nothing he'd ever seen before. The cat watched intently as J.D. struggled with the long track of tiny metal hooks. They were interlocked so tightly that two locomotives couldn't have torn them apart. Swearing under his breath, he reached for his pocketknife and thumbed open the blade.

"What are you doing?" Her eyes had shot open and were staring up at him in stark terror. Sensing her fear, the cat thumped to the floor and vanished under the bed.

"Nothing for you to get in a stew about," J.D. said. "Just trying to open up this damn fool coat so I can get it off you."

"Oh, good grief!" She pushed herself to a sitting position. Her fingers found a metal tag at the collar and jerked it downward. The infernal row of hooks parted like the Red Sea. "What's the matter with you?" she snapped. "Haven't you ever seen a zipper before?"

J.D. closed the pocket knife and folded his arms across his chest. "You've no call to get uppity with me, lady," he said in his steely marshal's voice. "It appears you're plumb loaded with things I haven't seen before. And since this is my cabin and you're here as an uninvited guest, I'd say you've got some fast explaining to do."

From where Emma sat on the low bed, the man looked about eight feet tall. His eyes burned through her like angry blue lasers. The fact that he was wearing long red underwear, worn to holes in spots where she didn't even dare look, made him no less intimidating.

He'd said his name was J.D. McNulty, and for all his disarray, he looked uncannily like the portrait of J.D. in his coffin—the chiseled, careworn features, the collar-length mane of silvered black hair and the Tom Selleck moustache J.D. had grown toward the end of his life.

But something was out of kilter. J.D. had been dead since 1872, and this was 2010. Either she was hallucinating or the man was

CHRISTMAS MOON                    19

some kind of nut case, like the brother in "Arsenic and Old Lace" who thought he was Teddy Roosevelt.

Since he'd already flashed a gun and a knife at her, she'd be smart to find another stick of firewood and keep it handy before he flashed something even scarier.

Her gaze darted around the cabin's cluttered interior, taking in the soot-stained rock fireplace with its raised hearth, the threadbare denims drying over the back of a handmade wooden rocker, the rough cut bookshelves stocked with dilapidated volumes of Shakespeare, Mark Twain, Charles Dickens, Edgar Allen Poe and James Fennimore Cooper. Everything she saw looked straight off Antiques Roadshow, from the rawhide-webbed snowshoes propped against the doorframe to the blackened iron pot that sat on a metal grate above the smoldering coals. The place bore no resemblance to a hangout for bums or druggies. It looked more like...a real old-time home.

The stranger had said she was in Glory Gulch, which sounded right in terms of the road and the steep terrain. But she'd hiked in to Glory Gulch just a few months ago. There'd only been a half dozen cabins standing, none of them fit to live in.

She stared at the fireplace, haunted by the impression that she'd seen it before. Even the jumble of mortared rocks, which looked as if they'd been gathered helter- skelter from the mountainside, pricked her memory, especially that hunk of ivory quartz that glittered with tiny flecks of what might be gold...

A clammy sweat bead trickled down Emma's spine as the realization sank home. This was the fireplace she'd seen in the ruins of J.D.'s cabin—or an exact duplicate, down to the very stones.

Maybe the cabin was part of some historical restoration project, like South Pass City had been; or a movie set, complete with a J.D. look-alike actor who believed in staying in character twenty-four-seven. Unless she was hallucinating, there was no other logical explanation.

These thoughts had fast-forwarded through Emma's mind, overshadowed by the stormy presence looming above her like some mythical thunder god—a god clad in nothing but trail worn boots and moth-eaten red woolies. What those woolies barely concealed was a hard, sinewy body with broad shoulders, a flatiron belly and an intriguing bulge where she knew better than to rest her eyes. Her cheeks flashed hot as she caught herself wondering whether the real J.D. had been so bodaciously hung.

His breath hissed out in exasperation. "I'm waiting, lady," he rumbled, "and I'm not a patient man."

That much Emma could believe. A calm and civil approach might work best. "M—my name is Emma Carlyle," she squeaked, then cleared her throat. "I took a wrong turn and ran my car off the road. To make a long story short, somebody stole it, along with my driver's license, my money, my checkbook, my credit cards and my cell. Is there a phone around here that I could use to call 911?"

He shook his rumpled head. "Lady—"

"My name isn't Lady. It's Emma. Or Miss Carlyle if you want to be formal. I'm a teacher."

His chest rose and fell, revealing a sheen of blackish hair where the buttons parted. His seething eyes flickered downward to Emma's belly. "Well, *Miss* Carlyle, you might as well be talking Transylvanian. The only word in all that balderdash I understood was *money*."

Emma sighed. She should have known what kind of person she was dealing with. "If it's cash you want, I can pay you a little but not till I get home. How much do you—"

"Oh, hell's bells!" Seizing her shoulders he hauled her to her feet. The smoldering tip of his cheroot wagged a scant two inches from her face. Its rank aroma made Emma's stomach roil.

"Listen to me, Missy," he growled. "You're half frozen and you've had a nasty bump the head. Now get that damp coat off and get yourself over by the fire while I heat up some coffee and scrape some beans off the bottom of the pot. Maybe after you warm up and get something in your belly, you'll start talking sense!"

Emma staggered backward as he released her, almost falling onto the bed. He was right about one thing, at least. She needed to get warm and dry. And she'd be a fool to turn down his offer of a meal, whatever it might be. For the baby's sake she needed to keep up her strength.

Willing herself to stay calm, she slid the parka off her arms and let it drop onto the tattered patchwork quilt. The split log floor felt splintery beneath her tender, swollen feet. What had become of her boots? Had this wild man taken them off so she couldn't run away?

Still groggy, she staggered to the rocking chair and sank down onto the thickly woven rush seat. Only as the warmth from the fireplace crept around her did Emma realize how cold she was. She leaned closer, hugging herself through her baggy red sweater.

"Put your feet up on the hearth," her host ordered. "They were damn near frozen when I pulled your boots off. I had to rub the circulation into them, and they could still use some warming."

Emma propped her heels on the stones and felt the heat spreading into her bare soles. At least he'd explained about her boots. But she had no memory of his massaging her feet. She must've been dead to the world not to remember that.

She stole furtive glances at his hands as he leaned past her to swing the iron pot off the fire. Like the rest of him they were uncommonly big, with long, tapering fingers and a faint white scar along the base of his right thumb. A shiver passed through Emma's body as she remembered the elegant hands in J.D.'s coffin portrait. It would be easy enough, she supposed, to find an actor with a facial resemblance to the legendary lawman. But what were the odds that his hands would be an exact match to J.D.'s as well, right down to the scar?

Emma could almost hear the "Twilight Zone" theme looping through her brain. Maybe that bump on her head had done more damage than she'd thought.

A mustard-colored cat had jumped onto the hearth and was taking Emma's measure with one saffron eye. The creature looked as if it had survived some run-ins with the neighborhood bully. Or maybe it *was* the neighborhood bully. Its permanently closed left eye was balanced by a cauliflowered right ear, and its tail was nothing but a stump. Still, with all the cockiness of its kind, it stalked over to Emma's feet and rubbed its head against her toe. When Emma reached out and scratched its back, it purred like a broken coffee grinder. At least something around here was friendly.

"Your cat?" she asked the stranger who called himself J.D.

"No." He leaned past her again to lay a log on the coals. It crackled into flame as its dry bark caught the heat. "Just a wanderer in from the cold. Like you, maybe. Here." He picked up a thick ceramic jug from the hearth, twisted out the wooden stopper and thrust it toward her face. "Have a swig. Nothing better for warming up your innards."

Emma sniffed the opening of the jug. The smell of sour mash whiskey almost made her gag. "No," she gasped. "No alcohol. Not with the baby."

"Well, then, excuse me while I help myself." He raised the jug to his mouth and tipped it high. His Adam's apple rippled in a mannish way as he took a leisurely swallow. Emma's heart sank. Right now, the one prospect worse than being marooned in a blizzard with a half-clad roughneck was being marooned in a blizzard with a *drunken* half-clad roughneck.

Lowering the jug, he jammed in the stopper and wiped his mouth with the back of his hand. "Takes the edge off, at least," he muttered. "Merry Christmas Eve, Miss Emma Carlyle. If you won't drink with a man, how about a cup of coffee?"

"That would be fine." She wasn't supposed to have coffee either, Emma reminded herself. But it was a lesser evil than whiskey, and the stranger didn't seem to have anything else to offer. Not unless there was a hidden fridge off camera stocked with assorted gourmet juices and Lean Cuisine.

Maybe she'd stumbled into one of those TV reality shows where contestants had to live in the past. Maybe, as an added twist, each player had been assigned the role of a historical character—a role they had to maintain in order to win. Farfetched as it was, the explanation made more sense than anything else she'd come up with.

But where were the cameras and the technical crew? Why hadn't she seen any vehicles, or even their tracks, on the road?

The baby shifted inside her, stretching, thrusting and finally settling head down against the cradle of her pelvis. Emma wrapped a protective arm around her belly. In this Mad Hatter's world she'd wandered into, only her child was solid and real. Only her child truly mattered.

The man who called himself J.D. McNulty filled a tin mug from a blackened coffeepot. "It's hot," he warned, shoving it toward her handle-first. Emma accepted the mug with a murmur of thanks. The coffee inside looked like molten tar.

"Do you have any milk?" she ventured. "Or maybe some sugar?"

"Sugar's used up, and the last cow in Glory Gulch busted its leg last fall. We had a dandy barbecue down at the Laughing Lady, but that was the end of the milk."

Emma forced herself to take measured sips. The coffee tasted as bitter as it looked, but its life-giving heat seeped through her body, warming her as she drank.

The cat had curled up on the hearth next to the whiskey jug. It watched with mild interest as J.D. scooped a lumpy brown mass out of the iron pot and slapped it into a pie tin. "Beans," he grunted, jabbing a fork into the middle. "Sorry I can't offer you biscuits but I ate the last of them for supper. As I told you, I wasn't planning on company."

Rankled by his manner, Emma glared up at him. "Excuse me, Mr. McNulty, or whatever your real name is. I didn't set out to impose on you. If I'd had a choice I would've checked into the local Holiday Inn, with vending machines and hot showers and cable TV. Unfortunately for both of us, I found you first."

"Now you're talking gibberish again." He handed her the beans. Then, nudging the cat away, he sat down on the hearth, took a deep draw on the stub of his cheroot and blew out the smoke in a lazy upward spiral.

"Must you smoke that awful thing?" Emma sputtered. "It's making me nauseous, and it's bad for the baby! Haven't you heard about the dangers of second-hand smoke?"

He scowled at her, then tossed the cheroot into the fire. "Touchy as a mare ready to foal, aren't you? But then I reckon that goes with being female."

Miffed beyond words, Emma stirred her beans. They smelled burnt and looked like something that ought to be scraped down the garbage disposal. She set the pie tin on the hearth. The real J.D. would have been a gentleman, not a hairy-chested, foul-mouthed Neanderthal, she told herself. And he would have treated her like a lady. He would never have compared her to a pregnant mare, even if she looked like one.

An unexpected tear trickled down Emma's cheek. Right now all she wanted was to wake up in her own bed and realize that this whole surreal encounter had been a dream.

"We need to have a serious talk, Emma Carlyle."

Caught off guard, Emma glanced up to meet his eyes. Reflected firelight glinted in their azure depths like flame trapped in dark water as he leaned toward her.

"So far all we've done is snap and snarl at each other like a couple of coyotes on a dead sheep. All I know about you is your name. Nothing else you've told me makes any sense. I'm willing to help get you back to where you belong, but first you need to tell me in plain English where you came from and how you got here."

Emma nodded wearily. "I'd like to do just that. But first I need to know where I am and what's happening with all...this." She encompassed the cabin with a gesture. "Is this a movie set? A historical replica of some kind? And what about you? Who are you in real life?"

He swore under his breath. "See what I mean? It's like we're speaking two different lingos. I already told you, I'm J.D. McNulty. You're in my cabin, in Glory Gulch, Wyoming Territory, United States of America. You came pounding on my door in the middle of a blizzard and that's all I can tell you."

Wyoming *Territory*? Emma stared at the man as the words sank home. "Wyoming is a state, not a territory."

"That's news to me. But then, what happens in Washington, D.C., can be slow getting to a place like Glory Gulch."

Emma felt herself sliding deeper down the proverbial rabbit hole. "Tell me one more thing," she ventured. "What date do you think this is?"

"December 24. Christmas Eve, for whatever the hell it's worth."

"The year." Emma felt as if her heart had stopped beating. "Tell me the year."

"It's 1871. Any fool knows that. Eat your beans before they get cold."

In the lamplit silence, Emma could hear the rush of wind beneath the eaves of the cabin. A coal in the fireplace burst into a shower of sparks.

For something she'd willed to be a dream, this place and this man seemed frighteningly real.

She cleared her throat. "Tell me something else. Who's the President of the United States?"

His eyes narrowed suspiciously. "Ulysses S. Grant, unless I've missed another bit of news. Why?"

"Because one of us is delusional, and the last time I checked, it wasn't me."

His nostrils flared. "Are you saying I'm crazy?"

"Listen to me. It isn't 1871. It's 2010, and out there in the world there are cars and telephones and computers and airplanes, and the president is Barack Obama. I don't know how to explain it, but you seem to be living in the past."

He shot to his feet and strode to the bookshelf. When he returned to the fireplace he was brandishing a folded newspaper. "Living in the past, am I? Explain this, then. It's two months old but it should prove that I'm not the one who's taken leave of their senses!"

He unfolded the newspaper and shoved it under Emma's nose. It was a well-worn copy of *The Cheyenne Daily Leader*. The front page stories included a hanging, a boarding house fire and the appearance of a popular singer named Matilda Appletree at a Cheyenne theater. "The date!" he snarled. "Look at the date!"

Emma leaned closer, blinking to make sure her eyes weren't deceiving her. There it was in black and white—October 22, 1871.

A sick little gagging sound emerged from Emma's throat. Could this really be 1871? And could this indecently clad, foul-mouthed ogre of a man really be J.D. McNulty?

Of course not. It was impossible.

The room had begun to blur. J.D. refilled the mug with coffee and raised it to her lips. "Drink it," he ordered. "You're as white as an undertaker's lily."

The coffee had cooled since the first cup, but the taste of it was enough to shock Emma back to her senses. She closed her eyes, letting the tarry brew slide down her throat.

"Better?" J.D. actually sounded concerned.

"Yes, thank you."

"Then you'd best chow down on those beans before that coffee eats a hole in your gut."

The man had a real way with words. Emma picked up the pie tin and speared a bite-sized portion of the beans. They were over-salted and definitely burnt. But then he had said something about scraping them off the bottom of the pot. At least he had no delusions about being a gracious host.

"Now, where were we?" He lowered himself to the hearth again, his back to the fire, his long legs extended and crossed at the ankles. "Have I convinced you that I'm not a raving lunatic?"

Emma forced the bite of charcoal-flavored beans down her throat and swallowed hard. "You have no idea what a stretch this is," she said shakily. "You say you're J.D. McNulty. Do you mean Jethro Darlington McNulty, born in Springfield, Illinois on April 20, 1827?"

"Now how in Sam Hill would you know all that?" He was staring at her as if she'd just sprouted horns.

Emma groped for another memory from her thesis notes. "You were a captain in the Union Army. You were wounded at Gettysburg and you have a scar on your left side to prove it. Am I right?"

He didn't speak. His bloodshot eyes drilled into hers, their gaze impaling her like hot nails. Without breaking eye contact, he reached up and began to fumble with the row of gaping, mismatched buttons that fastened the front of his underwear. Emma forgot to breathe as the ragged garment opened to reveal a dusting of black hair that tapered to form a silken line down the middle of his belly. Her mouth went dry as he slid his shoulders free and worked the fabric off his arms.

He had a warrior's body—there was no other word for it. His arms and shoulders, though not bulky, were knotted with the sinewy muscles of a seasoned fighter. His skin was pale gold, with a patina of small nicks and slashes.

Not until he turned his left side toward her and moved his arm clear did she see what he wanted her to see. There, just below the line of his ribs was an ugly walnut-sized pit of a scar that could only have been made by a rifle ball going deep. She remembered reading that the wound had become infected and nearly killed him.

"Satisfied?" He covered himself again, not hastily but with an economy of motion.

She nodded, drained of words.

"Then tell me one thing, Emma Carlyle." He leaned toward her, his voice a raw whisper. "Was it God or Satan who sent you here? Are you an angel or a devil?"

Emma licked her lips, struggling for the right words. "Honestly, I don't know where to—*oh*!"

The pain felt as if a giant fist had seized her body and was twisting her like a child with a handful of play dough. Gasping, she doubled over, her arms clutching her belly. Only as she felt the gush of warm fluid between her thighs did Emma realize what was happening.

J.D. was on his feet. "What the—" He gaped at her in horror. "Oh, Lord Almighty, don't tell me—"

"Yes!" Emma hissed at him. "It's the baby! My water just broke! I'm in labor!"

# CHAPTER THREE

J.D.'s mutterings could have been curses, prayers or both. How could this be happening? It was as if the demons he'd been dodging for the past seven years had finally run him to ground. If God was up there watching, it was a good bet He was enjoying this.

He could feel the sweat breaking out under his long johns. Facing a mob of screaming Sioux or an army of pistol-toting desperados would be less daunting than what lay ahead of him now. But there was no way out. Whoever she was and wherever she'd come from, Miss Emma Carlyle needed help. And with a December blizzard howling around the cabin, he was all the help she was going to get.

Reaching down, he clasped her upper arm. "Come on, we'd better get you into bed."

"Bed!" She stared up at him in horror. "For heaven's sake, this is an emergency! Call 911! Get me to a hospital!"

J.D. tightened his grip. "Stop talking foolishness. There's not a hospital within two hundred miles. We're going to have to make do right here."

"No!" She pulled away from him and reeled to her feet. "This silly charade is over as of right now! Get on the phone or the radio or whatever you have and get me some help! If there's no hospital nearby, I'll settle for an ambulance and a crew of paramedics!"

"There you go again! Speak English!"

"Do I have to draw you a picture? I'm about to have this baby!"

"Damn it, I know that!" J.D. exploded. "So let me draw *you* a picture! You're a good week from the nearest doctor, and that snowstorm outside would freeze a Montana mule in its tracks. I didn't invite you here, and I sure as hell didn't ask for the honor of having your baby born in my bed. But unless you want to give the cat a quick course in midwifery, I'm all the help you're going to get!"

Her eyes flashed a stricken look. Then she sagged against him and doubled over with pain. J.D. willed himself to stay calm. It wouldn't do to let the woman know how scared he was.

"Come on now," he said, walking her toward the bed and turning down the blankets to expose worn flannel sheets. "Stretch out here and we'll see about getting you out of those clothes. I ought to have an old night shirt stuffed away somewhere. Am I right in guessing this is your first baby?"

"I'm afraid so," she muttered through clenched teeth, "and I hadn't planned on having it in a place like...this." She let him ease her onto her back. For now, the pain seemed to be ebbing. She let out a long breath. "So how much experience have you had delivering babies?"

The question lanced J.D. with a pain that shimmered behind his eyes. Seconds passed before he found the breath to reply. "None that would do any good—unless you'd count watching a longhorn cow drop a calf."

Her pretty face was a study in helpless panic. "You said there were other people living here. Surely there's a woman, some miner's wife—"

"The only women in Glory Gulch work in the saloon—and above it if you get my drift. Mame, their boss lady, might know something about birthing. But there's no way for me to fetch her or anybody else in this storm. I'd have to leave you here alone, and there's a good chance I might not make it back." J.D.'s fingers raked his tangled hair. "Believe me, Missy, I'd rather be tortured by Comanche squaws than deliver a baby. If you think you can do the job without my help, I'd be happy to stay out of your way."

"Don't be silly!"

"Fine. I'll find you that nightshirt."

Leaving her, he crossed the room to the leather-bound trunk where his spare clothes were stashed. On the way he paused to pick up the whiskey jug and raise it to his lips for a long, burning swig. The proper Miss Carlyle probably wouldn't approve. She talked and behaved too much like one of those Temperance League ladies he'd known in Cheyenne. But there were times when a man needed a drink. This was one of them.

Emma's temper boiled as J.D., or whoever he really was, took his time lowering the jug. If he kept this up he'd be useless by the time she was ready to give birth.

"What do you think you're doing?" she demanded. "Take one more swallow and you're not coming near me!"

His cobalt eyes narrowed to slits. "Don't tempt me, lady."

"I told you, my name isn't lady. It's Emma."

"All right, Emma, there's something you need to understand. This is my cabin and my whiskey, and it's not your place to be giving orders." He set the jug back on the hearth. "So now that we've established who's in charge here, what d'you say you stop mewling like a sick heifer and let me try to get you comfortable?"

"Mewling like a sick heifer!" Emma's frazzled patience snapped. "Why don't *you* try having a baby sometime, you arrogant, chauvinistic son of a—"

Her words ended in a groan as another vise-like contraction closed around her. She curled onto her side, teeth clenched, hands clutching her rock hard belly.

"Now, that's better." He turned away from her and walked toward the chest. The cat leaped down from the mantel and followed him across the floor, it's bobbed tail raised like a stumpy yellow flag. As J.D. lifted the lid, it jumped into the trunk and began kneading the top layer of fabric with its claws. "This isn't your blasted bed," J.D. growled, sweeping the animal aside. "Stay out of the way if you know what's good for you."

After some rummaging he came up with a grayish wad of fabric. He shook it out to reveal a rumpled nightshirt. "Good thing I didn't rip this up for rags," he said, tossing it toward Emma. "Once you get it on we can hang those wet britches up to dry. I don't suppose you'll need any help changing."

"No. Just keep your back turned." Emma's contraction had passed. She was able to sit up and strip the baggy red sweater over her head. The nightshirt was the color and texture of dryer lint. It was soft and warm against Emma's bare skin and smelled faintly of mothballs. Pulling it down over her bra, she squirmed out of her damp black stretch pants and soaked pink polka-dot bikini briefs. They ought to be rinsed, or better yet, thrown away, she thought. But right now she had more urgent things to worry about.

Standing, she stepped out of the wet garments and let the hem of the nightshirt drop past her knees. J.D. was gazing at the cracked face of the cheap brass clock that sat on the mantel. At least he'd been enough of a gentleman to keep his back turned—a ludicrous gesture, now that Emma thought about it. Before the night was over she'd have nothing left to hide from him.

A furtive tear trickled down her cheek. Emma brushed it away. She'd planned on having her child in a safe, clean hospital with anesthesia to blot out the pain and a skilled medical team to make sure all went well. Instead, here she was, stranded in a mountain shack that didn't even have running water, let alone a decent bathroom. Her only human companion was a raving lunatic living in the wrong century. Worse, neither of them seemed to know any more about birthing babies than little Prissy in *Gone With the Wind*.

Feeling the start of another pain, she lowered herself to the bed and yanked the covers up to her chest. Why hadn't she forced herself to attend those childbirth classes at the hospital? The doctor had suggested it; but the thought of being surrounded by excited future mommies and daddies—some of them her former students—had been more than Emma could handle. She hadn't even read the recommended books. What was to know? You started having pains, you went to the hospital, the doctors and nurses did their job. You had ten minutes to kiss your baby goodbye and a long time to hurt.

*Oh, damn, damn, damn!*

"Are you all right?"

J.D. was standing over her, a worried frown on his long-jawed face. Her black maternity slacks and polka-dot panties dangled wetly from one hand.

Emma found her voice. "Yes...but not for long." This contraction was building slowly, like a big, deep sea wave. When it hit, she sensed, it would overwhelm her with the force of a tsunami.

"I'll just get these out of your way." He turned the back of the rocker toward the fire and shook out Emma's wet clothes. Color scalded her cheeks as he pondered the panties. "Right peculiar unmentionables you've got here," he mused aloud. "Can't say as I've ever seen the likes of them."

"It's what women wear these days," Emma snapped. "Where have you been?"

Ignoring her comment, he draped the garments over the back of the chair. After the way they'd gotten wet, Emma couldn't imagine wearing them without a good wash. Not that they were going to fit her after the baby was born.

The baby! Motherly guilt slammed her like a Mack truck. She had nothing to put on the poor little thing, not a blanket, not a nightie, not even a diaper! What was she going to do?

She could only pray that the search planes and snowmobiles would be out as soon as the storm cleared, that they'd be able to find her in this Brigadoon she'd stumbled into and get her back to civilization. Otherwise...

Emma gasped as the contraction peaked, squeezing and stretching her innards like so much putty. She'd experienced pain before—surely she had. But not like this. Her back arched off the mattress. Her head rolled back and forth on the pillow. Her hands clawed air—and met with something solid.

"Squeeze tight." J.D.'s long fingers closed around hers. His hands were warm and rough and strong. She caught at them like a drowning swimmer. "Scream if you want," he said. "Nobody can hear you but me and the old tomcat, and it might sound like music to him."

Emma wasn't a screamer by nature. But she gripped J.D.'s hands until the knuckles cracked. "It's all right..." his deep whiskey voice soothed her. "You're going to be fine."

"How do you know?" She stared up at him as the pain began to ebb.

"Damn it, I don't. But the good Lord made you a strong, healthy woman with hips like a mare's. If anybody can bring a baby into the world, you can."

Emma grimaced. Hips like a mare's. That just about said it all. A curvy size fourteen, she would never have made it as a fashion model. But she could only pray he was right about the baby. It wasn't as if she could have a quick C-section if something went wrong. As a historian, she'd visited her share of frontier cemeteries. The graves of women and babies usually outnumbered the men's three to one. It wasn't hard to understand why, especially now. The feeling of helplessness was heartbreaking—and terrifying.

She released his hands as the contraction slipped away. "Better?" he asked, pulling a wooden box close to the bed.

"For now."

"Good." He lowered his lanky frame onto the box, his red-clad knees jutting above his boot tops like sections of a carpenter's rule. Even sitting down, he loomed over her. "Since you're lying in my bed I hope you won't mind answering some questions."

"Ask away, I've nothing to hide. In fact I have a few questions of my own."

He leaned forward, his eyes glinting like two gun muzzles pointed at her heart. A burning pine knot snapped in the silence. Wind whistled around the frame of the small, high window. Snow peppered the glass.

"Before this baby of yours got us off track, you were telling me things I've always considered my own private business. I've never seen you before in my life, but you came here knowing my full name, my birthplace, my war record and heaven knows what else. I want the truth—now. Who are you, Emma Carlyle? Who told you about me and sent you here?"

Emma willed herself not to flinch under his steely gaze. "As I said, I have nothing to hide. I teach American history in Lander, Wyoming. And nobody sent me here. I found my way to your cabin by chance after my car disappeared—and believe me, I'm just as confused about some things as you are!"

"A teacher." His eyes narrowed. "That could fit. You've got the look of a schoolmarm about you—aside from the belly, of course. But I never heard of Lander, and I know the territory pretty well."

"Wyoming's a state now, remember? Lander's less than an hour's drive to the north, by car. I've been teaching there for the past ten years, at Esther Morris High School."

"Esther Morris, you say?" He rubbed his unshaven chin. "I met Esther when she was Justice of the Peace in South Pass City. Plain as an old Hubbard squash, but a right fine lady. Damned smart for a female. Didn't know she was running a school these days, but I'm not surprised."

"For heaven's sake, the school's named after her! The woman's been dead for more than a hundred years!"

He looked annoyed. "Either I'm Rip van Winkle, or you're talking gibberish again! And you still haven't answered my question!"

Emma felt another contraction welling from the depths of her pelvis. Maybe if she kept talking, it would take her mind off the pain. She might even convince this wild-haired ogre she wasn't crazy, although that was growing more doubtful by the minute.

As she gathered her wits against the pain, the clock on the mantle struck ten. The cat jumped down from the hearth and scurried off after some unseen prey.

"My answer to your question depends on your answer to mine," she said. "You claim you're J.D. McNulty, the marshal who gunned down the Cleary gang in Laramie?"

A shadow crossed his wind-weathered face. "Much as I'd like to give that honor to somebody else, the answer's yes."

"And tell me today's date again."

He swore under his breath. "How many times do I have to say it? It's Christmas Eve, Sunday, December 24, 1871."

She was hallucinating, that was it, Emma concluded. She'd focused so intently on her thesis that her brain had short circuited. She might think she'd wandered back in time and was meeting J.D. in person, but it was only her exhausted mind playing tricks. That would explain everything.

Relief swept over her as the pain ripped upward. The labor hurt too much not to be real. But the rest was all in her head. Play along, and she was bound to wake up soon—hopefully in the hospital.

"I'm waiting," he said. "Something here doesn't seem right, and I want to know what it is."

The contraction was cresting now. Emma rode with it, trying not to fight the pain. But it was too much for her. A moan escaped her tight lips. Without willing it, she reached out and caught J.D.'s fingers again, clutching them as if they were the only solid thing in a shifting universe. His hands were all bone and sinew, the pads leathered with calluses. But even as his touch comforted her, his eyes blazed with suspicion.

"You asked me how I know about you." She forced the words out as the tightness ebbed. "There's no mystery about it. The basic facts are public record. To get them, all I had to do was Google you on the internet."

"Blast it, you're doing it again!" he exploded, dropping her hands. "I've had a fair education in my life, but the words you're using don't make a lick of sense!"

"No, I don't suppose they would." Emma shifted her hips on the lumpy straw mattress. "I've been writing a thesis—a scholarly paper. It's about you. I've done a lot of research."

"The hell you say." He looked perplexed. "Why me?"

"Because you're a legend. People will want to know more about you."

"Sounds like a lot of bull to me. And what about that googly net thing you mentioned? Can you explain that, or is it just something that popped into your head?"

Emma sighed. This wasn't going to be easy. "I have a machine at home—it's called a computer. It looks like a window frame with lights behind it. The lights show letters and pictures, like pages in a book."

He folded his arms across his chest. One black eyebrow slithered upward.

"It's attached to a keyboard." She was stumbling now, and his expression showed it. "You push the keys with your fingers, and the letters or numbers you type appear on the screen. You can write, send messages and read what other people have written."

"Sounds like so much balderdash to me."

"Then you might not believe this either. Millions of people have computers, and they're connected to this...this huge, invisible library. It's called the internet. You can type in almost anything you want to know, like a question or somebody's name. Something called a search engine—that's what Google is—finds the information on the net and sends it to your computer."

"The hell you say." He shook his dark head. "And that's how you found out about me? With this internet hocus pocus? There are things written about me on it?"

She nodded.

"Well, how do I get them off?" he demanded.

"I'm afraid you can't." Emma felt the tightening, low in her belly.

"Damn it, a man's got a right to privacy!"

"Not in the year 2010. If someone's posted information about you on the net, there's not much you can do. Anybody with a connection can do a search to find out when you were born, where you lived, what you did and when you—*oh!*"

The pain closed around her, taking her breath away. This one meant business. She reached out for J.D.'s big, rough hands, found them and gripped them with all her strength. They were so solid, those hands; so *real*, right down to the sharp little hangnail on his pinkie and the ridge of scarring across the base of the left thumb. How could anything so vivid be a figment of her imagination? And how could this outrageous giant of a man with soul-piercing blue eyes be anyone except J.D. McNulty in the flesh?

Was it possible to fall backward through time?

Had she somehow done just that?

If the answer was yes, then the actual date was December 24, 1871. And the man...

Emma stifled a gasp as the realization struck her.

J.D. McNulty had died in a bloody poker game on February 17, 1872.

If the man holding her hands was the real J.D., he had less than eight weeks to live.

J.D. kept his eyes on the woman's face, watching the emotions that flickered like firelight across her features. His ability to read people had saved his life on any number of occasions. This time his instincts whispered that Emma Carlyle was hiding something.

Her story about the invisible library and the machine that could answer questions had been pure hogwash. Nothing like that could exist in the real world. But the things she'd known about him had all been true. She couldn't have pulled them out of thin air.

J.D. had come to Glory Gulch to escape his violent past. All he'd wanted was to be left in peace. But as a lawman and bounty hunter, he'd made more than his share of enemies. Some of those enemies were powerful. Given his reputation with the ladies, it made sense that one of them might send a woman to flush him out.

But *this* woman? Nine months along, dressed like a demented Chinaman and spouting nonsense every time she opened her pretty mouth?

She didn't fit the picture. Hellfire, she didn't fit any picture!

She was gazing up at him now, her light brown eyes so clear and honest that he would've believed her if she'd told him the sun rose in the north. What kind of game was she playing? One way or another, he was going to find out.

Her soft, strong hands relaxed their grip as the pain passed. Her breath whooshed out in a long exhalation.

"You say you're a schoolmarm?" he asked her.

"That's right—although that term would be an insult in my day. I'm a teacher."

"And since you introduced yourself as *Miss* Carlyle, would I be right in guessing there's no Mister?"

"You would. As the old saying goes, he done me wrong."

J.D.'s eyes traced the line of freckles that paraded across her firm nose. Her eyes were lightly creased at the corners. She was no longer young. But there was an air of tender innocence about her. Whoever had left Emma in this fix, it was a sure bet she'd loved the bastard with a pure and trusting heart.

"Any man who'd do you wrong would have to be a real son of a mule," he said, meaning it.

She gave him a wry smile. "Thanks. Something tells me his wife would have agreed with you."

Her honesty surprised and touched him. "So now you'll be raising a baby on your own. It's a hard lot for a woman, and it won't be easy for the little one either."

"I know that." She hesitated. Pain tightened her jaw. "I want the best for my daughter—a good home with parents who can give her everything she needs. That's why I arranged to have her adopted— signed the papers, everything." Her eyes squeezed shut. A tear trickled onto the pillow as she caught his hands and squeezed hard. He watched her face as the pain mounted, peaked and began to ebb. At last she released his hands.

"I had it all worked out," she said. "I was going to deliver my baby in the hospital, turn her over to her new parents and get on with my life. Then I got caught in a storm and took the wrong road. Now, here I am—but the words *now* and *here* have taken on whole new meanings. I don't know what's happened to me, let alone what I'm going to do."

"Looks to me like you're going to have your baby and let nature take its course," J.D. said. "No two ways about that. But one thing I don't understand. You keep talking about *her*. What makes you so all fired sure that youngster's a girl?"

"I've seen her sonogram, as they call it." She looked almost apologetic. "My doctor has a machine in his office. It uses sound waves to take pictures of unborn babies."

J.D. rolled his eyes. "Lordy, here we go again! Next you'll be telling me there's a machine that can fly folks to the moon! You're a right nice woman when you're not talking crazy, Emma Carlyle. Maybe you could use a swig of whiskey. I know I could!"

She shook her head. "No whiskey. And I'm not talking crazy. The baby's definitely a girl. You'll see when she gets here."

"See what? The odds are fifty-fifty either way. Just because your baby turns out to be a girl doesn't mean some doctor took a picture of her through your belly! Where do you come up with these wild ideas?"

She reached out and caught his hand again, although she didn't appear to be hurting. "Think about this, J.D. Imagine yourself living a hundred years ago, when America was still a colony. What if someone had told you about a machine that could capture your image and put it on paper—or wires that could carry messages, or a huge coal-burning engine that ran on iron rails and could pull a line of heavy cars all the way across the continent to the Pacific Ocean? What would you say?"

"Why, I'd probably figure they'd been out in the sun too long. Or that they'd had a bump on the head, just like you have." He could see the edge of another pain creeping across her face, tightening her pretty features.

"And yet you've seen those things with your own eyes. You know they're real. Can you imagine what kinds of things might be real in years to come? Carriages with motors instead of horses, wires that transmit people's voices, machines that can carry passengers through the air..."

J.D. stared down into her earnest face. No, the woman couldn't mean what he was thinking she meant. That bump on the head had addled her brain. Maybe he should venture out and get some snow to pack it and bring down the swelling.

"Do you think it's possible for a person to travel through time?" she whispered, voicing his own thoughts.

He shook his head, denying everything. "Only in stories. In real life, we're set down on this earth when we're born, and when our time's up, we die. Sounds like a sensible plan to me. Why complicate it?"

"I'm not asking if it *should* happen. I'm asking if you think it *could.*"

"If you're about to tell me there's a machine that can send people through time, I'm warning you—"

"No. Nobody's invented a time machine. I just—*oh!*" Her fingers dug into his hands, the bitten nails making little moons in his flesh. This pain was a long one and she took it hard, teeth clenched, back arched, hips writhing in agony.

J.D. murmured feeble comforts as the old, cold fear crept over him. Lord, could he do this? He'd failed once and lost everything he'd ever loved. Fail again, and he might as well put a gun to his head.

She lay gasping as the pain eased. The nightshirt had twisted around her body. Sweaty tendrils of hair clung to her damp face.

"Can I get you anything?" He hovered over her, dread clenching his gut.

"Maybe some water for later. I can't imagine this taking much longer, but it could on go all night." She had let go of his hands, but she reached out again. "I'm scared. What if I'm not up to this? What if something goes wrong?"

His fingers closed around hers as he voiced what she needed to hear. "Women were made to have babies. You'll be fine. So will your little one."

She closed her eyes, resting. "My little girl. I'm doing this for her, and she'll be worth it all, won't she?"

"If she takes after her mother, she'll grow up to be one fine lady."

Her eyes shot open. Her grip tightened on his hands. "Promise me something, J.D. If anything goes wrong—if I don't make it—"

"Don't talk like that!" Even her words were enough to make him sweat bullets. "Of course you'll be all right."

"No, listen. If something happens, and it comes down to my life or the baby's, promise me you'll save her first. And promise me you'll find her a good home—that you'll do it right away and not wait."

"Blast it, Emma—"

"*Promise!*" Her fingers dug into him. "Give me that much peace, at least."

He sighed. "Fine. I promise. But nothing's going to happen to you."

"Let's hope not." She released him with a feeble smile.

"I'll get you that water." J.D. rose shakily to his feet. He needed to take a piss before things got bad. And then, by damn, he needed one more drink.

# CHAPTER FOUR

As night deepened the storm moved out, sweeping down the slope of the mountains to fan eastward over the flatland. In the sky above Glory Gulch, thinning clouds unveiled the silver face of the moon. Its light glistened on a landscape blanketed in ermine. Lodgepole pines, shrouded in white, towered against the stars. Snow shimmered from a bare limb as a great horned owl took wing and floated into the darkness. It was a silent time. A magical time.

In the snow-buried cabin, the lamp had burned low. Glancing up, J.D. noticed that the hands of the clock had crawled past eleven. He had no memory of hearing the hour strike. More than likely he'd been gripping Emma's hands or bathing her face with a damp cloth. Her pains were coming harder and lasting longer. The woman even seemed to be talking less. Her attention was focused inward, on the job of bringing her baby into the world.

And what a hellish job it was. She lay resting now, her eyes closed, her hair plastered against her colorless skin. She was utterly spent, and the worst was yet to come. Lord help him, he wouldn't choose to be a woman for all the whiskey in Cheyenne!

J.D. lit a tallow candle to give light while he refilled the kerosene lamp and trimmed the wick. Fear gnawed at his innards—the fear of another ghastly failure. He craved a cheroot to steady his nerves, but Emma had said that smoke was bad for the baby. Another pull at the jug might take the edge off. But J.D. hadn't touched the whiskey in the past two hours. He'd been drunk the other time. If he'd been sober, it might have made a difference.

This wasn't the same, he reminded himself. Emma Carlyle was a robust woman whose full breasts and deep hips were fashioned for motherhood. His Maggie had been a fragile little porcelain doll. He'd likely sealed her doom the night he got her with child. Still, the doctor might have saved her—or at least saved the baby, if only J.D. had arrived home in time to send for him. As it was...

But he couldn't relive that night now. He would lose his mind if he did. He could only try to do for Emma what he hadn't done for his own wife and baby. Maybe in return, it would give him a small measure of redemption and shorten his sentence in hell.

Setting the lamp on the bedside table, he blew out the candle. Emma's pain-glazed eyes were open now. Her hands reached for his in a gesture that had become a reflex. Her grip was becoming weaker. If that baby didn't get here soon, she could be in trouble. Even the thought of that made his gut clench.

The long contraction was so intense that J.D. could almost feel it himself. As it passed, he lifted her head and gave her a sip of water from a tin cup. She sank back onto the pillow with a sigh.

"I'm getting tired," she murmured. "Why does this have to take so long?"

"You're asking *me*? I'm no doctor, but I've heard that first babies can be slow. You're doing fine." J.D. could only hope it wasn't a lie.

"Were you ever married, J.D.? Did you have children?"

"You mean your damn fool google net didn't tell you that? Yes, I was married. My wife died. She's buried back East."

"I'm sorry."

He felt the blade twist. "It was a long time ago, the year after the war. I don't talk about it—or about her."

"So you came west after you lost your family?"

"I thought you knew everything about me."

A wan smile lit her face. "Not by a long shot. That's why I've had such a struggle with my thesis. I can only get so much from books and old papers and the internet. There are gaps in my research you could drive a truck—excuse me, a wagon—through. For instance, why did you leave Laramie after the big gunfight? How did you wind up in a dead-end mining camp like Glory Gulch?"

J.D. didn't like questions unless he was doing the asking. And since she planned to publish his answers, he especially didn't like *her* questions. There was something unsettling about Emma Carlyle—something he neither understood nor trusted. "I came here because I won the cabin in a poker game, and it seemed as good a place as any to hole up for the winter. As for Laramie, that's nobody's business but mine."

"That's what Tilly said—the woman who runs the bookstore in

South Pass City. As she put it, you play your cards close to your vest."

"There's no bookstore in South Pass City. If there was, I'd be the first one in the door."

"The building was a barbershop in your time. Now it's a bookstore, about halfway down the main street on the north side. The owner's name is Tilly Farson, and she talks about you as if you were an old friend. Of course, that's not really possible—"

"Whoa, there. Hang on an all-fired minute." J.D. stared down at her. "You said it was a barbershop in my time. Hellfire, this *is* my time! And there's a barbershop in South Pass City. I got a shave and haircut there this past October. But I didn't see one book and I've never heard of this Tilly person. Make some sense!"

"I'm...trying to!" She ground out the words as another pain tore into her. This one seemed to be the worst yet. Little grunts of agony emerged through her clenched teeth. Her stubby nails clawed his hands as her body arched upward. "Get something under me..." she muttered. "I think it's...happening!"

Pain ripped through Emma with the fury of a tornado. Low in her body, she felt something shift. She bore down with all her strength but the contraction ebbed, leaving her frustrated and gasping.

J.D. had stuffed a folded sheet under her hips. She hadn't thought to ask him how clean it was. Her concerns for modesty had fled as well.

"Can you see anything?" she demanded.

"See anything?" His face was white. If he got sick or fainted, by heaven, she was going to kill him!

"I assume you know where babies come out! Take the blasted lamp and look!"

His hands were shaking. Emma couldn't see them, but she could see how the shadows quivered as he pulled the covers down and lifted the hem of the nightshirt. Emma stared up at the log rafters, pretending she was in the gynecologist's office. The cat watched the drama from its perch on the mantel.

"Don't see anything out of the ordinary," J.D. said. "No baby, at least."

"Never mind, then, it can't be much—" Her words ended in a grunt as Mother Nature and her own instincts took over. The pain was powerful, the urge to push all-consuming. Beads of sweat stood out on her face. Her neck cords bulged with effort.

"I see something—" J.D. sounded transfixed. "It's...Lord Almighty, it's the top a little head! Not much hair—"

"She's coming!" Emma gasped. "Help—"

She could feel his hands fumbling between her wet thighs. "Push," he was urging her. "Push, damn it!"

"I'm ... pushing!" She ground out the words, her strength flagging as the contraction ebbed.

"Well, push harder! If a blasted cow can do it, so can you!"

"Of all the stupid, asinine—" Fury-fueled adrenalin surged through her spent body. She dug into the next contraction, bearing down with everything she had.

"That's it! Keep it up—"

With one last push and a gush of fluid, Emma's child slid into the world.

"Well, I'll be damned, you were right! It's a little girl!" J.D. sounded as overcome as if he'd had the baby himself.

"Is she breathing?" Emma struggled to rise off the pillow but she was too spent. "Pick her up! Spank her bottom, like they do in the movies!"

"Like they *what*?" Emma heard him muttering. In the eternity of silence she heard the faint chime of the clock. Then the hush was broken by a two sharp slaps and an operatic shriek that sent the cat scurrying for cover. Emma's daughter had found her voice and was expressing her outrage at the whole miserable experience of being born.

Emma had seen enough reruns of "Dr. Quinn, Medicine Woman" to know that a knife and a length of string would be needed for the umbilical cord. These J.D. had placed on a box beside the bed. "A cow would just bite it in two," he remarked as he wrapped and knotted the string. "And then she'd eat the afterbirth."

"I'm not a blasted cow!"

"I'm aware of that." J.D. removed the lamp's glass chimney, passed the blade of his knife through the flame, then cut the cord. He'd been a nervous wreck before the birth, but now that the baby was safely here, he seemed surprisingly at ease with her. She screamed like a little wildcat while he sponged her off, but once she was wrapped in Emma's soft, red acrylic sweater, she snuggled greedily into its warmth.

He stood beside the bed, a ludicrous, rumpled scarecrow figure in ragged long johns, cradling the tiny red bundle in his huge hands. Something shrank inside Emma. She'd spent months preparing herself for the moment when she'd hold her baby for the first and last time. But nothing could have prepared her for this.

Somewhere in the outside world, a wealthy Cheyenne attorney and his TV newscaster wife—decent people—were waiting to take their new infant home to a designer nursery, complete with electronic surveillance and a full-time nanny. They had all the papers—papers Emma had signed in good faith, telling herself it was for the best.

So what now? How could she love and care for this baby when, at any time, she could be hauled back to Lander and forced to give the child up? Did she even have a choice?

J.D. was waiting. He cleared his throat. "Take your little girl, Emma. She needs you."

Emma forced herself to hold out her hands. There were times when choices didn't matter, she told herself. This was one of them.

J.D. laid the baby in Emma's arms. "Merry Christmas," he said.

Emma shifted higher on the pillows so she could look down at her daughter. The baby was tiny and perfect with huge dark blue eyes and a head of damp, blond fuzz, so light and fine that it looked like no hair at all. She bore no resemblance to her biological father, and not much to her mother. She was simply her own small, unique self.

Almost timidly, Emma touched one doll-sized hand. The tiny fist closed around her index finger and hung on. Emma fought back a surge of tears. Surely heaven had made some mistake, placing this precious little person in her care. What was she going to do with her? She didn't know the first thing about babies.

"Hello, little stranger," she whispered. "Where do we start? I hope you're a good teacher because your mother's got a lot to learn."

"She needs a name," J.D. said. "What are you going to call her?"

"Why...I don't know." Emma had blocked the idea of a name.

Naming the baby would have only made it harder to give her up. Now her mind had gone blank. She shook her head. "What do you think, J.D.? You took us in and helped her into the world. What would you name her?"

J.D. rubbed his sandpaper beard. He looked dead on his feet.

"She's a pretty little mite," he mused. "I've always thought Ruby was a pretty name. How does that strike you?"

Emma studied her daughter, the wide eyes, the beautifully shaped cupid's-bow mouth, the stubborn chin with its tiny dimple. Ruby wasn't what you'd call a trendy name. But somehow it seemed to fit. "Hello, Ruby," she said. "How do you like your new name?"

The rosebud face puckered and reddened. The pink mouth opened in a wail of distress. There was certainly nothing wrong with Ruby's lungs.

Emma glanced up at J.D. "I'm sorry. It's a lovely name. I'm sure she'll get used to it."

"I don't think it's the name that's got her riled. More than likely it's her belly. Sounds to me like she needs to be fed."

"Fed? Now?" Panic rushed over her. "But I don't have anything to—"

She broke off as she saw his face. J.D. was looking at her as if she were a backward child. "Hellfire, of course you've got something. You've got two somethings. And if you can't figure out what they're for, that's your problem. I'm going to do a little cleanup here and then get some shut-eye."

He gathered up the soiled sheet from the foot of the bed, sopped up some wet spots and stalked toward the door. A blast of icy air swept into the cabin before he closed it behind him.

Cheeks scalding, Emma laid the screaming baby on the quilt, unbuttoned the nightshirt and fumbled with her bra. How on earth did women do this? She'd seen nursing mothers, of course. One woman had even fed her infant during a parent-teacher conference. A stalwart mother of six, she'd draped a blanket over her shoulder and gone on with the conversation about her teenaged son's homework as if it were the most natural thing in the world.

So how hard could it be?

Emma managed to slip a strap off her shoulder and free one swollen breast. She'd seen catalog photos of nursing bras. Now she understood why those odd-looking flaps and hooks might come in handy. But there was no point in wishing for what she couldn't have. Not with Ruby's screams growing more assertive by the second.

Tilting her daughter's head closer, Emma used her free hand to work the nipple within range. Ignoring it, Ruby kept right on with her tirade.

Emma tried again. This time she managed to shove her nipple into the baby's open mouth. Ruby turned her head away, punctuating her screams with hiccups.

A tear of frustration rolled down Emma's cheek. She was raw and damp and hurting like blazes, and so far she was a total failure at motherhood.

She gazed down at the demanding little stranger who'd just taken over her life. "You poor little thing," she murmured. "It wasn't in the plan, but for now we seem to be stuck with each other. What in heaven's name are we going to do?"

J.D. had closed the door and stepped off the porch before he felt the chill and realized he'd forgotten his coat. He muttered a curse. The wild night must've addled his brain. But at least the worst was over. Emma was all right and so was her baby. God hadn't chosen to punish another innocent woman and child for J.D. McNulty's sins.

The cold bit through the threadbare fabric of his long johns, raising goose bumps on his skin. He was literally freezing his ass off. But he wasn't about to go busting back in while Emma was trying to nurse her baby for the first time. He had that much sensibility, at least.

Who was she? The question was driving him crazy. The woman didn't appear to have any family, any money or even a change of clothes. And the stories she told! His first guess would have been that she was somebody's demented sister, escaped from a locked room somewhere. But that picture didn't fit. She was too aware, too intelligent. And too much of what she'd said rang true, especially the things she'd said about him.

For now, that mystery would have to wait. More urgent was the question of what to do with her. The last thing he'd counted on was sharing his tiny cabin with a woman and child. But she had no place to go and nothing for the baby. She didn't even seem to know how to care for the little thing. How could he turn them out in this winter weather? They wouldn't last a day!

Shivering, he stowed the fluid-stained sheet in the lean-to that served as a woodshed. Tomorrow he'd burn it or bury it, so the smell wouldn't attract critters, but tonight the shed would have to do. A lot of things would have to do. Maybe after a few hours of sleep he'd be able to think his way out of this mess.

Slowly he walked back to the porch. The powdery snow drifted around his boots, glittering like diamond dust. Overhead, the sky was bright with uncountable stars. The hush of Christmas newly born lay over the land.

Most years J.D. did his best to ignore Christmas. It was a holiday for happy people, not for regret-steeped loners like himself. But tonight it had crept up on him, catching him unaware with its beauty.

Maybe the magic had something to do with the new baby in his cabin. Whatever it was, he wanted nothing to do with it. After Maggie's death, he had hurt like he never wanted to hurt again. Over time he'd learned that the easiest way not to hurt was not to feel. He'd grown skilled at it, this business of not feeling. And anytime a vulnerable emotion threatened to break through, there was always the numbing power of alcohol.

Come to think of it, he could use a drink right now.

J.D.'s teeth had begun to chatter. Scooping up an armload of wood from the pile on the porch, he rapped on the door. "You decent, Emma?"

It struck him as a silly question, since he'd just delivered her baby; but now there would be new rules in place. Until he understood what they were, he'd be smart to err on the side of caution.

"Yes, come in." He could barely hear her words above the cries of the baby. Evidently, things weren't going well.

Stomping the snow off his boots, J.D. opened the door and stepped inside. Warmth rushed around him, prickling on his chilled skin as he piled the wood on the hearth. Emma was sitting up in his bed, the top of the sheet draped over her bosom. Her eyes were smudged with exhaustion. Her hair framed her face like a tangled string mop. Young Ruby was caterwauling at the top of her brand new lungs.

"Sounds like trouble," J.D. observed.

Emma's bloodshot eyes narrowed murderously. "If you're about to tell me a cow could do this, I'm warning you—"

"Now, you know me better than that, Miss Emma Carlyle. But it does strike me that you could calm her down a bit before you try to feed her. The way I figure, babies come into the world with the same instincts most animals have. If you're out of sorts they can sense it, and it gets them upset, too."

"In other words, she's crying because she knows I'm scared to death of her."

"Makes sense to me. Maybe the two of you ought to get better acquainted before you give her the tit."

Her eyebrows shot up, and J.D. figured he'd said something unseemly. But he was too damned tired to apologize. "You're holding her like she might break," he said. "Snuggle her up. Maybe sing to her a little. Let her know the world's not such a rotten place after all. I'll leave you to it."

He turned away and busied himself with starting the sourdough for tomorrow's breakfast flapjacks. But it was already tomorrow, wasn't it? It was the dark dawn of Christmas morning. He wouldn't have chosen to spend the holiday with a contrary woman and a squalling infant, but it might be more tolerable than drinking himself into a sodden mess alone.

Emma's daughter was still fussing. Her baby cries tightened something in J.D.'s chest, but he squelched the temptation to turn around and look. Emma wasn't his woman and young Ruby wasn't his child. The less he got involved with them the better.

Emma struggled to settle the baby against her shoulder. Ruby's body had gone as stiff as a board, and she was sobbing herself into exhaustion, which couldn't be good. Emma rubbed the rigid back, her feeling her birdlike spine and ribs through the thickness of the sweater. J.D. had suggested singing. But what were you supposed to sing to a baby? She couldn't recall her mother ever singing anything to her, let alone a lullaby.

Taking a deep breath she began with the first song that came into her head. "*I can't get no...satisfaction...I can't get no...*"

Ruby stopped crying. Her damp head sagged into the hollow of
Emma's throat. Scarcely daring to move, Emma kept on singing.
"...*though I try...*"

Ruby's mouth had found the collar of the borrowed nightshirt.
Getting her gums around its edge, she began to chomp contentedly.

J.D. shot her a glance over his shoulder. "What the hell kind of
song is that?"

"It seems to be Ruby's kind of song. Maybe she heard it on the
radio in the car."

"There you go again!" He shook his head and went back to
puttering in the cluttered corner that served as a kitchen.

Still singing, Emma eased her baby downward. Ruby whimpered
when she had to let go of the collar but this time, when Emma
offered her the nipple she clamped down and began sucking like a
hungry little piglet.

Emma felt the pull of that tiny mouth all the way down to her
toes. At first it hurt so much that tears welled in her eyes. But as the
seconds passed it became comforting. A slow, warm contentment
crept over her as she gazed down into her daughter's lamplit face—
the eyes blissfully closed, the sweet lips working furiously against
her breast. How could she have even thought of giving her up—
this small, precious person who was so much a part of her? How
could she have chosen not to experience this astonishing love?

The past eight hours had been the most confusing time of
Emma's life. Even now, she wasn't sure where she was or how she'd
come to be here. But she couldn't deny the feeling that she was
here for a reason, and that maybe Ruby was here for a reason, too.
Maybe time would reveal more. For now, at least, she was safe and
warm, with her baby in her arms. It was as much as she dared ask.

Her finger coaxed the damp blond fuzz into a curl. Roused by
her touch the little girl opened her dark blue eyes.

"Happy birthday, Ruby," Emma whispered, "and merry
Christmas."

J.D. gave her a few minutes before he turned around. "I see the
two of you finally figured it out," he said.

"Finally." Emma managed a tired smile. "I don't know how
much nourishment she's getting, but at least she's quiet."

"She'll get what she needs. Trust nature to take care of that." J.D.

picked up the jug from the hearth and twisted out the cork stopper. Emma said nothing as he raised it to his mouth and took a long swig; but her silence was scathing.

"When she's finished eating, you'll need to get the air out of her stomach," he said. "Do you know how to do that?"

She shook her head as he replaced the jug on the hearth. "She seems to be finished now. Why don't you show me?"

Show her how to burp a baby? Where in Sam Hill had this woman been brought up? With a sigh, J.D. walked over to the bed and took the warm bundle from her hands. Ruby gazed up at him from the folds of the red sweater. Her trusting azure eyes could have melted basalt.

"You do it like this." He raised the baby to his shoulder. Her tiny body curled against him. Her toothless gums chomped the salty skin along his collarbone. J.D. battled a surge of tenderness. He'd be damned if he was going to let himself get attached to this little mite.

His hand was big enough to cover her whole back. Gently but firmly he began to pat her. She fussed for a few seconds, then emitted a belch that would've done credit to a muleskinner.

"That's all there is to it." He eased the baby off his shoulder and thrust her back at her mother. "You'll need to do that every time you feed her. Otherwise her stomach won't settle."

Emma cradled the baby in her lap. "For a man who never raised a family, you seem to know a lot about children."

"My father died when I was six. When I was nine, my mother got married again and had four more babies. I did my share of tending and then some."

"Not me." Emma gazed down at the little girl as if she'd just unwrapped her first Christmas doll. "It was only me and my mother, the whole time. I've never taken care of a baby before. I'm going to need some lessons from you."

"What's to learn? If she's hungry you feed her. If she's dirty, you wash her. If she's sleepy you put her to bed. And speaking of bed..." J.D. covered a yawn.

She looked startled. J.D. wouldn't have minded the idea of what she was likely thinking, but he knew it wasn't practical. He'd built his bed extra long but it wasn't wide enough for two adults and a baby.

"Don't worry, I'm not going to crawl in with you," he said. "I'll be fine in the rocker. Heaven knows I've bunked in worse spots."

"I'm sorry about taking your bed," she apologized. "I'll be out of your way as soon as I can."

J.D. was tempted to ask her how she planned to manage that. But it was well past midnight and they were both punchy with exhaustion. "That's fine," he said. "Now let's all get some sleep."

Without giving her time to bring up anything else, he snuffed out the lamp. The embers in the fireplace gave enough light for him to find his way to the rocker. J.D. moved her damp clothes out of the way and sank into it, working off his boots so he could rest his stocking feet on the hearth.

In the darkness he could hear the whispery rush of Emma's breath, in and out. Lordy, but he loved the sound of a woman breathing in the night. There was something about it, so soft and feminine and comforting. It had been far too long since he'd had the chance to listen.

Slumping into the hard pine chair, J.D. leaned back, closed his eyes and let her sweet rhythm lull him into sleep.

# CHAPTER FIVE

Emma awoke to the tantalizing aromas of bacon and fresh coffee. Raising her head, she could see J.D. crouched before the fireplace, tending an iron skillet that rested on the grate above the coals. This morning he wore faded denims over his long johns, with leather suspenders that crossed between his broad shoulders.

He glanced up as Ruby began to fuss. "Good morning," he said.

Emma stirred and stretched. She was sore and sticky and her swollen breasts felt as big as watermelons. She probably looked even worse than she felt. "Good morning," she mumbled. "I hope you got some sleep."

At the sound of voices, Ruby began to howl. She'd slept through the night, thank heaven, but now it was time to let the world know she had urgent needs.

"First things first." Emma pulled the sheet over her shoulder and unbuttoned the nightshirt. The baby rooted for the nipple and clamped onto it, making happy little chomping sounds as she fed. Emma could feel each tug of the small, strong mouth as a contraction, low in her body. She was feeling something else, as well—something totally and shockingly unexpected.

As J.D. squatted by the hearth, turning the bacon in the skillet, his posture stretched his blue jeans across his hips, giving Emma a view of his lean, taut rear end. The heat rose in her face as she imagined slipping up behind him, trapping him with her arms and rubbing her body against those hard buttocks until she went off like a Roman candle.

Good grief, what was the matter with her? Enjoying the sight of a nice, firm butt was one thing. But she was ready to rip those jeans off the man with her bare hands. It had never occurred to her that nursing a baby could heighten her libido.

Not that it mattered. She'd just given birth, and she was a mess.

Seduction was *not* on her agenda. It wasn't even at the bottom of the list.

She cleared the thickness from her throat. "Coffee smells good. I've got quite an appetite this morning."

"I figured you might have," he said, straightening to his full height. "Sorry, there's not an egg to be had between here and South Pass City. But I've got flapjack batter mixed. Soon as the bacon's done I'll fry some up for you."

"Thank you—and Merry Christmas, J.D."

He quirked one black eyebrow. "So it is," he said in a flat voice. "Soon as you're fed, I plan to snowshoe down the trail to town and see what I can scrounge up for you and the baby. Can't promise what I'll find, but you're going to need some cloth for diapers and for wrapping, and some kind of box for a cradle. We'll just have to make do."

"Thank you again." Fumbling beneath the sheet, Emma switched Ruby to her other breast. The soreness made her wince, but it soon eased. "I know you didn't plan on taking us in. I'll try not to impose on you any longer than I have to."

"Do you have a place to go? Friends? Family?"

The question hung over Emma, its implications threatening to crush her. Had anybody back in Lander missed her? Would anybody be looking? The couple who'd planned to adopt her baby wouldn't be expecting her at the hospital for another week. The few friends she had were accustomed to her wandering off without telling them. Unless her car had been found, no one would even realize she was missing.

And even if they knew, where would they look? How would they find her when she seemed to have fallen off the map? For all she knew, she could be over the rainbow, in the land of flying monkeys and broom-riding witches—and her without a pair of ruby slippers to her name.

"For now, I seem to have lost my bearings," she replied to his question. "But once I'm on my feet, I'll manage fine. If nobody comes for me I can always get a job. Surely some little town can use a teacher, or maybe a waitress—I got pretty good at juggling plates while I was in college."

Clearly unimpressed, J.D. shook his head. "Give it some time,

Emma. It's cold enough to freeze hell out there, and you just had a baby. Take care of your little girl, get your strength back and give things a chance to work themselves out. True, I didn't invite you here. But I'm not the kind of man who'd throw a woman and a newborn baby out in the snow."

"That's reassuring. But I won't mooch off your hospitality. I mean to repay you as soon as I can."

"You can do that by leveling with me." He scooped the cooked bacon into a pie tin and poured a dollop of flapjack batter into the sizzling grease. "You've been talking in circles ever since you walked through that door. I want the straight story, the whole story—who you are, where you came from and what you're doing here."

"Fine. You'll get it as soon as I figure it out for myself. That may take a little time."

He shot her a sharp glance. "All right. But don't take too long. I'm apt to lose my patience, and when I do, I can get downright testy. It's not something a lady would want to see." He worked a fork under the edge of the flapjack and turned it over. While the second side cooked he filled a mug with hot coffee.

Ruby had finished her meal and was examining her fist. Emma rearranged her bra and lifted the baby to her shoulder. The belch came easily, but the red sweater that served as a blanket was wet through. Ruby's bladder seemed to be as healthy as the rest of her. Emma sighed. What she wouldn't give for a carton of newborn-sized Pampers!

"Here." As if he'd read her mind, J.D. tossed her a piece of clean flour sacking. "You'll have to tie it on her for now. With luck, maybe one of the girls in town will have a pin."

Emma put her daughter on the bed, tucked the sacking around her bottom and managed to knot the corners. As she remembered hearing, the only "girls" in town worked in the saloon. Given J.D.'s reputation as a ladies' man he probably knew them well, in ways she didn't even want to think about.

But never mind. If one of them could come up with a safety pin, then bless her heart!

J.D. had slid the flapjack onto the pie plate and drizzled a little honey on top. After arranging the plate, the coffee and a single fork onto a battered tin tray, he carried it to the bed and placed it on

Emma's lap. The bacon was slightly charred, the flapjack probably laced with enough cholesterol to put Lance Armstrong into cardiac arrest, but it smelled wonderful.

"Thank you. I don't recall that anyone's ever brought me breakfast in bed before."

"Not even your mother?"

Emma shook her head. "More often than not, I did it for her. Coffee, at least."

"She was an invalid?"

"She was addicted to pills and alcohol. Eventually they killed her."

"I'm sorry."

"So am I. Especially now." Emma glanced down at Ruby. Her daughter had kicked the folds of the sweater aside and was testing her legs, flexing and stretching them like a little swimmer.

J.D. buttoned a wool shirt over his long johns, shrugged into a heavy sheepskin coat and lifted his rifle off the rack above the door. "Just put the tray on the floor when you're done. If there's anything left over the cat will finish it. I'll take care of the rest when I get back." He tugged on leather gloves and picked up the snowshoes. "The thunder mug's under the bed and it's empty. Use it. You're not in any shape to make it outside to the privy, let alone make it back. Hear?"

"I hear." Was this the sort of conversation he usually had with a woman? Emma had expected J.D. McNulty to be a charmer. That notion had flown the way of her modesty. "Don't worry about us," she added. "We'll be right here."

"Fine. Bolt the door when you're able to get up. If you need rags, there's a box of those under the bed, too. I'll try not to be too long." He stepped out the door and closed it behind him. Emma could hear the faint thud of wood on wood as he strapped his snowshoes onto his boots. Then there was nothing outside but winter silence.

Without J.D.'s presence, the cabin seemed larger and much quieter. While Ruby dozed, Emma attacked her breakfast, leaving some flapjack and a few bites of bacon for the cat. The coffee was strong enough to eat the enamel off her teeth, but she drank it all. It shocked her fully awake, filling her with a restless energy.

J.D. would be gone for a couple of hours, at least. His absence would give her the chance to go through every inch of the cabin. If the place—and the man—weren't what they appeared to be, she needed to know. Her very life, and Ruby's, could depend on it.

She sat up and eased her legs over the side of the mattress. Her slack belly fell into her lap like a lump of dough. Maybe those black stretch pants were going to fit her after all.

The thunder mug J.D. had mentioned was under the bed. It was a two-gallon-sized metal pot, finished inside and out with white enamel. Emma was grateful to find it. J.D. had been right about one thing. She was in no condition to make it outside to the privy, or anywhere else for that matter. And she was glad he'd told her about the box of rags. Both she and Ruby were going to need them.

She took a few minutes to arrange herself. Then, wincing with every step, she tiptoed across the floor. In one corner, a crude washstand held a mismatched pitcher and basin. Above it, a small, cracked mirror was nailed to the log wall. Avoiding her reflection, Emma poured a little water into the basin, scrubbed her hands with a sliver of soap and splashed her face. What she really needed was a bath, but there was no sign of a tub, or even a washcloth. Personal hygiene didn't seem to be one of J.D.'s priorities—if the man who'd taken her in was truly J.D. McNulty.

Marooned here, in this isolated cabin with a forceful stranger, she'd begun to believe the things he was telling her. But she could be falling into a dangerous trap—dangerous, even if it was only in her mind. Hard, cold reasoning told her that what appeared to be happening was impossible. There had to be a logical explanation. If the answers were here, she was going to find them.

Struggling to organize her thoughts, she made a mental list. One of four possibilities could be true.

1. She was hallucinating.
2. Everything here had been cleverly staged.
3. The man who claimed to be J.D. was a demented hermit.
4. In defiance of all reason, she'd traveled back in time, to the year 1871, and her reluctant host was the real J.D. McNulty.

Emma started by gazing up into the rafters, searching for any place a camera or microphone might be hidden. Seeing nothing,

she checked the walls. The pine logs were solid, the chinks filled
with dried mud that looked to have been in place for years. There
were no wires, no hidden devices, nothing that didn't belong in the
nineteenth century.

Pausing, Emma glanced back to check on her sleeping daughter.
Her pulse lurched.

Curled on the quilt next to Ruby's warm little body was the
bob-tailed cat. As Emma approached, it raised its head and stared
at her with its single golden eye.

Ruby was fine. Clearly the beast hadn't harmed her. But Emma's
protective mother instincts flashed red alert. Backing up, she
fumbled for the iron poker that leaned against the hearth. Raising
it, she edged back toward the bed.

That was when she heard it—a low, breathy rumble that seemed
to vibrate through the whole cabin. The cat was purring, its claws
gently working the fabric of the quilt. Snuggled against its fur and
lulled by the sound, Ruby dreamed away with a milky little smile
on her face.

Still shaking, Emma lowered the poker. She would need to
watch the cat around her baby. But for now, the two of them made
a picture of contentment that tugged at her heart. As long as she
stayed close by, she saw no need to disturb them.

Bracing herself against the cold, she opened the door a crack.
If she could spot vehicle tracks, power lines, a search plane or
helicopter, or even the distant vapor trail of a jet, she would know
she was still in her own century. That would take care of item
number four.

As the opening inched wider, the glare of sunlight on pristine
snow stabbed into her eyes. Emma squinted, inhaling the frigid
air as her pupils shrank against the brightness. The emerging vista
of blazing blue sky, snow-clad mountains and towering pines was
Christmas card perfect. Where the land sloped away she could see
the trail of J.D.'s snowshoes leading down into the canyon. There
was no other sign of human life.

She listened, straining for the sound of searchers. But the winter
silence was so pure, so absolute that it almost hurt her ears. Only
the call of a crow broke the stillness.

Shivering, Emma backed into the cabin and closed the door.

Remembering J.D.'s admonition, she slid the heavy bolt home. No matter what century this was, there could be dangers outside, and she had a baby to protect.

Ruby was still napping. Beside her, the cat opened a watchful eye, then settled into a doze.

Emma laid a fresh log on the fire and resumed her search, starting with the bookshelf. If even one volume had a copyright date later than 1871, she would know that nothing in this cabin was what it appeared to be.

The books were yellowed with age and moisture, their leather spines softened from years of handling. Some of them dated back to the early 1800s, but the most recent copyright she could find was 1862. So far, it seemed, she had wasted her time.

Next she did a careful inspection of the cabin's furnishings. Anything manufactured from plastic, resin or aluminum, or bearing the imprint, *Made in China*, would be a dead giveaway. But even after she'd washed and stacked the breakfast dishes, Emma hadn't found so much as a teaspoon that wasn't consistent with the late 1800s.

She rechecked her mental list. Maybe it was time to cross off number two. The cabin and everything in it appeared to be genuine. As for number three, she'd never given it much weight. A mentally ill recluse, living in the twenty-first century, would be surrounded by a hodge-podge of junk, not well-used antiques. She might as well cross that choice off, too. But before she passed final judgment she would look inside the leather-bound wooden chest where J.D. evidently kept his clothes.

By now Emma's strength was flagging. Her watery knees gave way as she knelt on the rug in front of the chest and raised the lid. The faint aroma of mothballs rose to her nostrils as she gazed at the folded garments. Gooseflesh prickled the back of her neck. If there was anything to find, she sensed, she would find it here.

She would have to remove things carefully and put them back in the same order. If anything was out of place, J.D. would know she'd been snooping. With his penchant for privacy, it was a sure bet he wouldn't be happy about it.

His everyday clothes were on top—a half dozen flannel shirts, a single pair of jeans and a motley assortment of worn-out woolen

socks. Beneath them were two faded sets of long underwear, one
of cotton, the other of scratchy-looking gray wool. Setting these
carefully on the rug, Emma picked up a leather vest—unremarkable
except for two small but distinct pinholes on the left front side.

Her pulse slammed. They were exactly the sort of holes that
would be made by the pin on the back of a badge. J.D. had been
wearing a similar vest, with his marshal's star, in the famous poster
photo—the one that gave her hot flashes every time she looked at it.

Her hands had begun to tremble. But she couldn't stop now.
The vest didn't prove anything. She needed more.

Beneath the vest was a well-made black woolen overcoat, of the
sort that a man might wear to church or to a winter funeral. It
appeared to have had little wear. When Emma checked the pockets
she found a single coin—a copper Indian-head penny, dated 1866.

Refolding the coat she laid it next to the vest. Beneath it, at the
bottom of the trunk, a layer of muslin covered a black suit jacket
with matching trousers and a plain white shirt. The loose ends of a
black string tie emerged from under the shirt's collar.

Something rose in Emma's throat, choking off her breath. She
could swear she'd seen this suit before, seen the shirt, seen the tie.

Could she really be looking at J.D.'s burial clothes, the ones he'd
worn in the infamous coffin portrait?

One thing would tell her for sure. While studying an enlarged
version of the photo, she'd noticed a single mismatched button on
the jacket. It was black like the others, but it was slightly smaller
and had four holes instead of two, as if the original button had
been lost and replaced with the closest thing available.

She stifled a little cry as she found it—the odd button, third
from the top, exactly where it had been in the photograph. It was
final, irrefutable proof, the proof she'd wanted and dreaded with all
her heart. This was J.D.'s suit—the suit that, in her own time, lay
buried under six feet of earth and snow in South Pass City.

With shaking hands, Emma smoothed the fabric of the coat,
preparing to cover it again. She had her evidence. There was no
point in looking for more.

Just then her fingers touched a hard edge. There was something
else in the trunk; and even though she'd told herself not to look,
she knew she had to see what it was.

Reaching under the suit she pulled out a small object bundled in a white silk shawl. Unwrapping it, she found herself gazing at a silver-framed photograph of a man and a woman.

Dressed for her wedding, the woman was dark, petite and as pretty as a spring violet. Her eyes were large and expressive, her black hair swept up into a nest of curls that anchored her gauzy wedding veil. Over her shoulders she wore a fringed silk gypsy shawl—the same shawl that Emma now held in her hand.

The man beside her was seated, most likely because his towering height would have dwarfed his tiny bride. In the uniform of a Union officer, the younger J.D. was a dazzling figure. Emma could imagine women swooning at his feet. But the expression on his face made it clear that he had eyes only for the delicate beauty he'd married.

Emma turned the frame over. A notation was engraved on the back. *Jethro and Margaret, November 2, 1863.*

Feeling like an intruder, she rewrapped the picture and slipped it back into its hiding place. Only one man would own that photograph and that white silk shawl. The tall stranger who'd taken her in, saved her life and delivered her baby was the real J.D. McNulty. And if he was real, so was everything else.

Emma doubled over, clutching her belly as if she'd just been struck by a cannonball. Her breath emerged in airless gasps as the truth sank home. She was never going to be rescued. She was never going to finish her thesis or go back to her teaching job. She and Ruby were trapped in the year 1871 with a man who was destined to die in less than two months—to die senselessly and miserably, in a barroom brawl over a silly poker game.

And there was nothing she could do about it.

By the time Emma had repacked the trunk, Ruby was awake and fussing. Fleeing the racket, the cat had retreated to the mantel. Emma tottered over to the bed and propped the pillow so she could nurse. She sighed as she slipped beneath the warm quilt. It was a relief to be off her feet.

She settled back into the pillow as her baby found the nipple and began to suck. It was December 25, 1871. There were no cars, no phones, no radios or TVs, no computers and no Seven-Elevens.

If the cabin caught fire, she wouldn't be able to call 911. And if Ruby got sick, there would be no antibiotics to make her well. That prospect alone frightened Emma half to death. How did people survive in these times? The sad truth was, many of them didn't.

In the stillness of the cabin, Emma could hear the ticking of the clock and the little swallowing sounds her daughter made as she drank. Unless some magic whisked them back to the future, Ruby would be a child of the nineteenth century. She would be a young matron when the first airplane took off from Kitty Hawk. If she lived to be a very old woman, she might even watch Neil Armstrong step onto the surface of the moon. But she would never know the frenetic, overcrowded, technology-driven world her mother had left behind.

Maybe that was all right. It might even be best not to tell her about it.

But Emma could make that decision later. For now, her one purpose in life was to take care of her little girl. The future would have to take care of itself.

Ruby had finished nursing. Emma raised the baby to her shoulder and brought up the familiar belch. Then she settled back into the bed. The fire whispered in the fireplace. The aromas of bacon and coffee lingered in the air. The one-eyed cat jumped onto the bed to curl at her feet.

Warm and exhausted, Emma drifted into sleep.

# CHAPTER SIX

The sound of voices jerked Emma out of deep slumber. From outside she heard the snort of a horse, followed by a pounding on the barred door.

"Emma! You in there?" J.D.'s voice boomed through the heavy planks.

She mumbled an incoherent reply and staggered to her feet. Tucked next to the pillow, Ruby began to fuss.

"Slide back the bolt and let us in!"

*Us?* The word penetrated her foggy brain as she worked the stubborn bolt. Had the wretched man brought company? She imagined his bewhiskered cronies swilling whiskey around the fire. That was the last thing she needed today.

The bolt clattered free. The door swung open. The cat squeezed past Emma and raced around the corner of the cabin, keeping to the shelter of the eave where the snow wasn't so deep.

Beyond the porch, a brown horse, wearing loaded canvas panniers, stood in the trampled snow. J.D. was helping a cloak-wrapped figure down from the saddle—the figure of a woman with a bulging carpet bag.

Hidden by her dark blue cloak, she appeared to be short and sturdily built. Only after she'd stepped to the ground and flung back her hood did Emma get a better look. The first thing to capture her gaze was the woman's hair—a garish shade of vermilion that Nature might have saved for some tropical bird. Styled in cascading ringlets and miniature sausage curls, it was almost certainly a wig. Below the hair, the lavishly made up face was plump, middle-aged and unremarkable except for the eyes. They were a startling absinthe green, their hue so intense that if this had been the twenty-first century Emma would have assumed she was wearing contact lenses. They were outlined in kohl like the eyes of a Hindu goddess.

Those eyes looked Emma up and down. The rouged lips pursed

and spoke. "Goodness, my dear, what are you doing out of bed? Mame is here to see that you behave yourself." Mounting the porch she ushered Emma back inside and closed the door. "While J.D.'s unloading the horse, you and I can get acquainted. I can't wait to see that baby girl of yours!"

It would be a waste of breath, Emma decided, to explain that she'd gotten up to unbolt the door. She was already being guided firmly back to bed. If memory served, Mame was the proprietor of the local saloon and brothel. She certainly looked the part. But she had a kind manner and she'd come a long way up the snowy trail to help. This was no time to be judgmental.

Mame draped her cloak over the back of the rocker. The dress beneath was of plain dark worsted, cut to accommodate her immense bosom. Beneath it, the mother of all corsets cinched her ample body to spider-like proportions. A silver brooch, its design resembling an intricate Celtic knot, was pinned over her left breast.

"Why, there's the pretty girl now! May I?" She'd spotted Ruby next to the pillow. As her plump hands reached out, she paused to glance at Emma, as if waiting for permission. Emma nodded.

"Oh, my, just look at her!" Mame scooped Ruby up from the mattress, carefully supporting her head. Ruby stopped fussing to stare up at her in fascination. "Isn't she the most precious little thing? It's been such a long time since I've held a baby in my arms. You forget how tiny they are, and how innocent." Her odd green eyes seemed to mist for a moment. Then she laughed. "I can't believe that big lummox J.D. delivered her! It's a wonder he didn't pass out cold!"

"I was worried about that myself," Emma said. "But he's actually been a lot of help. I'm afraid I don't know anything about babies."

"So J.D. told me. He said you'd made plans to put her up for adoption."

Emma eased her body lower in the bed. "That was before I held her. Now I'd fight an army of wildcats to keep her. Do you have children, Mame?"

"Not me, dearie. But I've learned a few things about birthing and babies over the years. That's why I said I'd come when J.D. asked me. I don't suppose he knew enough to knead your stomach, did he?"

"What?" Emma's head shot off the pillow.

Mame sighed. "I thought as much. Lie back and I'll put your little one next to you. This is bound to hurt a bit but it needs doing—best while J.D.'s still outside. I asked him to give us a little time. Men can be so squeamish."

With growing trepidation, Emma settled Ruby beside her and watched as Mame rummaged in the rag box and came up with an old plaid shirt. "Just try to relax, dear. This won't take long." She pulled the covers down and wadded the flannel layers beneath Emma's hips. Then she placed her palms on Emma's slack belly. "We need to get rid of the blood clots inside you. Otherwise they could fester and make you sick. This will help you get your figure back, too. That's always good for a woman, especially when she's got a man around."

"But he isn't—*oh!*" Emma yelped as Mame's strong hands pumped into her flesh. The contraction they triggered was excruciating. She felt a gush.

"It's fine if you scream," Mame said. "But if J.D. hears you, he's liable to come charging in. The man's right protective of you and that little one. To hear him talk you'd think he'd planted the seed himself!"

Emma tried to ignore the heat that scalded her face. Her own impression was that that she and the baby were nothing but a bother to J.D. If he felt differently, he certainly hadn't shown it. She braced herself as Mame repositioned her hands. "You sound as if you know J.D. pretty well," she said.

"Oh, we're old pals. Three years ago, when he'd had a good run at the tables, J.D. lent me the cash to buy the Laughing Lady. I had to stiff him when the gold played out here, but he never held it against me. Why, I'd cut off my arm for the man!"

Mame shoved her fists into Emma's flaccid belly like a baker kneading a lump of dough. Emma swallowed a scream. What if this was the wrong thing to do? What if it was some barbaric practice that had gone out of fashion with the dawn of the twentieth century?

She felt another gush, then a sense of release as she fell back onto the pillow with a moan. Contractions rippled through her body. Her insides felt as if they'd been trampled by a herd of buffalo.

"That should do nicely." Mame reached into her bag and pulled out a roll of winding strips. With these, she wrapped Emma's hips and belly. Then she sponged Emma's legs and replaced the flannel pad. Finally she helped her into a clean muslin nightgown and sat her in the rocker to nurse Ruby while the bedding was changed.

"I feel almost human again," Emma sighed as she settled back onto fresh sheets. "I don't know how to thank you, Mame."

"You can thank me by doing the same for some other poor girl who needs tending to. That's the only way we women survive in this country, by sticking together." Mame rummaged in her bag and came up with a rosewood-backed oval brush. Moving to the bedside again, she began stroking Emma's tangled hair back from her face. It felt heavenly.

"What lovely, thick hair you have," she chatted. "Mine's hopeless. That's why I wear this silly wig. But yours will be beautiful when it grows out. If you're still here, the girls and I can show you some ways to style it."

It struck Emma as odd that Mame hadn't questioned her shoulder-length bob and strange-looking underthings, or anything else about where she'd come from and how she'd arrived here. But then, J.D. had probably told her what to expect. In any case, if the woman was an old friend of J.D.'s this might be her one chance to learn more about him.

"J.D.'s something of a puzzle," she ventured. "Does he talk much about his past?"

"What has he told you?" The brush strokes paused.

"When I asked him about family he said that his wife had died. But that was all he'd tell me. And when I mentioned Laramie, he closed up like Fort Knox."

"You've already heard more than he'd tell most folks." Mame resumed brushing. "J.D. keeps things to himself, and he doesn't welcome prying. But I can't help thinking you and your little one could be good for him. A man who's alone too much tends to get dark and gloomy. He loses interest in living. After a while he gets plain tired of it."

The newspaper account of J.D.'s death played through Emma's mind like a scene from a silent movie. Maybe that's how it had happened—or would happen. A man wearied of life, unarmed and refusing to back down, almost inviting the gambler to kill him.

Did she have the power to change anything in the time that remained, or was history a thing carved in stone, unchangeable even while it unfolded? She bit back the urge to confide in the woman. Given Mame's profession, she'd likely heard her share of wild tales. But Emma's story was one she would never believe.

"Hey, in there!" J.D.'s gravelly baritone rumbled through the closed door. "How long are you two going to make me stand out here and freeze? If somebody's not decent, I'll just close my blasted eyes!"

"Keep your britches on, McNulty!" Mame bustled to open the door. Her easy manner with J.D. triggered more questions. Mame could have been a seductive woman in her younger days. Had these two been more than friends? Would it be Mame who was destined to cradle the dying J.D. in her arms? The newspaper article had mentioned an unnamed "girl," but in a saloon setting, that word could refer to almost any female.

The door swung open and J.D. stormed in, followed by the cat, which made a beeline for the hearth. J.D.'s battered felt Stetson and sheepskin coat were dusted with snow. His arms lugged the loaded panniers he'd taken from the horse. Staggering a little under their weight, he dropped them in the middle of the floor. "Merry Christmas!" he growled.

His presence seemed to shrink everything in the cabin. Shrugging out of his coat, he hung it by the door, along with his hat. Then, reaching for the jug, he twisted out the cork. His throat rippled as he took a long swallow. "That's better," he muttered, licking his lips as he lowered the jug. "It's cold enough to freeze hell out there!"

Mame had filled a kettle from the water bucket and set it on the grate over the fire. Purring now, the cat jumped down from the hearth to rub against her skirts.

J.D. raised one sooty eyebrow. "Your cat, Mame?"

She reached down and scratched the scruffy head. "He's nobody's cat. I've fed him a few scraps from the kitchen, that's all. The girls tried to make a pet of him but he disappeared. I was wondering where he'd gone to."

"He's not bad company." J.D. sank into the rocker with his boots dripping snowmelt on the hearth. "Lives on mice and scraps. Goes outside to do his business. And he doesn't try to talk my ear off or reform my bad habits. What more could a man ask?" His eyes flickered toward Emma. Was that a twinkle she'd glimpsed in their cerulean depths? Impossible she told herself. J.D.'s legendary charm was just that, a legend. The real J.D. McNulty was an irascible, hard-drinking curmudgeon. If she ever got the chance to finish her thesis she would make that fact known.

But what was she thinking? Her thesis, if it even existed, was lost in the year 2010, somewhere between her computer and a bookstore in South Pass City.

"Why don't you show Emma what we brought from town?" Mame suggested.

"It's mostly woman things. Better you do it. Besides, I lugged them off the horse and brought them in here." J.D.'s fingers fumbled for a cheroot. Then, as if in recollection of what Emma had told him about smoke, his hand dropped to his knee.

"Men!" Mame shook her head. Finding the wooden whiskey crate that served as an extra seat, she settled next to the panniers and began pulling out their contents.

First to emerge was a stack of faded flannel and calico pieces, freshly torn to diaper size. Attached to one of them was an honest-to-goodness treasure—a rusty, thumb-sized safety pin. A murmured "*oh*" rose in Emma's throat. In this place where possessions were few and precious, the residents of Glory Gulch had combined their scant resources to help a needy mother and her newborn. There were no baby clothes, but there were larger flannel pieces for receiving blankets (was that what they were called?) and some odds and ends of toweling. How many people had sacrificed their shirts, sheets and nightgowns for the sake of her baby?

But there was more.

"J.D. said that Ella Rose was about your size. These are her spares." Mame upended the second pannier and dumped out a tangle of women's clothes. One by one she held them up for Emma's inspection.

There were three pairs of dingy-looking, open-bottomed drawers, a threadbare chemise and a petticoat with a ruffled hem, as well as some cotton stockings with garters and two faded calico housedresses. At the bottom of the pile was a yellowed satin corset. "Granted, it's had a little wear, but the busk is genuine whalebone, real quality," Mame announced, dangling the garment for display. Emma could have sworn she heard J.D. snicker, but his face remained as impassive as marble.

As a historian, Emma was familiar with the clothing of the period and knew what to expect. But knowing was one thing. Wearing was another. Bulky underthings without an iota of spandex? Ground-dragging petticoats and rib-crushing stays? They were going to be miserable. As for what those drawers had been through—no, she didn't even want to think about it.

But beggars couldn't be choosers. She was helpless and destitute, totally dependent on the charity of others. Until she found a way to support herself and Ruby, she could only accept the gifts and be thankful.

"These are from my other girls, Angel and Petunia." Mame opened a washed flour sack and dumped out its contents—a comb and brush, some hairpins, a red ribbon and a bar of lavender scented soap.

Emma accepted them gratefully, knowing they were precious. But what she really missed was a toothbrush and some toothpaste. Her mouth tasted like stale garbage and probably smelled worse. Alas, according to a bit of trivia she'd read, toothbrushes hadn't been—or wouldn't be—mass-produced in America until 1885. She had more than a decade to wait. Meanwhile she would have to make do with a stick and some baking soda, or whatever it was people used in this place.

A hiss of steam announced that the water in the kettle was hot. Mame rose. "How would Miss Ruby like a nice warm bath? Come on, little lady, let's show Mama how it's done."

Taking the kettle off the fire, she mixed hot and cold water in the basin, testing the temperature with her wrist, not her fingers. When it satisfied her, she brought the water for Emma to feel. It was pleasantly lukewarm.

"After her cord drops off, you can put her in the water," Mame said. "She'll like that. But for now we'll just sponge her off." She laid a strip of toweling on the foot of bed and placed the squirming Ruby on it. The makeshift diaper was soaked by now, as was the red sweater that had served as a blanket. How did one go about doing laundry here in the middle of winter? Emma felt like a child herself, newly born into a world where she could barely perform the simplest tasks.

Ruby had yowled when J.D. cleaned her with cold water. But when Mame soaped her head and body and rinsed her with a warm wet cloth, she kicked her tiny legs in a show of pleasure. The next time she needed bathing it would be up to Emma to do it. Right now, even that challenge seemed daunting.

"Mame owns the only bathtub in Glory Gulch." J.D. had wandered over to the kitchen counter, where he appeared to be rubbing something in his hands. "She charges a dollar for a warm bath, fifty cents for a cold one. When you're feeling chipper enough, we'll pay her a visit. You can have yourself a nice soak."

"That would be lovely." Emma didn't have the money for a cold bath, let alone a warm one. Maybe she could sweep the saloon floor to pay for it. She was beginning to understand how homeless people must feel.

Ruby had started to fuss again. "Shush," Mame soothed as she dried her with a towel. "Almost done, little lady. J.D., have you got some bacon grease?"

Reaching under the counter, J.D. handed her a battered Arbuckle coffee tin. Mame dipped her fingertips inside and came up with a dab of grease, which she smeared over Ruby's rosy bottom and thighs. "Best thing ever for keeping the rash away. Strain it through a cloth first. That way the grease won't be so dirty looking."

Emma remembered the flowery lotions the women in Lander dabbed on their babies. Ruby would smell more like a BLT sandwich. But at least the cat didn't seem to mind. It had jumped onto the bed to sniff at her well-lubricated little bum. Mame shooed it away as she doubled a scrap of plaid flannel and folded it into a neat triangle.

Emma watched her sure movements, struggling to remember each step. Today even the simple process of folding a diaper seemed beyond her. And she was still cramping from the rough treatment Mame had given her belly. What if she started hemorrhaging? She remembered the headstones in the old cemeteries, the weathered names of young mothers gone before their time.

Another fear seized her. She saw herself waking up to discover that she was back in the 21<sup>st</sup> century. She imagined groping for her child, her panic mounting as she realized Ruby hadn't returned with her. She and her daughter belonged to different times. The mysterious force that had plucked her out of 2010 could just as easily fling her back again, leaving Ruby marooned in the past.

It could happen tomorrow. It could happen anytime.

Mame had fitted the diaper around Ruby's tiny body. Even folded, the cloth looked too large. J.D. handed her the safety pin, which he'd cleaned and polished. Then he turned away to putter with the fire. Mame held the three overlapping points of the diaper in place, leaving the umbilical cord exposed. "You'd best fasten this yourself," she said, handing Emma the pin. "My eyesight isn't the best, and I don't want to stick her."

"How many times have I told you to get some spectacles, Mame?" J.D. muttered. "Hells bells, is your vanity worth going around half blind?"

"Ignore him, dear," Mame said sweetly. "He goes on like this from time to time."

Emma managed the pin with shaking hands. Ruby looked so small and helpless, lying there on the blanket. She was going to need so much care. If anything went wrong, it was urgent that she have someone prepared to look after her.

"Mame—" Emma reached out and laid a hand on the woman's forearm. She'd expected softness and was surprised at the solid strength beneath her fingertips.

"What is it?" Mame's painted eyes narrowed. Her gaze flickered toward J.D.'s back.

"Just—if anything happens to me, would you take Ruby and find her a good home?"

"What silliness! Nothing's going to happen to you, dear. You're strong and healthy. Everything's fine."

"But you never know. Just in case, I need to know she'll be looked after." Emma kept her voice just above a whisper. "Promise me Mame, please. There's nobody else."

"There's J.D."

"But he won't—" Emma stopped herself. There was no way she dared explain why she couldn't leave her child with J.D. "He's good with her, but he's a man. A little baby needs a woman. You're the only woman I've met here."

"You know what I do for a living, don't you?"

"Yes, and I know you're a good person. I'm not asking you to raise her, just to find her a good family."

Mame reached for the roll of winding strips and began wrapping Ruby's body, first around the belly and under the arms, crossing the shoulders like a little shirt; then down and around the legs. Swaddling bands, Emma realized.

"Babies like being wrapped," Mame said. "It makes them feel secure, so they're less apt to fuss. Ask any Indian mother." She split and knotted the end of the strip, then draped a red flannel blanket around Ruby and laid her in Emma's arms. "Here's your girl, all sweet and tidy. For now, at least."

Ruby lay in the folds of the blanket like the furled heart of a rose. Wisps of golden fuzz framed her translucent face. Her fathomless eyes gazed up at her mother with pure innocence and complete trust.

Emma had never felt so inadequate in her life.

"There's no need for promises," Mame said. "Of course I'd look after her if it came to that. But it won't. I feel it in my bones, and my bones are never wrong."

"I hope that's true." Emma toyed with her daughter's hand, not daring to voice her deepest fear. If she wanted to be accepted by these people, and others, she would be wise to keep her story to herself. There could be no more talk of cell phones and sonograms and computers. She would have to come up with a more plausible explanation for her being here.

J.D. straightened and cleared his throat. Doubtless he'd heard every word of the conversation. "If either of you ladies would like a bite of Christmas Dinner, I can offer you leftover bacon and cold flapjacks," he said.

Mame was stuffing dirty sheets and clothes into one of the panniers. "Not me, thanks. I need to get back to the Laughing Lady. With so many men wanting a bit of Christmas comfort, the girls will be too busy to tend bar." She reached for her cloak and fastened it around her shoulders. "I'll drop your horse off at the livery stable, J.D. And I'll give this laundry to the Chinese folk down by the creek. They'll be glad for the extra work."

J.D. fished in his pocket and came up with some coins. "Here's a little extra to pay them," he said, slipping the money into Mame's carpetbag. "I'll see you out."

"Thanks." She glanced from J.D. to Emma. "Don't depend on this galoot to see that you eat and rest. You take care of yourself, girl. If you need anything, ask him for it and don't take no for an answer. I'll be back to check on you and the little one in the next day or so."

"You're a godsend, Mame. I can't thank you enough." Emma watched the woman bustle out of the cabin. J.D. ambled after her, shutting the door behind him. Ruby had fallen asleep. She lay in a thin ray of sunlight that fell through the window. Her lips made little sucking sounds as she dreamed.

Emma settled the baby against her side. She was tempted to drift off herself. But J.D. would be back inside any minute, and she sensed a confrontation brewing.

The first time he'd tried to back her into a corner, she'd gone into labor. After that, Ruby and Mame had kept the issues between them at bay.

But this time there'd be no stopping him. The legendary lawman would bully and batter her with questions until he was satisfied that he'd learned the truth.

And the truth was the one thing Emma couldn't give him.

# CHAPTER SEVEN

J.D. had found the wooden cartridge box behind the building that had been Glory Gulch's general store. It had been buried by rubble from a collapsing shed and was wet and dirty. But it was the right size and shape to serve as a cradle for little Ruby. It just needed some cleaning up.

He'd carried it under one arm as he led the horse up the trail to the cabin with Mame and the panniers. It had been too muddy to bring into the cabin. Now, with Mame headed down the trail, he bent to cleaning it with a scrub brush and handfuls of snow. Left on the hearth to dry, it could be usable by tonight.

When the mud had been cleaned off to his satisfaction, J.D. picked up the box and rapped on the door. In the past twelve hours his whole quiet bachelor existence had been turned upside down. It was time he found out why.

Last night, when he'd questioned her, Emma Carlyle had spouted a line of gibberish that would put Jules Verne to shame. J.D. had chalked it up to the bump on her head. This morning she seemed better. Maybe now she'd be able to give him some rational answers.

Picking up the box, he reached for the latch. He was just opening the door when he remembered the new rules for entering his own cabin. Closing the door again, he rapped lightly on the planks. "Emma?"

"Come in,"

J.D. opened the door, stepped inside and closed it behind him. Emma was sitting up against the pillows with Ruby snuggled against her side and the cat curled at her feet. Even last night he'd conceded she was a good-looking woman. Now, in that clean white nightgown with her taffy-colored hair brushed back from her face she looked downright fetching. Her skin glowed in the flickering firelight. Tiny reflected flames danced in the depths of her sarsaparilla eyes.

J.D. swallowed the tightness in his throat. She wasn't his woman, he reminded himself. And the little mite beside her wasn't his baby. Like the cat and most other things in his life, they were just passing through. He knew better than to get attached to them.

He held up the box. "I found a cradle for Miss Ruby," he said. "Once it's dried out, it should do her fine."

A smile lit her heart-shaped face. "Thank you, J.D. I've worried about crushing her in my sleep. Now I'll rest better, and she'll be safe."

J.D. set the box end-up on the hearth where the heat would dry the inside. "Feeling better?" he asked.

"Much. Your friend Mame did wonders for me. And the things she brought..." Her throat choked with emotion. "I never knew there was so much kindness in the world."

"Most folks are decent at heart," J.D. drew the wooden crate up beside the bed and lowered his haunches onto it. "The trick lies in knowing which ones aren't."

The baby stirred in her sleep, wrinkling her little puckered face. Emma smiled down at her. The woman had a lovely mouth. But this was no time to wonder how those ripe lips would taste.

"Feel up to answering a few questions?" He fixed her with his lawman's gaze.

"I did promise you answers, didn't I?" She was too charming, too compliant, probably getting ready to lie through her pretty teeth.

"All I want is the basics," he said. "Who you are, where you came from and how you got here. And no gibberish, understand? Just plain English will be fine."

She hesitated, her eyes studying the pattern on the patchwork quilt—not a good sign by any measure.

"I'm waiting," he said.

"I'll try. But the thing is, there's a lot I don't remember. I think I must've stepped off the edge of the road and tumbled down the slope. That's how I hit my head."

"What were you doing on the road in a storm? It's not like you fell out of the blasted sky."

She looked confused. "I'm sorry, but that's exactly what it felt like. Falling out of the sky. I woke up in the snow, climbed back to the road and found my way here. That's all I remember."

J.D. chewed at the edge of his moustache. It didn't take a genius to know she was hiding something. Her memory loss was too damned convenient to be believed. If she'd been a man and he'd been wearing his marshal's badge, he might have roughed her up a little. But how was he supposed to pry the truth out of a sweet-face woman with a baby?

"Let's backtrack some," he said, struggling to be patient. "Last night you told me you were a teacher. Is that right?"

"Yes. A history teacher."

"And when I opened the door you recognized me. Had you ever seen me before?"

"Only in photographs. And I'd read about you in the papers. You're a famous man, J.D."

Was she trying to flatter him? Hellfire, fame was the last thing he wanted these days. That was the reason he'd come here.

Something here smelled like moldy fish. The woman knew too much. Maybe she was one of those God-cursed reporters, one who'd taken the trouble to delve into his past by way of old records back east. One who'd take advantage of her condition to insinuate her way into his life.

What kind of woman would risk her baby to find him in a blizzard? He'd get to the bottom of this mess if it took him all night!

She was watching him quietly, her eyes velvet soft in the firelight. Damn her to hell, what was she trying to do? Seduce him?

"You must've been on that road for a reason. How did you know where to find me?" he demanded.

"I didn't. I don't recall that I was even looking for you. I found you by pure happenstance."

And pigs could fly, J.D. thought.

The cat opened a sleepy golden eye, turned in place and resettled itself next to her feet. Cats had good instincts about people. This half-savage creature had taken to Emma like some long lost kin. But that didn't mean he should trust her. The woman wanted something. Everybody did. In her case, he just had to find out what it was.

If she was one of those damned, snooping reporters, she'd be out in the snow as soon as she could walk down the trail.

"Let me get this straight," he said. "You'd read about me, knew my birth date and birthplace from memory, knew about the war wound...and then you stumbled onto my cabin, in the middle of nowhere, by pure *accident*?" He fixed her with a glare that would have turned the likes of John Wesley Hardin to calf's foot jelly. "You're lying, Emma Carlyle. And I'm running out of patience. I want the truth, and I want it now."

His blue eyes blazed into her like bullets. Emma willed herself not to cringe. If any doubts had remained that she was seeing the real J.D. McNulty, those doubts had fled. The man was formidable, and he wasn't acting.

He'd demanded the truth. Maybe the truth was all she had left.

The slow tick of the clock filled the silence. A pine knot sizzled in the fireplace as J.D. waited.

Emma cleared the tightness from her throat. "You'll think I'm crazy," she said.

"Try me, lady."

She took a deep breath and plunged over the precipice. "I know you won't understand this. I don't understand it myself. But until last night I was living in the year 2010—in the future, from your perspective. I got lost in a snowstorm, fell off the road and woke up here, in your time."

"Mmm-hmm." His voice dripped sarcasm. "And that's how you came by those stories about the giant invisible library and the machine that takes pictures of unborn babies?"

"Yes. But I'm not going to talk about those anymore. I'm quite aware that in this time—your time—such things don't exist."

"Well, that's a step in the right direction." His eyes were narrow slits of suspicion. "You said you were writing about me. Are you one of those mud-sucking reporters who's tracked me down to get a story?"

"I'm a teacher. And I was writing a scholarly paper to qualify for my Master's degree at the University of Wyoming. But everything I've written is lost now. I lost it when I traveled through time. In fact, I lost everything except the clothes on my back. And Ruby. She's all that matters now."

He snorted, shaking his head. "You traveled through time? That's the biggest crock of bull I ever heard."

"Yes, I'm sure it is. I couldn't believe it myself, at first. But I know where I was—and I know where I am. I'm here, J.D. That's the one thing neither of us can deny."

He swore under his breath. "But it doesn't make sense!"

"Then what does? Look at my hairstyle. And look at what I was wearing when I got here. A nylon jacket and stretch polyester pants. Those fabrics were made from chemicals, in big factories. They don't exist in this time! And what about the underwear you found me in—what woman in the 1800s would wear underwear like that?"

His mouth twitched at one corner. "I'll confess I kind of liked those skimpy little britches of yours. And that strappy thing that holds up your tits, that's a right clever device. I wouldn't mind getting a better look at it."

Emma sighed. "It's called a bra—a brassiere. And you're getting off track!"

He rose to his feet, looming above the bed. "Let's assume, for the sake of argument, that you're telling the truth. The next question is, what in Sam Hill are you doing here?"

"I don't know."

"*You don't know?*" His soot black eyebrows met above the bridge of his nose.

"You think I sent myself here? It was Christmas Eve and I was driving home from South Pass City. I realized I'd left my briefcase in the bookstore and turned around to go back. The storm came roaring out of nowhere, and here I am."

"But, damn it, there has to be a reason! You were writing about me and you ended up on my doorstep? That's a bit too much of a coincidence for me to swallow."

"I'm sorry, but it's all I can give you. If I was sent here for some purpose, I don't know what it is."

"No, this is too much. I'd be a fool to believe you, and an even bigger fool to trust you." He paced to the window and stared out at the snow, his big hands jammed into his hip pockets. "One of us is crazy, Emma Carlyle, and the last time I checked it wasn't me." He swung back to face her. "You say you're from the future and you know everything about me."

"Not everything. I was still looking for information. That's the reason I went to South Pass City."

"But you had access to the basics. When and where I was born, my military record, my time as a lawman, my—" The words broke off abruptly. He swung around, his eyes drilling into hers.

That was when she knew he'd guessed the truth.

If Emma was really from the future, she would know the time and circumstances of his death.

Would he ask her? Would he demand to know?

Would telling him make any difference in the outcome?

She watched, trying to second-guess the emotions that flickered across his face. Doubt? Uncertainty? A hint of resignation? At last he turned away, walked toward the fireplace and picked up the whiskey jug. She watched as he twisted out the cork and took a prolonged swallow.

Ruby had awakened and started to fuss. Pulling the quilt over her shoulder, Emma unbuttoned her nightgown, worked down her bra strap and put the baby to her breast. She sank back onto the pillow as the sweet sucking sensations trickled through her body. Her womb contracted, clenching like a fist. The cat stood up, stretched and padded over to the hearth.

J.D. jammed the cork stopper back into the jug. Behind him, he could hear the little rooting sounds the baby made as she nursed. They triggered forbidden images of Emma's swollen breasts, their warm satiny texture, like loaves of risen bread, the dark, puckered nipples. He could almost imagine burying his face between them, pressing his lips into the damp hollow, filling his senses with her sweet-hot woman smell, and then...

*Damn!*

He was almost beginning to accept her craziness. The idea that she'd traveled back in time had to be pure balderdash. But nothing else made sense. Emma's clothes, her hairstyle, her stories of fabulous machines that beggared the imagination—they hadn't come from nowhere. It was as if every piece of the puzzle that was Emma Carlyle had fallen into place. But the picture they made was too frightening to be believed.

A person from the future, especially a teacher of history, would know what had happened in the past. Emma had studied his life, all of it, including when and how that life would end.

Something in those earnest light brown eyes of hers told him she knew—and that it wasn't far off.

What if he were to ask her—to seize her by the shoulders and demand the truth? Would she tell him? Would he want her to?

J.D. reached down to stroke the cat. Its back was bony beneath the thick winter fur. The creature was getting old, and so was he. Forty-four was ancient for a man who'd lived by the gun. By then the reflexes were slowing, the senses were dulling, and arthritis was seeping into lightning quick fingers. If the end was near, what of it? He wouldn't care. Even if Emma could tell him, he'd just as soon not know the time and circumstances. Let death sneak up on him, the way it did on most folks. That was nature's way.

But what in holy hell was he thinking? Emma Carlyle was either a lunatic or a charlatan with an extremely vivid imagination. She'd read a few things about him and blown them up into a story. He'd be a fool to be taken in by her medicine-show babble.

Wandering over to the kitchen, he laid the leftover flapjacks and bacon in the big iron skillet. Emma needed to eat. The least he could do was warm the food.

"Coffee?" he asked her.

"Please. And not too strong."

J.D. watered down the tarry brew in the pot and set it on the grate. Whatever the circumstances, it was Christmas Day, little Ruby's first and possibly his last. Maybe it wasn't too late to make a celebration of it.

Crossing to the door, he shrugged into his coat. "I'm going out for a bit," he said. "I'll be back by the time the food's warm."

Emma shifted Ruby to her other breast and sank back into the pillows. She'd lost track of the day, and she couldn't see the clock, but the slant of sun through the window told her it must be late afternoon. She'd be wise to rest while she could. The days ahead would be exhausting and filled with uncertainty. She couldn't continue to impose on J.D. Sooner or later she'd have to strike out on her own, starting with a place to live and a respectable job. Respectable would likely mean that she'd have to leave Glory

Gulch. So many needs and so few resources. How on earth was she going to manage?

The cat had jumped back onto the bed. Now it walked up along her legs to investigate Ruby's little feeding noises. Cocking its scruffy head, it edged closer until Emma nudged it away. "Shoo! You've got your own dinner!"

The cat jumped down and padded over to the fireplace, where the flapjacks, bacon and coffee sat warming on the grate. The food was beginning to smell good, and Emma realized she was ravenous. The fact that she'd be eating breakfast leftovers hadn't dulled her appetite in the least.

Ruby spat out the nipple with a gassy little belch. Emma raised the tiny girl to her shoulder and patted away the rest of the air bubble. As a mother, she had a lot to learn, but at least she'd mastered feeding and burping.

But her daughter was about to give her another lesson. Her little doll face wrinkled and reddened . There was faint bubbling sound from the region of her diaper. An aromatic cloud rose around her. Emma groaned. At least Ruby's bowels were as healthy as the rest of her. Just her luck it would happen for the first time when J.D. wasn't around to help.

Rummaging through the rags, she found a piece of clean toweling and spread it on the quilt. Then she gathered a cup of water, a flannel washcloth and the tin of bacon grease. The diaper and washcloth would need to be scrubbed clean by hand. Heavens to Betsy, what she wouldn't give for a packet of baby wipes!

She was in the middle of the job when J.D. rapped on the door. "Come in!" Emma snapped as she struggled to keep Ruby's kicking feet clear of the mess. The door swung open, and J.D. staggered in with a small, freshly cut pine tree and a bucket.

"Good Lord!" He sniffed the air. "Smells like somebody turned a skunk loose in here."

"Very funny. What am I supposed to do with this?" She wadded the soiled diaper and held it up.

"Here." He held out the empty bucket. "I brought it in for the tree, but there seems to be a more urgent need for it."

"You brought us a Christmas tree!" Emma gazed at the bushy little pine that J.D. had set against the bookshelf.

"It's for Ruby." His face was ruddy with cold. "I figured this being her first Christmas, we shouldn't let it pass without some kind of celebration."

"You're full of surprises, J.D. McNulty." Emma dropped the diaper into the bucket. How long had it been since she'd had a real Christmas tree? The one at her house in Lander was made out of plastic and wire. Most years she didn't even take it out of the box.

She finished diapering Ruby while J.D. set the bucket on the stoop. With the diaper mess gone, the tree smelled heavenly. It filled the whole cabin with the scent of Christmas.

J.D. set the tree in the far corner and propped it up with a few firewood logs. The bucket might have made a better stand, but the logs worked well enough. After all, the tree wouldn't be inside for more than a day or two. But what would they do for decorations?

The wooden box J.D. had found for Ruby's bed was already dry. Lined with soft rags and a folded piece of flannel blanket, it made a sturdy cradle. When Emma laid Ruby in it, fresh and clean once more, she fussed for a few seconds and promptly went to sleep.

"Now for Christmas dinner!" J.D. stacked the flapjacks and bacon onto Emma's plate and filled a mug with coffee. The bacon was burnt, the flapjacks were stale and the coffee tasted like watered-down turpentine, but Emma wolfed it down. She was hungry, and beggars couldn't be choosers.

Was J.D. going to grill her again? Emma waited, bracing herself for another barrage of questions. It didn't come.

J.D. ate in silence, seated in the rocker next to the fireplace. Emma sat propped against the pillows, studying him furtively over her plate. She'd told him as much as she dared. The question was, did he believe her?

Light from the glowing fire cast his rugged features into stark relief. Thoughts seemed to flicker across his face, reflected in shifting lines and shadows. J.D. was a highly intelligent man, and she'd given him plenty to think about. If she could peer into his mind, she'd likely see it working like an efficient machine, sorting facts, weighing each piece of evidence, discarding anything that rang false.

Would he dismiss her as a harmless lunatic? Or would J.D.

accept the unacceptable—that she'd come here from a future time, knowing things that no one on earth had the right to know?

Outside the window, the sky glowed with the first rays of winter sunset. The fragrance of pine drifted into every corner on the cabin. Emma inhaled, filling her senses with its sweetness. Nothing was going to be resolved tonight, she told herself. It was Christmas, and there was a new life to celebrate.

Finishing her dinner she set her plate and mug on the bedside table. "That's a right fine tree," she declared in a voice loud enough to startle him. "But it needs decorating."

He glanced up. "Fine. Any ideas?"

She thought fast. "Do you have anything? Beads? Ribbons? Yarn?"

He shook his head.

"Well, then, let's see..." Her gaze darted around the cabin and came to rest on some old magazines, piled on the bottom row of the bookshelf. Emma's fifth grade teacher, Mrs. Kleppman, had taught her students origami. Emma had loved it at the time. Maybe she could remember a little of what she'd learned.

"Can you spare me a one of those magazines, just a few pages? "she asked.

"Why not? I was only saving them for the privy." He rose, lumbered over to the shelf and tossed her the topmost magazine. "What do you plan to do with it?"

Emma grinned mysteriously. "Magic."

J.D. watched in amazement as Emma's hands worked, folding torn-out magazine pages into intricate little figures. Birds, butterflies, animals and flowers emerged under her fingers. The cat trailed J.D. as he carried each one to the tree and set it carefully on the branches. The makeshift decorations lacked color, but they looked festive in a whimsical way. It took less than a dozen of them to cover the small tree.

"Watch this!" Emma's quick hands fashioned a new and different figure. This one took her only a few seconds. It was wedge-shaped, like an arrowhead, with tapered folds emerging flat on either side. Lifting it above her head, she flung it with a quick motion. Like a darting bird, it sailed the length of the cabin, looped crazily and came to rest at the foot of the tree.

"What in Sam Hill—" J.D. picked it up, studying its simple folds.

"It's an airplane. A toy."

"Do it again." He returned the object to her and watched as she sent it sailing again. He took the precious seconds to study its flight—the way the wings caught the flow of air, the way the slight weight of the folded tip kept it hurtling forward. Bigger, with some kind of lightweight engine to keep it going, J.D. could almost picture it in the sky.

No, damn it. He wasn't going to be taken in by the woman's tricks. It would take more than a silly piece of paper to convince him that Emma Carlyle had come from the future.

Annoyed with himself, he picked up the airplane where it had landed on the floor. Crumpling it in his fist, he tossed it into the fire.

She was staring at him in stunned dismay, her eyes large and liquid in the firelight. J.D. felt as if those eyes could see right through him, all the way to his cowardly, hesitant heart.

"Stop it right now, Emma," he said. "You and your baby are welcome to stay here as long as you need to. But whatever mumbo jumbo it is you're selling, I'm not buying it."

He had wounded her. He could tell from the way her gaze dropped to the tattered magazine in her lap. For the space of a breath she was silent. Then her head came up. Her eyes glittered with proud defiance.

"Fine. I can't blame you for refusing to believe me. That makes everything easier for both of us, doesn't it?"

"Emma—" An apology quivered and died on the tip of his tongue. It would only make things worse.

"There'll be no more questions about where I came from," she said. "If you ask me, I won't answer. I'm me. I'm here. And nothing counts except the present—and Ruby. Understood?"

He scowled, hesitating just to make her squirm. It was his way. "Understood," he said at last. "So now, what do you say we finish our Christmas tree? I just thought of something to brighten it up."

"All right, let's see it." She put the magazine aside and sank back against the pillows. He'd drained her enthusiasm, and part of him, at least, was sorry.

Rummaging on a shelf above the kitchen counter, he found the battered tin canister, shoved to the back and forgotten. Working off the rusty lid, he checked the contents, then walked over to the bed. "Take a look," he said.

She peered in cautiously. "Oh! Peppermint sticks! I love peppermint!"

"Then help yourself." J.D. had never cared for peppermint. The candy was a long-forgotten gift that he'd never bothered to sample. Why he'd even kept it was a mystery.

Abandoning her pique, she took a peppermint stick and sucked on it. Her eyes lit up like a child's. Lord, but she was beautiful when she was delighted.

"In the trailer park—" She stopped herself, then started over. "In the place where I grew up, the woman next door used to pass these out to neighbor children at Christmastime. She always gave me extras. It was one of my best memories."

"I take it other memories weren't so good."

She glanced up at him, her eyes darkening, then, forced a smile. "Don't even ask. It's better that way. And now, Mr. J.D. McNulty, let's get these candy sticks on the tree!"

She eased out of bed and sat in the rocker to supervise while J.D. arranged the peppermint sticks on the branches. Her feet, showing below the hem of the nightgown, were pale and neatly groomed. Still J.D. couldn't help wondering about those flecks of red paint on her toenails. He bit back the urge to mention it. Emma was right about one thing. For now, at least, some questions were better left unasked.

By the time they'd finished it was dark outside and both of them were yawning. The tree looked quaintly festive, its dark green needles contrasting with the red and white peppermint sticks. It was a shame that Ruby, whom the tree was meant to honor, was too young to appreciate it.

Emma leaned back in the rocker and studied the tree. She'd eaten three of the peppermint sticks, and the taste of childhood lingered fresh in her mouth. "It's missing something," she said. "What it needs is a star on top."

J.D. massaged the small of his back with one hand. His eyes were bloodshot, his jaw rough with stubble. He'd had about three hours of sleep since her arrival, and those had been in the rocking chair. Maybe she should give him a turn at the bed. It wouldn't hurt her to sit up for a while.

"Can't you make a star out of paper?" he asked wearily.

"I could try. But it wouldn't look right. A star should be shiny."

He rolled his eyes toward the ceiling. "A shiny star, the lady says! As if I could go outside and pluck one out of the blasted sky!"

Emma giggled. "Oh, never mind. It doesn't—"

"Wait! I've got it!" He bent over the leather-bound chest where he kept his spare clothes. Emma held her breath as he raised the lid. Would he notice that anything had been moved?

J.D. rummaged through layers of clothing until he reached the leather vest, the one with the holes where a badge would have been pinned. When he lifted it clear Emma noticed for the first time that the vest had a small pocket on the right side.

His long fingers fumbled in the pocket. "As I remember, it should be right..." He pulled out a slightly tarnished marshal's badge—a simple silver star. He took a few seconds to polish it on his flannel shirt. "I knew there was a reason I forgot to give this back when I left Laramie. Here's your star, Miss Emma. Made to order."

He fastened the badge to the top of the little tree, using the pin on the back to secure it in place. It was the perfect, crowning touch. Emma clapped softly, not wanting to wake Ruby. It had been a silly venture, setting up a Christmas tree when Christmas was nearly over. But the diversion had released some tension. It had been good for both of them.

J.D. yawned, rubbing the back of his neck and flexing his broad shoulders. "I don't know about you, but I could use some shut-eye."

"You're welcome to the bed," Emma said. "I've been napping half the day."

"You just had a baby. Take the bed. I'll make out fine." He fumbled for a cheroot and opened the door. "I'll be right outside if you need me," he said, stepping out into the darkness.

Ruby was sleeping like an angel in the cartridge box. Emma

took advantage of the privacy J.D. had given her to use the chamber pot and change her padding. Tomorrow Christmas Day would be over, and the rest of her strange, new life would begin. The uncertainties she faced would overwhelm her if she stopped to think about them—where she would live, how she would support herself and her child, how she would keep Ruby safe and healthy. These challenges could be dealt with over time. J.D. McNulty was another matter.

Even before she met J.D., she'd been half in love with the idea of him. But the image on the poster paled next to the man. Every trait the real J.D. possessed came in a giant-sized package—his physical presence, his stubbornness, his temper, his vices, his loyalty, to say nothing of his tenderness and his damnable all-fired sexiness.

Was she falling in love with him?

But she didn't even want to go there. After the way love had kicked her in the teeth, she never wanted to go there again.

Did she want him?

Jumping his bones was an unqualified yes. But right now that was out of the question. Even if it were possible, Emma knew better than to think it would last. Like the one-eyed cat, J.D. wasn't a creature to be kept. He'd given his heart once and tragically lost it. Something in his manner told Emma he had no heart left to give.

But that wasn't the issue here. The issue was his life.

J.D. had rejected her story about traveling through time. He'd made that clear enough when he'd flung the paper airplane into the fireplace. Given that, how could he believe that she knew he was going to die?

Telling him outright would be useless. J.D. would laugh in her face.

And even if he believed her, even if she could stop him from going to the saloon, did she have the power to change history? Did she have the right?

Even if the answer was no, somehow she had to try.

# CHAPTER EIGHT

The tip of J.D.'s cheroot glowed red in the shadows of the overhanging porch. He leaned against the rough log wall of the cabin, closing his eyes as he inhaled the bitter smoke and let it drift out between his lips.

Lord Almighty, what a day it had been. The Christmas he'd planned to ignore had turned into a blasted three-ring circus.

As a former army officer and long-time lawman, being in charge came naturally to him. But newborn babies came into the world giving orders, not taking them. And how in hell's name could he corral and hogtie a woman who insisted she'd traveled here from the future?

As he saw it, he had two choices. He could believe her story or resign himself to the fact that she was crazy. The first choice was more than his rational mind could accept. As for the second—J.D. swore under his breath. Aside from her wild tales, Miss Emma Carlyle seemed as sane as any woman he'd ever met. She was bright, logical, tender and quick with a witty comeback—all traits he found appealing in a woman. And it didn't help that she was as pretty as a ripe plum. Most mentally unstable women he'd known had haggard faces, unkempt hair and haunted eyes. When he pictured Emma, the first thing that came into his head was the notion of kissing those soft, pink lips or cupping those lovely, swollen breasts in his woman-hungry hands and...

*Damn!*

J.D. flung the stub of the cheroot into the darkness, watching as the red dot arced and vanished into the snow. The last real Christmas he remembered was the only one he and Maggie had spent together as man and wife. They'd decorated a beautiful tree and invited friends and family members over for roast goose with all the trimmings. After the feast, everyone had gathered around Maggie's elegant little spinet and sung Christmas carols while she played. The two of them had ended the day nestled in the big armchair in front of the fireplace, surrounded by the happy clutter of the day. That was when she'd told him about the baby.

By the next Christmas Maggie and the baby were gone and he was passed out dead drunk behind a Dodge City saloon.

After that he'd pretty much managed to ignore Christmas. Until this one.

The cabin had gone dark and quiet. Through the window, the tin star on the little Christmas tree caught the glow of the dying firelight.

The tree had been an impulse—a foolish one at best. He'd cut it for Ruby, in the belief that a new life deserved a celebration. But decorating the tree with Emma had stung him with forgotten memories. He'd be glad when they could take the tree down and forget the holiday for another year. For him, Christmas had ended with Maggie.

The waning moon had risen above the peaks. It hung like a silver teardrop in the inky sky. A snowy owl, down from the North, floated like a ghost above the pines. J.D. stirred. It was time to go in and spend another half-sleepless night in the rocking chair. Maybe tonight he'd try the floor instead. It couldn't be any worse.

He opened the door, stepped inside and bolted it softly behind him. Firelight cast the interior of the cabin in a soft amber glow. Emma's paper birds and animals stirred in the lingering draught from the door. The star-shaped marshal's badge glimmered on the top of the tree. There were memories there, too. Memories he'd willed away forever. He should have flung that star into the dust when he rode out of Laramie. After what had happened there, it had made no sense to keep it.

Ruby lay on her back in the cartridge box, her out flung hands balled into tiny fists. Her golden lashes curled darkly against rose petal cheeks. J.D. brushed the downy little head with one callused fingertip. He remembered the slickness of her newborn body, squirming in his hands, the sudden gasp that had been her first breath. His throat tightened. Ruby was probably the closest thing he'd ever have to a child of his own. That didn't mean had any claim on her, of course. But bringing her into the world had been an experience J.D. would never forget, a privilege and a blessing.

Emma had already fallen asleep, curled loosely on her side with her back to the outside wall. Her breathing was a silken sigh in the darkness. J.D. imagined sliding in behind her, fitting his bony frame to her soft curves, his knees spooning her thighs, her ample rump nested against his crotch. He wouldn't even need to make love to her. Just cradling her in his arms, filling his senses with her musky aroma and her little womanly sleep sounds would be enough to send him over the brink of heaven.

J.D. liked women, always had. As far as he was concerned, females were God's gift to a rough, lonely uncivilized world. In the years since Maggie's death, he'd enjoyed them as friends, lovers and even adversaries. But he'd long since given up on the idea of another wife and family. He was no fit husband for any wife, no fit father for any child.

Remembering a task to be done, he slid the chamber pot from its place under the bed, carried it outside and emptied it in the trees beyond the house. The white owl had perched in the top of a scraggly pine. Its eyes followed him as he trudged back to the porch, stomped the snow off his boots and entered the cabin again.

Emma hadn't stirred. J.D. replaced the chamber pot under the bed, eased out of his boots and, after a moment's deliberation, rolled his coat into a pillow and stretched his lanky body in front of the fireplace. In his younger days he'd boasted that he could sleep anywhere. But these days he had less meat on his carcass. The floor felt as hard as granite against his spine and hip bones. It was a good thing he was so tired. Otherwise he might never get to sleep.

The cat prowled the darkened cabin, eyes and ears alert for any mouse foolish enough to venture into sight. J.D. lay awake, listening to the sound of Emma breathing, imagining her in his arms, warm, sexy and healed from the birthing. Even that wasn't enough to help him drift off. Maybe the rocker would been a better choice. Either way, it was going to be a long night.

Emma woke to the sound of Ruby fussing in her box. She sat up. Her nipples were leaking fluid, soaking through the fabric of her bra and her nightgown. Now she knew what nursing pads were for. Too bad she didn't have any.

Still muzzy, she twisted off the mattress, picked up her daughter and lifted her onto the bed. Ruby was wet and hungry. Her bedding was probably soaked, too. Good grief, what time was it? Was this going to happen every night?

Feed her first, that would be the thing to do. Otherwise her crying would wake J.D. She could just make out his long body stretched in front of the fireplace. It couldn't be very comfortable. If he'd managed to get to sleep, the last thing she wanted to do was wake him.

Ruby's gums clamped onto her tender nipple. Emma winced at the soreness, then settled back as the pain eased. Something told her she might as well get used to this routine. It was going to last a long time.

J.D. stirred and sat up. Either he'd been awake or he was a light sleeper. "Everything all right?" he asked.

"Fine. She's just hungry. You can go back to sleep."

"Can't say as it's worth the bother." He stood and stretched, massaging the small of his back with one hand. Sometime in the night he'd taken off his shirt and trousers. He was wearing nothing but his long johns.

"I'm sorry," she said. "We've really got to do something about this sleeping arrangement, or you're never going to get any rest. Maybe we can take turns with the bed."

He muttered something she couldn't quite catch and ambled to the hearth, where he unstoppered the jug and raised it to his lips. After a brief swallow, he lowered it again and wiped his mouth with the back of his hand.

"Do you always drink in the middle of the night?"

"Only when I wake up." He laid a fresh log on the coals, sank into the rocker, rested his bare feet on the hearth and leaned back. Emma finished feeding Ruby on one breast and switched her to the other. The clenching sensation low in her body was painful but not unpleasant, and it was having its usual effect. Thoughts of J.D. in his long johns stole into her mind. She pictured the threadbare holes and the male body she'd glimpsed beneath. How would the man look entirely naked?

The cabin was cool, but she'd begun to sweat. What was wrong with her? She'd just had a baby, and she was a mess! Even if she gave him a blatant invitation, there was no way anything was going to happen between them.

While Ruby nursed, Emma caught herself looking at the bed. It was an odd size—either J.D. had made it himself or someone had made it for him. Its frame was six or seven inches longer than usual, to accommodate his height. But it was the breadth that interested her now. Narrower than a double bed, it was still wider than common twin size. If they lay straight and didn't sprawl, two people could definitely sleep in it. And now that Ruby had a safe little bed of her own...

But what was she thinking? Some things just weren't done.

By the time Ruby finished her midnight snack and burped up the air bubble, J.D.'s head had drooped to one side and he was snoring softly. Glad she hadn't embarrassed him with an invitation, Emma changed her daughter's diaper, wrappings and blankets and laid her gently back in the box.

But Ruby was in no mood to sleep. No sooner had her back touched the blanket than she let loose with a howl that would have done credit to a Wagnerian Valkyrie. The noise sent the cat streaking for the mantel. J.D. snorted and raised his head.

"What the—"

"Sorry. Oh, I'm so sorry." Emma cradled her daughter. Ruby appeared to have startled herself. She was screaming now, and butting her head against Emma's chest.

"Oh, hells bells!" J.D. staggered to his feet. He was wild-haired, wild-eyed and looked plain terrifying. Emma resisted the urge to cringe as he walked toward the bed. "Here," he muttered, reaching out with both hands. "Give her to me."

Emma's eyes widened. Her arms tightened around her precious offspring.

"Blast it, just give her to me," he growled. "I'm not going to hurt her."

Slowly Emma released her hold. J.D.'s huge hands lifted Ruby up to nest against his shoulder. His arms jiggled her lightly as he began to walk with a rolling motion, like a sailor on a deck. He seemed to be singing low, under his breath, but if there were words, only Ruby could hear them.

As seconds passed, Ruby's cries diminished to little hiccuping sobs. She relaxed in J.D.'s arms. Within minutes her head was lolling in sleep. Little by little he shifted onto her back, lowered her into her box and tucked the blanket around her.

"That was amazing," Emma whispered. "How did you do it?"

"Just my way with the ladies. Even works on little ones. Now maybe we can both get some sleep." He turned wearily and walked back toward the rocker.

"J.D."

He turned back to look at her. Emma had shifted to the outside edge of the bed, leaving a space against the wall. She could feel her heart pounding as she spoke.

"I think there's room for both of us in your bed. I'll take this side, since it's closest to Ruby."

For an instant he seemed to freeze. Then an ironic smile tugged at the corners of his mouth. "You have my word I'll be a perfect gentleman."

"You won't have much choice. Just try not to snore."

"Now that I can't promise."

She moved aside to let him climb into the bed. He lay straight against the wall, giving her as much space as his broad shoulders would allow. "Thank you, this beats the floor," he muttered.

"We might as well be practical. After all, it *is* your bed. Goodnight, J.D." She stretched onto her side with her back to him. The bed seemed smaller than she'd estimated. There was no way to sleep without touching. But they were responsible adults, Emma reminded herself. They were more or less decently clothed, both dog tired—and in any case, her condition ruled out any untoward behavior.

*Drat!*

She doubled the thin pillow and closed her eyes. It would've been bliss just to drift off. But every cell in her body tingled with awareness of the big, warm male animal beside her. His unwashed winter long johns smelled of pine smoke, tobacco and good, healthy man sweat. The light contact of his hip against her bottom sent whorls of heat spiraling along her nerves. Nursing Ruby had come with its usual side effects. Emma swallowed a moan. Heaven help her, she'd never felt more awake in her life.

* * *

J.D. lay plastered against the rough log wall. His aching joints and wearied brain cried out for sleep. But one part of his body had other ideas. No sooner had Emma slid into bed than the damn blasted imp between his legs had sprung awake, all perky and ready for play.

J.D. swore silently, struggling to ignore the strain at the crotch of his long johns. If he'd been alone, he might have reached down and taken care of the problem himself. But that sort of behavior wouldn't set well with a lady like Emma—and she *was* a lady. He had no doubt of that.

Now she lay quietly beside him, her round, nightgown-clad bum resting lightly against his hip. Her shallow breathing told him she was still awake, but she clearly meant to mind her own business. He had no choice except to do the same.

Opening his eyes, he stared up into the rafters. To divert his mind, he recited the entire Declaration of Independence, which he'd memorized in fifth grade. Nothing changed, and his thoughts began to wander. He imagined turning on his side and spooning himself against her back, his swollen cock resting against her gloriously plump buttocks, his hand cradling her breasts. Making love to her would be out of the question. But there was a lot to be said for good old fashioned snuggling.

Damn it, he could use a drink. He could use something else, too, but there was no help for it. He couldn't get out of bed, or even turn over, without disturbing her. Time crawled as he lay with his eyes closed and his huge erection tenting the blankets. He could only hope she wouldn't sit up and look. That would scare her out of bed in a hurry.

The clock on the mantel struck two. Emma's breathing had slowed to the dreamy cadence he was coming to love. Lulled by the sound of her, he felt his own tension beginning to ease. He drifted into her warmth, in the sweetness of her milky aroma, deeper and deeper until at last he sank into blessed sleep.

Emma opened her eyes to early dawn. An instant of confusion swept over her. What day was it? Where was she? Then the sound of gentle snoring crept into her senses and she remembered everything.

J.D. lay next to her, his arm flung across her chest. He was sprawled on his side, his bony knees jutting against her legs. His big body had crowded her to the edge of the mattress.

Twisting slightly, she turned her head to look at him. He slept like a tired child, eyes closed, lips parted, dark hair spilling onto the pillow. The snore that quivered in his throat was like the contented purr of a lion.

The bed was an island of warmth in the chilly cabin. It would be heaven, she thought, to wriggle against him and just lie there, in a warm tangle of arms and legs. But he'd been exhausted last night. It would be thoughtless to disturb him. Besides, J.D. had never laid a hand on her, or given her any other sign that he'd welcome physical contact between them. The last thing she wanted was to invade his space and make him feel uncomfortable.

Ruby was awake, stirring in her box and making little morning sounds. By now she'd be hungry. Emma eased out of bed and gathered her up. Her clothes and blankets were damp but she gazed at her mother with a blue-eyed serenity that hinted at some inner wisdom.

"Good morning, Sunshine," Emma whispered, aching with love. "Welcome to the second day of your life."

Settling herself in the rocker she opened her nightgown, let down her bra strap and put Ruby to her breast. The rosebud mouth chomped down hungrily. Emma leaned back in the chair, letting the day's realities seep into her mind. She felt stronger than she had the day before, and she could tell that her bleeding had slowed. She knew it was customary for 19th Century mothers to have their "lying in" period after the birth of a child, often lasting for weeks. But that practice had since been found to do more harm than good. In what she still thought of as her own century, most healthy woman left the hospital the day after birthing and were up and around in no time at all. She was looking forward to being on her feet, taking care of her own needs and doing her best to fit into this strange world.

The sun was rising, its light rosy pink through the windowpanes. Emma's gaze wandered to the Christmas tree she and J.D. had decorated last night. The star he'd placed on the topmost branch glimmered in the dawn. Christmas was over. It was time to get on with the rest of her life, and Ruby's.

What would she tell her daughter in years to come? Ruby was bound to have questions—about her birth father, her extended family and her mother's origins. There was plenty of time, of course, but the answers would be more believable if she had a solid story in place. The sooner she started building her new identity, the better. And the first thing she needed to do was erase any impression that she'd come from the future. She didn't want anyone telling Ruby that her mother was crazy.

So much to think about! Emma switched Ruby to her other swollen, leaking breast. Whatever she did in the days ahead, whatever half-truths and outright lies she told would be for the sake of her daughter.

J.D. stretched, yawned and opened his eyes. Emma's side of the bed was empty, but he could see her sitting in the rocker, nursing her baby. Her hair was tousled, her breast uncovered. A ray of rose-gold light, falling through the windowpane, illuminated her like a figure from a Renaissance portrait. Raphael himself couldn't have painted a more fetching Madonna.

Her eyes widened as she caught him watching her. She fumbled for the blanket that wasn't there. J.D. sighed.

"Emma, if I had a nickel for every woman I've seen nursing her baby, I'd be a rich man. Don't worry about a little flash of bare tit. If it bothers you, I'll just look the other way."

"You're not looking the other way now."

He turned his head, averting his eyes. "Better?"

"Fine."

"How did you sleep?" He stepped into his pants where he'd dropped them on the floor and pulled them up to his waist. He felt raw and grumpy, but at least he'd gotten a little rest.

"You snore."

"I warned you." He tugged the suspenders over his long johns. His boots and socks were on the hearth. He'd leave them for now. Opening the door, he let the cat outside. The air was crisp and clear, promising a sunny day. Maybe he'd go after deer or rabbit for the pot and give Emma some time to herself. He wasn't much for conversation in the morning.

"You'll be happy to know I'm feeling better," she said. "That bump on my head must have affected my mind. I apologize for the wild tales! I'm coming to my senses now, but I still must have a touch of amnesia. There are so many things I can't remember."

J.D. rolled his eyes toward the ceiling. He liked Emma well enough. In fact he was growing right fond of her. But he was long past believing anything the woman told him. She'd fed him so many versions of her story that he wouldn't recognize the truth if it bit him in the ass. Yesterday it had been time travel. Today it was amnesia. Tomorrow it would be something else.

The baby had finished nursing. Emma burped her, then laid her on a towel and proceeded to give her a gentle sponge bath. After twenty-four hours she was becoming a competent mother. He'd known all along she had it in her.

While Emma took care of the baby, J.D. put on his boots and started breakfast. Bacon, flapjacks and coffee again. Until he shot some game, or a midwinter thaw allowed a wagon to bring in some canned goods and potatoes, that would be pretty much all they had to eat.

He hoped Emma wouldn't complain. By rights, she shouldn't. She and her baby wouldn't have survived without his help. All the same, he found himself wanting to do right by them, to protect and provide for them as best he could. He'd been a loner most of his life. Yet, caring for this woman and her newborn came as naturally to him as breathing.

But he couldn't let himself get used to it, J.D. reminded himself. Given the life he'd lived and the reputation that followed him everywhere, he was a walking target. Sooner or later he'd find himself in some gunslinger's sights. He couldn't afford to let a woman and child get in the line of fire. If anything were to happen to Emma and little Ruby because of him, he would never forgive himself.

While the road was blocked by snow, they'd be safe enough. But with the first thaw, the danger would return. Then it would be time for the three of them to part company.

Emma settled Ruby in her box and sat down on the hearth to eat. J.D. frowned at her from the kitchen counter. "You've been up a while. Shouldn't you be back in bed?"

She shook her head. "I'm feeling fine. Since Mame left me some clothes, I thought I might try getting dressed. Then, if I can figure out how, I'll make myself useful and do some laundry."

"Oh, no, you don't!" He loomed above her like a thundercloud. "The last thing I need is you having complications because you didn't rest."

His bossiness was beginning to rankle her. "Where I come from, healthy women who've had babies don't stay in bed more than a day or two. They do just fine."

"Oh?" One black eyebrow slithered upward. "Well, around here, women have more sense. Now get back in that bed!"

"I'll stay up as long as I want to. You can't tell me what to do, J.D. McNulty."

"Can't I, now?" He snatched away her plate and, with a single lightning movement, swept her up in his arms. Her mug went flying, spattering coffee on the hearth as she kicked and flailed. Emma wasn't a small woman, but he held her as if she weighed no more than a feather. The man was a powerhouse.

"Put me down you...you cave man!" Emma sputtered.

"Fine." He strode to the bed, yanked down the covers and deposited her on the bottom sheet. "Now, stay there," he growled. "I won't have it on my conscience that you bled to death because you were up trying to do the wash when you should have been resting."

Emma glared as she pulled the blankets up to her chest. Common sense whispered that he was right. In a world where doctors and hospitals were minutes away, it might be safe to push the limits. Here, if anything went wrong, there'd be no one qualified to help her. J.D. had reason for concern. But that didn't give him the right to manhandle her.

"Don't you ever lay a hand on me again!" she snapped.

"Don't give me reason to, and we'll get along fine." He refilled her coffee cup and handed her the plate. "Now eat your breakfast. I'd planned on some hunting, but I'm going to stay around the cabin today, just to make sure you behave."

"The laundry—"

"The damned laundry can wait. If you need to wash your face and hands or use the thunder mug, it's fine to get up. But if I see you running around like a silly damned chicken, there'll be hell to pay. If you need anything, call me. Understood?"

"Fine." She fell to eating her breakfast, which had cooled in the interim. She was well aware that until the 20th Century, women were considered little more than breeding stock, and men had the right to order them around as they pleased. But that didn't mean she had to accept it, let alone like it. J.D. had won this round on brute strength and logic. But he had a few lessons to learn.

By the time Emma finished eating J.D. had put on his coat and gone outside. She could hear the ring of his ax as he split a massive log and chopped it into firewood. He was probably pounding out his frustrations with her. Well, too bad. She hadn't chosen to be here, and she didn't have to stay. She could pass herself off as a widow and find a town that needed a teacher, or a family that needed a tutor for their children. If that didn't work out she could scrub floors, take in laundry, whatever it took to survive. J.D. McNulty could have his precious peace and quiet back. He could go to blazes for all she cared!

She sank back onto the pillows, the sound of J.D.'s ax ringing in her ears. She pictured his big, callused hands gripping the hickory handle, his arm and shoulder muscles bunching and stretching as the steel blade crashed into the wood.

Another picture drifted into her mind—one she'd studied closely enough to memorize every detail. J.D. lying in his coffin, dressed in the black suit with the odd button, his eyes closed, his unruly hair slicked down with pomade and his strong, giving hands—the hands that had delivered her daughter—crossed lifeless and cold over his chest.

An unforeseen tightness rose in Emma's throat. No, she wouldn't be leaving. Not anytime soon. She owed it to J.D. to see this thing through and do whatever she could to save him. If his fate was sealed, at least she could be here for him until the end.

At least she could see that he didn't spend his last days alone.

Emma gazed past the bookshelf to the corner where the little Christmas tree stood. It was still fresh and fragrant, but its time was already over. Common sense dictated that it be thrown out soon, before its drying needles became a fire danger. But she would leave it for now, with its paper ornaments and peppermint sticks and the tarnished tin star on top. She and J.D. had created it together to celebrate a memorable day—Ruby's birthday and her first Christmas.

And, very likely, J.D.'s last.

Emma's daughter gave her an hour's peace before she started fussing again. Emma remembered reading somewhere that newborn babies should nurse every four hours, and that any mother with a modicum of discipline could get them on a regular schedule. But no one had bothered to inform Ruby of that. It was barely 9:00 and she was screaming like a little diva. When Emma put her to the breast, she rooted for the nipple and sucked as if she'd been put out to starve. No sooner had she finished than she filled her diaper with odoriferous yellow-brown goo, which she managed to get all over her kicking feet.

It was one of nature's miracles, Emma reflected, that these yowling, demanding, smelly little creatures managed to be so loveable.

Outside, she could hear J.D. rearranging things in the woodshed, making more noise than necessary, she thought. Maybe he was still upset with her. Or maybe he just wanted to remind her that he was around.

Suddenly the noise stopped. The silence was so startling that the cat, who'd been dozing next to J.D.'s whiskey jug, raised its head and pricked its ears.

Emma had finished washing Ruby for the second time that morning. She was just wrestling the clean diaper into place when she heard J.D.'s rap on the door.

"Emma?"

She yanked the pin from between her teeth. A lock of hair had tumbled into her eyes, blurring her vision. "It's fine. Come on in!"

He opened the door and thrust his head inside. "Seems we've got company—a bunch of folks coming up the trail."

"Coming *here*?"

"Appears that way. Don't worry, they look friendly enough. I'd say it's just a social visit."

"A social visit!" Emma smeared bacon grease on Ruby's bottom, overlapped the ends of the diaper and struggled to force the dull pin point through layers of plaid flannel. "Look at me, J.D. McNulty! I'm a mess, and so is the cabin! How can I think of having visitors at a time like this? Don't people call ahead?"

"Call ahead?" He gave her a puzzled look. Only then did Emma realize what she'd just said. Of course people didn't call ahead. If she wanted to fit in, she would have to watch her tongue.

"Never mind. Stall them outside for a few minutes, all right?"

"Fine. But don't try cleaning up. You just had a baby. A few dirty dishes aren't going to bother anybody!"

"But we don't even have any refreshments!"

"Sure, we do."

He closed the door, leaving her alone with the baby.

Just a social visit.

Emma fought rising waves of panic. She'd always been shy about meeting new people. But whether she liked it or not, she was about to experience socializing, Glory Gulch style.

# CHAPTER NINE

The cabin smelled of bacon grease, stale coffee and dirty diapers with a faint undertone of Christmas tree. Emma wrapped Ruby in a clean blanket. Then she reached up and unlatched the window. Cold, fresh air poured in.

Rushing now, she laid Ruby in her box, splashed her own face clean and slicked the rosewood brush through her tangled hair. It wasn't as if she'd be entertaining high society, Emma reminded herself. But she did want to make a decent first impression on her new neighbors. She could only hope they weren't expecting much.

Through the open window she could hear the sound of men's voices. J.D.'s was the deepest among them. He sounded relaxed, almost jovial. Maybe this was his company behavior.

She glanced down at her nightgown. Wet milk stains dribbled in twin streams down her chest. She sprang for the bed, jerking the covers up under her arms, just as J.D. wrapped on the door.

"Emma, can our friends come in for a visit?"

She lifted Ruby out of her box and readjusted the blankets. "Come on in," she called out.

Booted feet stomped snow on the porch as J.D. opened the door. The three men who entered were ragged and tired-looking, with heavy, resoled boots and bruised hands. Emma had seen enough old photographs to recognize them as miners, probably working their played out claims to the last grain of gold. They gazed at her shyly, as if they'd just walked into a cathedral and come upon a statue of the Madonna. J.D. closed the door quietly behind them.

One of the men, his head covered by a raveled knit cap, approached the bed and spoke. "Ma'am, could we see the baby? It's been a long time since we set eyes on a little one."

Emma laid Ruby on the foot of the bed. "Would you like to hold her?"

"Oh, could we, Ma'am?" At Emma's nod, he slid his work-roughened hands underneath Ruby's blanket and lifted her into his arms. Ruby was on her best behavior. Her dark blue eyes gazed up at the miner with heart-melting innocence. His throat moved as he swallowed.

"Here, let me take her." The second man moved in, stretching out his arms. "Lord Almighty, will you look at that? Such a little bit of a thing! And as pretty as a butterfly!"

"We brung her some presents. Not much but they's all we had." The first man reached into his pocket and brought out a teacup-sized figure of a bear, freshly carved from aspen wood. Emma imagined the man sitting up late by lamplight to finish the little animal shape. Her eyes misted as she thanked him.

"Not much she can do with this now, but maybe you can put it away for her later." The second man, who'd passed Ruby to his companion, fumbled for something in his pocket. When he opened his fist, Emma saw a nugget the size of her little fingernail, pure gold.

"But this is valuable!" Emma protested. "You could sell it!"

The man flushed. "More where that come from," he mumbled. "All a man's got to do is dig in the right place."

The first two men joined J.D. by the fireplace, where they passed around the jug. J.D. had been right about refreshments. No worries there.

The third man lowered Ruby to the bed and drew a brown paper bundle, tied with string, out of his threadbare vest. "I bought this to send to my sweetheart," he explained shyly. "But then a letter come sayin' she married another, so I never put it in the mail. Now I got no sweetheart and no use for pretty things, so I hope your little girl can use it. And when she gets a sweetheart, I hope she's true to him, not false-hearted like mine was."

Emma opened the package. Inside was a lacy pink lambs wool shawl, a true treasure in this remote country. Bundled around Ruby, it would be warm, soft and beautiful.

After the miners had drunk and Emma had expressed her heartfelt thanks, they left. But more visitors were coming up the trail. For the rest of the morning, the citizens of Glory Gulch—miners, tradesmen, cooks, and even the Chinese brothers who ran the laundry—trooped up the snow-packed trail to see the tiny miracle that was Ruby. They were hungry for the sight of an infant's face and the warm weight of a tiny body in their arms. One by one they held her and brought out their little gifts—a piece of furry sheepskin for her bed, a hand-made rattle, a length of calico, carefully trimmed squares of woolen blanket., a child-sized piece of an old rain slicker.

J.D.'s supply of whiskey was getting low by the time Mame and her three girls, riding double on a pair of mules, appeared through the bare aspens. Emma, who'd just taken time out to nurse her baby, watched through the window as they came closer. Beneath their drab cloaks, their petticoats fluttered like tattered rainbows.

J.D. went outside to help them dismount. Mame's girls were laughing, joking and flirting with him, and he was giving as good as he got. Clearly, when it came to women, J.D. enjoyed being the center of attention.

But why should she be surprised? Accounts of the time had described him as a ladies' man. But he'd been so gruff and bossy with Emma that she'd been ready to dismiss those accounts as rumor. Only now, with four soiled doves as his audience, did he turn on his legendary charm.

He certainly hadn't displayed any of that charm with her! Maybe he didn't consider her worth the trouble.

They came onto the porch together. Mame had brought another whiskey jug. J.D. was holding it up, laughing. The shortest and plumpest of the girls was clasping his waist. The blonde one, tall and full-figured like Emma herself, was leaning on his shoulder. She would be Ella Rose, who'd donated her cast offs. The third girl, thin and dark, trailed behind with Mame. Angel and Petunia—no doubt she'd soon discover which was which.

At the rap on the door, Emma scrambled back into bed. The last thing she wanted was to let them know she'd been spying on them.

"Come in." Her words sounded as prim as if they'd been spoken by Queen Victoria. What was wrong with her? Surely she couldn't be jealous!

They spilled through the doorway, the girls laughing and chattering. Up close, Emma could see that the term "girls" was misleading. Not one of the trio looked under thirty-five. Their painted faces were road maps of the hard lives they'd led.

Under their coats they were dressed for work. The low-cut satin gowns, in shades of burgundy, teal and mustard, showed signs of heavy use. The bustled skirts were faded and stained, the bodices frayed at the tightly fitted seams. The dresses were not unlike their owners, Emma observed. But then, who was she to judge these women and what they did to survive in a rough world?

"How are you today, honey?" Mame put down her carpet bag and swept off her cloak. She was wearing the same plain gown as she had the day before, but when she moved, Emma glimpsed a flash of tangerine petticoat beneath the skirt. Her absinthe eyes, outlined like Cleopatra's today, studied Emma carefully. "You're looking good, girl. Nice color in your cheeks. Are you feeling any stronger?"

"Hellfire, she was talking about getting up and doing wash this morning," J.D. growled. "I had to threaten her with mayhem to keep her in bed."

"You wouldn't have to threaten *me* to keep me in bed, J.D." The shortest of the three girls gave him a flirtatious wink. She was far from beautiful, but her pug nose and plump little chin gave her an air of sauciness that any man would find appealing.

"Mind your manners, Petunia," Mame said. "You're not at work."

Petunia. Porky's girlfriend. Emma was a believer in mnemonics and the old cartoon idea worked. The other girl, dark and thin, with faint pockmarks under her makeup, would be Angel. She looked Hispanic—although that word wasn't in use yet, Emma reminded herself.

"And you, young lady—"Mame turned her attention back to Emma. "You just had a baby. Don't get rambunctious and think you can take on the world. At best, you'll wear yourself out and be slow to heal. At worst, you could make yourself sick and lose your milk, or even bleed to death. So behave yourself for a few more days. You hear me?"

"Loud and clear. But I don't want to impose on J.D. any longer than I have to."

"Believe me, having a pretty woman in his bed would never be an imposition on J.D." Mame shot him a sly wink. "Give yourself till the end of the week. By then, if you take it slow, you should be ready to get dressed and help out a little. And, J.D., I'm charging you to see that she doesn't overdo it. Keep her in that bed."

"My pleasure." His grin tempted Emma to slap him.

Ella Rose had discovered Ruby, asleep in her box on the floor. "Oh, will you look at that?" she squealed so loudly that Ruby started, woke up and began to fuss.

"Oh, no! I'm sorry! Come here, little baby!" Ella Rose reached down to pick up the squalling infant. There was a sudden yellow flash and a savage hiss. Ella Rose jumped back, muttering curses and nursing a red scratch on the back of her hand.

The cat stood between Ella Rose and the baby's bed, its scruffy back arched, its teeth bared showing one broken fang. Mame chuckled. "Well, it appears young Ruby's got herself a protector. Did he hurt you Ella Rose?"

"Not too bad, I guess. I usually get on fine with cats. I used to feed that one-eyed devil. He never came at me before. Don't know what got into him."

Emma reached down from the bed and picked up Ruby. This time the cat didn't object. "Would you like to hold her now?" she asked Ella Rose.

The woman shook her bleached curls. "Maybe another time, when that cat isn't around."

"I'll take her." Angel spoke for the first time, her voice small and shy. Her thin face framed a pair of haunting dark eyes. "*Por favor.* Please."

She held out her arms and gathered Ruby close. Turning away, she walked over to the tree. Emma could hear her talking and singing in Spanish. Ruby had stopped fussing and snuggled down in her arms.

When Angel turned around a moment later, tears were trickling down her scarred cheeks. "I had a little girl once," she said. "It was a long time ago. But the memory is sweet."

"What happened to her?" As soon as she asked, Emma was sorry."

"*Viruelas*—you call it smallpox. It took almost a hundred lives in our village. My husband. My child. They were luckier than me. "She gazed out the window. Sunlight etched her ravaged features into stark relief. "After that I tried to get work as a maid. Nobody would hire me with my face. Then a man took me north. He said my scars wouldn't matter in the dark."

"Oh!" Emma pushed herself upright in the bed. "No woman should have to go through that. Surely there are laws—"

Angel shook her head. "It's not so bad. I'm used to the work now. And The Laughing Lady is a good place. Mame is a kind boss. The other girls are my friends. Even the men, the ones who know me, are gentle. There's no need for you to feel pity."

Defiance flashed in her black eyes, warning Emma not to say more. Hers was a degrading, miserable life. But Angel had her pride—even if that was all she had.

"My turn!" Petunia had been paying more attention to J.D. than to the baby, but now she held out her arms. Ruby, who'd had a long morning of being passed around, took to the change without a fuss. "Oh, just look at you!" she warbled. "Look at those eyes! You're going to break hearts, little girl! And Petunia's just the one to teach you!" She raised Ruby to her shoulder and danced around the floor with her, humming a spritely waltz and glancing back over her shoulder to see if J.D. was watching her. Was Petunia the unnamed saloon girl who would hold the dying J.D. in her arms? Seeing her now, Emma wouldn't have bet against it.

"Who'd like some lunch?" Mame opened her carpet bag and passed out venison sandwiches wrapped in a big linen napkin. They were little more than meat and bread, with none of the fixings Emma was used to. But the bread was fresh, the meat tender and flavorful. After two days of bacon, sourdough flapjacks and J.D.'s bitter coffee, the sandwiches tasted divine—and the apple pie Mame had brought for dessert tasted even better.

While the others ate wherever there was space, Emma sat up in bed, balancing her plate on her knees. All she need now was a Diet Coke. But unless the time warp yanked her back into the 21$^{st}$ Century, there was no way she'd live long enough to enjoy a single sip.

Maybe she could invent iced mocha lattes—open a coffee shop next door to the saloon and expand it into a franchise. Given some cheese, tomatoes and bread dough, she could invent pizza, too. She could invent hamburgers, French fries, Monopoly games, panty hose, even—wonder of wonders—disposable diapers! Why settle for teaching school? For a woman who knew the future, the possibilities were endless!

But her mind was playing a dangerous game, Emma warned herself. Introducing new ideas before their time could violate some unwritten cosmic law and lead to chaos. She had no right to change history. This was 1871, and she'd be a fool not to live by the rules.

Her eyes found J.D., where he sat on the hearth, talking with Ella Rose. She studied the craggy lines of his profile, the contours of his long, expressive hands. Did living by the rules mean that she had to let him die?

Did it mean that a proud, intelligent woman like Angel had no choice except to earn her living on her back?

Did it mean that her own daughter, her bright and precious Ruby, would grow up with limitations? Limitations imposed on her because she was a girl?

How could that be right?

How could it be right in any century?

After lunch, Mame packed up her girls and headed back to town to open the saloon for the evening. Emma got out of bed long enough to thank them for coming and bid them goodbye. She stood in the doorway as J.D. helped them mount their mules and saw them off down the trail. When he turned around and came back to the porch she was still there, waiting for him.

"Why don't you go with them?" she asked. "I hate to keep you from having a good time with your friends."

He gave her a pained look, ushered her into the house and closed the door. "It's fine, Emma. I can go to town anytime. Now go on back to bed. I'll clean up."

"Really, I can help. I'm fine."

His scowl was thunderous. "Bed. Now."

Emma sank onto the edge of the mattress. The day had been long and hectic, and she was too strung out to nap. "Thanks for playing host. I hope the people who came know how much I appreciated their gifts."

"It was a treat for them to see the baby. Probably reminded them of home." He gathered up the tin plates and cups, stacked them on the counter and added some hot water and soap slivers to the dishpan. "You'll find the folks here are good neighbors. All of them."

Emma knew he was talking about the women. "Yes. I already know that."

The strain that lay between them was heavy with the question she knew better than to ask. J.D.'s back was rigid as he washed the dishes.

"I know what you're thinking," he said at last. "The answer is no. I haven't patronized any of those girls. It's a personal rule of mine. I don't pay women to sleep with me. Never have. Put that in your thesis if you want, Miss Emma Carlyle. It should make for some juicy reading."

"I'm assuming you never needed to. Pay, I mean."

"No comment. A gentleman doesn't tell."

"And I suppose a lady shouldn't ask."

"Now you're getting the right idea."

Ruby had begun to whimper. Emma lifted her out of the box, freed her breast and let her daughter nurse. "What's going to happen to those girls?" she asked J.D. "They're not getting any younger. Where will they go after the Laughing Lady?"

"That depends. Some whores get married and turn respectable. In country like this, where wives are hard to come by, that happens a lot. Generally, folks don't hold it against them."

"What about the others? The ones who don't get married?"

"Some of them, the smart ones, save up enough to open up their own business, like a shop or a boarding house. Or they hire some girls and start a place of their own. There's good money for those who can stomach the trade."

"Like Mame?"

"Mame's a good friend." There was a note of warning in his voice. "She bought the Laughing Lady to run as a saloon. The girls came with the place. She didn't have the heart to throw them out. And they're luckier than most. Mame's opened bank accounts for them in South Pass City, and puts away twenty-five percent of their earnings, so they'll have something for a new start when they leave. "

"Oh. Like a 401-K."

"A *what?*"

"Never mind. It's nothing you need to know about."

"Then I won't bother to ask." J.D. kept his back discreetly turned. He could hear the faint sounds of the baby nursing, and he knew that Emma would feel more comfortable if the didn't look directly at her.

She'd done all right today, with the stream of visitors. Tired as she was, she'd managed to be pleasant and courteous to all of them, even Mame's girls. He imagined taking her to town when she was stronger, parading her around dressed in something pretty, with the baby in her arms. Almost as if she was his woman.

She wasn't his woman, J.D. reminded himself. But she was sure as hell *somebody's* woman. And she'd sure as hell come from someplace. Wherever it was, she'd have folks there who were worried about her—maybe even a husband. The last immaculate conception he was aware of had taken place more than eighteen hundred years ago, and he'd known since he was knee high to a billy goat that you didn't find babies under cabbage leaves!

She'd told him the baby's father was married, but that didn't mean she was telling the truth. Some women got strange notions when it came their time to give birth. She wouldn't be the first female to run away from home, pop up in a strange place and concoct some cockamamie story to cover her tracks.

J.D. considered himself an honest man. If he found a lost wallet with money in it, he'd make every effort to get it back to its owner. How much more important was a lost woman with a baby?

No two ways about it, he needed to learn the truth about Emma Carlyle. So far all he'd established was that she was pretty, warm, funny and a damned poor liar. Only a fool would believe the crazy stories she'd told. And J.D. had never considered himself a fool.

But what about the clothes she'd been wearing? Like that puffy green coat with its infernal fastener? And those intriguing little drawers that barely seemed big enough to cover a woman's backside? Except for the contraption that held up her tits, Mame had taken everything down the gulch to the Chinese laundry. Otherwise, he might not mind having a closer look—especially at those drawers.

Ruby had finished nursing. J.D. could tell by the sound of her belch. But the little mite was still fussy. When he turned around, he saw that Emma was rocking the baby in her arms, singing in a breathy, off-key contralto that J.D. found downright sexy.

"Down in the valley, the valley so low...Hang your head over, hear the wind blow..."

Now there was a good song. But Ruby didn't seem to like it. Her cries rose to a crescendo of howls. Evidently she fancied herself a music critic.

Emma switched to the song he'd heard her sing earlier. The one about getting no satisfaction. It wasn't much of a song, J.D. observed. The words didn't amount to anything, and the tune wasn't even hummable. But Ruby seemed to like it. Her cries subsided to whimpers. Moments later she drifted off to sleep with her tiny pink fist in her mouth.

"Where'd you get that dad-blamed awful song?" J.D. asked Emma as she lowered the sleeping infant into her box. "I thought I'd heard just about every song there was, but I never heard that one."

"There's a lot of songs you've never heard," she said. "And right now I'm too tired to sing any more of them."

"If they're anything like that one, don't bother."

"Some of them are worse." She giggled.

"Is that the kind of songs they sing where you came from?"

"It's one kind. There are other kinds you might like better."

"So what kind of place *do* you come from, Emma?" He swung the rocker around to face her and sank into it. "I'll confess, you're the damndest woman I've ever met. Just when I think I've got you figured out, you come up with a new trick that leaves me scratching my head."

"Don't, J.D.," she said, suddenly serious. "I told you, I'm me and I'm here. That's all you need to know. Anything else you say will only confuse things."

J.D. eased lower in the chair. He could tell he wasn't going to get far with her today. "You look worn out," he said. "Why don't you get some rest?"

"It's starting to get dark outside. It'll be bedtime in a couple of hours. I'll wait. What do you do to pass the time up here, J.D.? Besides drink whiskey, I mean?"

"When you showed up on my doorstep I was about to start reading a new book. This one's thick enough to keep me out of trouble for weeks. He reached for the shelf and pulled out a heavy volume. Most of my books are old. But I bought this one from a traveler in South Pass City. It's supposed to be about whaling.

"Really? What's the name of it?"

He glanced at the cover of the book, whose odd title had slipped his mind in the confusion of the past two days. "Moby Dick."

She brightened. "Oh, yes! I read it about fifteen years ago, for my high school English class. It's an amazing story. The part where Captain Ahab harpoons that huge white whale just gave me goose bumps..." She trailed off, as if she'd just realized she'd said something wrong. "Anyway, I know you'll enjoy it."

He frowned at her. "I'll enjoy it more if you don't give away the story! And what business did your teacher have, letting you read a book like this? From what I was told, it's no story for girls. It could give them bad dreams, or strain their weak young female minds with all those long words."

"Bad dreams? Weak minds?" She looked as if she wanted to reach under the bed and fling the chamber pot at him. "I'll have you know, where I grew up, girls could read anything they—"

She broke off as she realized he was struggling not to grin. "Oh!" she gasped, realizing she'd been had. "Oh, you beastly man! You had me going!"

He let the laughter out in a single burst. Lord, but she was beautiful, he thought, with her face flushed and her eyes dancing. Under different circumstances he'd be tempted to crawl under the covers with her, kiss her silly for starters, and show her what real lovemaking was like. Something told J.D. she needed to know. She had the look of a woman who'd had her heart broken and believed she deserved nothing better. He wanted to show her the truth— that she was a queen, a goddess. He wanted to worship her body in bed.

That it wasn't possible made it all the more tantalizing. Emma wouldn't be recovered from Ruby's birth for weeks. And that aside, J.D. preferred to know about his lovers. If a woman was on the run or had a husband waiting in the wings he didn't want to discover it after the fact. In Emma's case, either possibility could be true.

Meanwhile, the woman was driving him to a fair frenzy.

Needing a distraction, he sank back in the rocker and opened the book. He thumbed past the cover page and the preface to the first page of the story.

"Would you mind reading to me?" Her words startled him. He glanced up at her.

"Just for a little while," she said. "Just long enough to help me relax."

"Did your mother read to you when you were young?"

She shook her head. "My mother took pills and drank booze and chased any man who'd help her get them."

"That's why you don't like my drinking? Because of your mother?"

"I've never had the time or money for psychoanalysis. Just read. For a little while. Please."

He sat up a little in the chair, holding the book so that the page caught the fading daylight through the window. Emma had settled back against the pillows, looking soft and mussed and pretty.

Clearing his throat, he began. "Call me Ishmael..."

Emma sat back and let the familiar words flow over her. J.D.'s deep voice was rich and expressive, with a gravelly undertone that plumbed the depths of sexiness. This was what she'd been craving all day, she realized—to listen to that voice without having to pay attention to what he was saying or scramble for a clever retort.

Her research hadn't done him justice, she reflected. He was rougher-looking than his photographs, with a rawness around the edges that rendered him both fearsome and vulnerable. No words could have described his looming, rumpled presence, and nothing could have prepared her for the voice that trickled through her body like hot fudge over ice cream, with lazy, delicious warmth.

If he'd called her on the phone in the 21st Century, she would have fallen in love with him sight unseen.

Not that she *had* fallen in love with him. Her research had shown her a man who was a product of his times, impulsive, forceful, even violent. And his attitude toward women was somewhere between Neanderthal and Cro-Magnon. Even so, she couldn't help wondering what it would be like to have such a man make love to her.

Emma had lost her virginity her freshman year in college, after some ham-handed fumbling in the back seat of a Chevy Malibu. Subsequent encounters, what few there were, hadn't been much better. The job in Lander had pretty much put a damper on new possibilities—as a teacher she had a reputation to maintain. But then she'd met Derek at a church singles dance, and everything had fallen into place. For a woman who'd been starved for love all her life, three simple words were all it took to get her into bed.

For Emma, the affair—which was what it turned out to be—had made up in emotion what it lacked in pyrotechnics. She'd made love with all the pent-up need of her lonely years. In her euphoria, she'd failed to notice the way he always kept one eye on the clock.

A more experienced woman would have recognized the signs. All Emma knew was that she'd found love at last. The phone call from Derek's wife had blasted her out of denial and left her with a shattered heart.

A part of her was still angry, more at herself than at Derek. What a trusting, sappy-eyed cow she'd been! As if any man, even a complete jerk, could ever fall in love with her!

But at least one thing had come out right. Whatever else she could say about Derek, the lying bastard had given her one priceless gift.

He had given her Ruby.

J.D. paused in his reading. His cobalt eyes glanced up at her, probably hoping she'd nodded off. She smiled and nodded, allowing him no mercy. It wouldn't have mattered if he'd been reading *Bloom's Taxonomy of Educational Objectives*, a book she'd hated in college. She craved the sound of that voice flowing through her like dark, wild honey. What a shame she couldn't have the rest of him to go along with it.

Sex with J.D. would be raw and honest. No lies, no promises, no useless emotions—not on his part, at least. It would be a roll in the hay, a rollicking romp that would probably blow her socks off and leave her with a 500-watt glow. And when it was done he would tip his hat and do-si-do off in some other direction like a partner who'd swung her around in a square dance.

But why was she even thinking about it? There was no way it was going to happen. Apart from her condition, the timing was bad for them both. For her it was too soon.

For J.D., she suspected, it was too late.

# CHAPTER TEN

Emma had finally drifted off, her head sagging against the pillows. J.D. stopped reading and closed the book, using a broom straw to mark the page. He hadn't minded reading to her. It had taken him back to the winter evenings when he used to read to his younger brothers and sisters—books like *Gulliver's Travels*, *Uncle Tom's Cabin* and *The Last of the Mohicans*. He remembered how they would beg him for one more page, then another, until their eyes began to droop and their small heads began to nod.

When he married, he'd looked forward to reading to his own children. Then the worst had happened. After Maggie's death he'd sworn off any desire to have a family. He'd compiled a mental list of excuses—he was on the move too much; he hadn't saved enough money yet; a lawman's job was risky, and being an ex-lawman was even riskier. J.D. had made all of those excuses to women, to his friends and to himself. After a while he'd come to believe them. It was easier by far than facing the truth. A family demanded love. Love walked hand in hand with loss. And he'd had all the loss he could stand.

Walking over to the bed, he stood gazing down at Emma. She lay back on the pillows, her hair tousled like a young boy's. Why would anyone cut such beautiful hair? Maybe she'd lost it to a fever, as some women did, and was still in the process of growing it back. He imagined it long, falling around him like a silken tent as she leaned above him, her knees straddling his hips, his shaft planted deep and hard inside her. Heat flowed to his loins as he pictured her swollen breasts hanging over him like ripe pears, the nipples brushing his lips as she rode him to a frenzied, pumping climax.

J.D. cursed under his breath. That kind of thinking would only get him in trouble, and he was in enough trouble already. The pressure against his crotch wasn't going away. Neither were the images in his mind. Resigned, he stepped out onto the porch and finished what Nature had started. It was a piss poor substitute for the real thing, but at least he felt sane again.

He came back inside, bolted the door and washed his hands in the basin. Ruby lay in her box, eyes closed, thumb in her mouth. Leaning down, J.D. brushed a fingertip along her downy cheek. Instinctively, she turned her head toward his touch. Her lips made little sucking motions. Not wanting to wake her, J.D. withdrew his hand. Maybe tomorrow he'd scour the town for some paint to fancy up that battered old cartridge box. A pretty little girl deserved a pretty bed.

Emma stirred on the pillows. The stack behind her was too high for comfortable sleep. J.D. supported her with his arm while he slipped out the extra pillow. Then he lowered her to the mattress. She slept on, not even stirring as J.D. slipped his arm out from under her. She'd had a long, tiring day and she'd handled it well. He'd been proud of her.

On impulse, he leaned over and brushed a kiss across her closed eyelids. "Sleep tight," he murmured, wishing he dared do more. Her lips were so close, so soft and full. And they would fit so nicely below the edge of his moustache.

He would go back to the rocker and read until he couldn't keep his eyes open maybe if he let himself get sleepy enough, he could crawl in beside her and drift off without lying awake, feeling her warmth against his side as he imaged all the things he'd like to do with her...and to her...and on her...and under her...

Hellfire and damnation, it was happening again!

Swearing under his breath, J.D. sank back into the rocker. It was a good thing *Moby Dick* was a long book. It could turn out to be a very long night.

New Year's Day, 1872, had come and gone without fanfare. By the week's end, Emma was more than ready to be up and dressed. Her bleeding had all but stopped, her belly had shrunk noticeably, and she was brimming with restless energy.

"You're sure you're ready to do this?" J.D. asked when she'd requested some privacy to get into regular clothes.

"I'm more than ready. If I have to spend another day in that bed I'll be climbing the walls!"

"Climbing the walls? How in Sam Hill do you manage that?"

"It's just an expression. It means I'll be antsy—half crazy with boredom."

"Antsy?" His eyebrows met above the bridge of his nose. "You've got a whole head full of expressions I've never heard before, Miss Emma Carlyle. I'm tempted to start writing them down. Folks must have a right peculiar way of talking where you came from." He shook his head. "Where did you grow up, if you don't mind my asking?"

"Cheyenne. I lived there until I was eighteen." The truth came without forethought. "It was before you were there," she added, tasting the bitterness of the lie.

"Well, I've spent plenty of time in Cheyenne, and I never met a blessed soul who used words the way you do."

"What can I say?" She turned away and began rummaging through the pile of clothes Mame had left. Mame had visited the cabin twice since the day she'd come with her girls. Emma had to confess that the more time she spent with the owner of the Laughing Lady, the more she liked her. Mame seemed to accept her strangeness without question, maybe because she was so unconventional herself.

On her last visit, Mame had returned Emma's laundry from the Chinese brothers, nicely cleaned and folded. The down parka, which she hadn't meant to send in the first place, had come out as flat as Mexican tortilla—of course there'd been no way to tumble it dry. Maybe it could still be punched it into shape. But at least she had a fresh supply of clean wrappings and diapers for Ruby. Mame had also brought back her black stretch pants, red maternity sweater and polka dot panties, all without comment. Looking at them now, Emma realized she mustn't put them on again. Whether she liked it or not, it was time to start dressing like the locals.

"I'll confess I've been curious to see you got up like a regular woman. "J.D. said as he prepared to go out and chop firewood. "Call me, now, if you need any help."

"I'm a big girl. I can dress myself, thank you."

He went outside whistling. Emma didn't recognize the tune, but guessed from the twinkle in his eyes that it must be something bawdy. Ruby and the cat watched her from the bed as she stripped down, gave herself a light sponge bath and readied herself for the ordeal. There was no getting around it. She would have to get used to this unaccustomed way of dressing.

Did the drawers or the stockings go on first? Emma had prided herself on her knowledge of historical costumes, but she had no experience putting them on. Drawers and chemise before stockings, she resolved. At least that way she'd be starting out decently covered.

Shaking out the threadbare muslin drawers, she stepped into them, pulled them over her hips and tightened the drawstring around what would be her waist when she got her figure back. The frayed string was a pain to knot and would be an even bigger pain to untie. The person destined to invent elastic deserved a Nobel Prize!

The drawers were slit from stem to stern and revealed more than the skimpiest hospital gown did. But once she got the knee-length chemise over her head, Emma felt less exposed. Her stretched-out bra was almost beyond wearing. She would put it away and save it. Maybe at some later time she could use it as a pattern for a new one. But without spandex, it wouldn't be the same.

Sitting on the bed, she pulled the woolen stockings up to her thighs. The well-used cherry red satin garters were trimmed in lace, with attached strings that could be tightened to adjust the fit. How did women keep the scandalous things up without cutting off the circulation in their legs? Maybe that was why so many of them ended up with varicose veins.

While she was sitting down she pulled on the flat-heeled boots Mame had brought her. Emma had been grateful for the lucky find. The lightweight boots, which had probably belonged to a man, fit comfortably on her size nine feet. They were scuffed and in need of resoling, but at least she wouldn't have to clomp around the cabin in her heavy snow boots.

When Emma stood, she felt as if she were wearing a combination of crotchless pajamas and hobbles. How in heaven's name had women won the West dressed like this? The petticoat, at least, was uncomplicated. But the real challenge lay ahead—the corset.

Outside, she could hear the intermittent blows of J.D.' ax as he split kindling off the larger pieces he'd cut. Ruby had dozed off, but the cat watched with interest as Emma loosened the laces, raised her arms and slipped the contraption over her head. She would need to lace it tightly. Otherwise, she'd never be able to fit into Ella Rose's hand-me-down dresses. But how was she supposed to accomplish that on her own?

From the looks of it, the corset laced down the back. The front featured a stiffened strip called a busk, designed to flatten the wearer down the middle. That in itself wasn't a bad idea. But most corsets Emma had seen unhooked in the front. This one, with its sturdy whalebone busk, appeared to be all one piece.

She already had it around her body. But the only way to reach the laces would be to twist the corset around, bringing the laces to the front. Then, once they were tightened, she'd have to twist it back again.

With effort she worked the corset around to a backwards position with the laces in front. But she swiftly discovered two problems. Pulling the laces away from her body put her arms at a disadvantage. She couldn't tug hard enough to do much good. And even if she cold lace the corset tightly enough, how would she manage to twist it back to the proper position? Wearing the corset backside-front wasn't an option either. Not if she wanted to bend over.

The cat closed and opened its single amber eye. If cats could laugh, this one would probably be in hysterics. Emma could feel the sweat dripping between her breasts. She swore out loud. There was only one thing to do—swallow her pride and call for reinforcements.

Slipping on her parka, she went out onto the porch. The morning sun glinted on crystallized snow, blinding her for a moment. She could hear J.D. chopping wood. When she called his name, he came striding around the corner of the cabin. His hair was damp and wind-tousled, his cheeks ruddy with the cold. He looked like a mountain man, strong and wild and sexy.

"Is everything all right?" In the sunlight, his eyes were the color of the lakes that formed at the foot of melting glaciers, a deep, unimaginable blue.

"Not quite." Emma tried not to sound flustered. "I just need your help for a minute. Come on inside."

He followed her into the cabin, yanking off his gloves and

shrugging out of his coat at the door. Emma turned her back to him. He'd seen more of her than her underwear, she reminded herself. Her out-of-shape body would be nothing new to him. Slowly she let the parka slide off her shoulders. The moment of silence was broken by a half-strangled chuckle.

Emma shot him a glare over her shoulder. "Go ahead and laugh. I just can't figure out how women get these things on alone."

"Generally they don't. Not that style, at least. For starters, the laces go in the back."

"I know that."

"Then turn it around and I'll give you a hand."

She yanked the corset around and lined up the busk with her sternum. Behind her, she could feel his hands adjusting the laces and hooks from the top down. He worked competently—maybe a little too competently.

"You've done this before, haven't you?" Emma couldn't resist asking.

"Are you going to put that in your thesis, Miss Emma Carlyle?"

"No. Just an observation. Am I right?"

"No comment. Let's just say I've lived an interesting life. If I were to kick the bucket tomorrow, I'd be damned good and ready."

His words sent sudden chill through Emma. She went rigid.

"Is something wrong?" he asked.

"No," she lied. "It's just your hands. They're a little chilly."

"Sorry. I'll try to be more careful."

She could feel the tightening around her middle as his fingers untwisted and tugged their way to the bottom of the corset. "Now comes the fun part," he said, glancing around. "Unfortunately, this bed didn't come with corner posts. Close the door and hang onto the handle. That should work."

Emma had seen enough period movies to know what would happen next. She'd just never expected it to happen to her. While she gripped the door handle with all her strength, J.D. pulled backward on her laces. The stays inched inward, molding her middle. She could feel her insides shifting with the pressure. It was getting harder to breathe.

The famous scene from *Gone With the Wind* came back to her— Scarlett O'Hara clutching the bedpost while Mammy tugged on her corset strings. "You done had a baby, Miz Scarlett," she muttered the remembered line through clenched teeth. "You ain't never goin' to be no seventeen inches again!"

"What are you mumbling about?" J.D. braced his knee against her lower back for the final pull.

"Nothing. Just a line from an old mov—an old book. I—*oof*!" The air whooshed out of her as he yanked the strings and tied the ends. Emma's breathing felt shallow, as if the air could only fill the top part of her lungs. This couldn't possibly be good for her. What had women been thinking, wearing these torture devices for so many generations?

Staggering a little, she stepped back from the door and cast a downward look at her body. Her waist, if not tiny, at least had a nice inward curve to it. And the top of her corset thrust her breasts upward and outward like no bra she'd ever tried on.

She looked good.

"Too tight?" J.D. asked.

"No...no, it's fine." Maybe he'd pull it even tighter if she asked him. But what was she thinking? She could scarcely breathe as it was.

Not that it was easy to breathe anyway, with J.D. looming behind her. She could feel his nearness like a warm aura that crept over her skin. She could feel the blood racing through her body, the subtle, weighted throbbing in forbidden places. His fingers brushed the back of her shoulder. Their touch jolted through her like a subtle electric current.

Late at night, with his long, hard body stretched out beside her, it was all she could do to keep from turning over and settling into his arms, her head cradled against his shoulder, her knee resting between his thighs. She was still sore from the baby. But she wouldn't say no to a little snuggling.

As for the rest, she was as raw emotionally as she was physically. It would take time to heal her battered psyche and get her get her bearings before she was ready to take the plunge again. Months, at least.

Months that J.D. didn't have.

"Will you be all right?" His voice startled Emma out of her reverie.

"I will be—if I can get used to the oxygen deprivation. On the up side, I look like I just had liposuction and a tummy tuck, or spent six months working out at the gym."

"Like you just had *what*?"

"Never mind." Emma sighed. She really needed to get in the habit of thinking before she opened her mouth.

"In that case, I've got wood to chop."

"Go on then. I'll keep an eye on the stew."

J.D. had shot a rabbit and skinned it the day before. Emma, who had a soft spot for furry little animals, had been dismayed at first. But now that the meat was cut up and simmering in the iron pot, with sourdough dumplings, a few bacon slices and the last of the onions, she had to admit it smelled downright decadent. Rabbit stew would be a welcome change from flapjacks.

Earlier that morning, she'd watched as J.D. seared the meat in bacon grease, browned some flour and added enough water to make a bubbling gravy. After that he'd mixed the dumplings and spooned the dough into the stew. Emma had taken mental notes of each step. As soon as she could be up and around, she wanted to take over her share of the work. Back in Lander she'd barely mastered heating frozen dinners in the microwave. She had a lot to learn about cooking over an open fire, using whatever ingredients were at hand. Running to the supermarket at the last minute to buy what she needed would be a thing of the past—or to put it more correctly, a thing of the future.

Emma checked the stew, stirred it and moved it toward the edge of the fire grate, where it was less likely to burn. Ruby was beginning to fuss. Emma took the time to change and feed her. Then she tucked her back into bed and resumed the lengthy process of getting dressed. She could only hope she'd master it in the next few days. Otherwise, looking presentable was going to take up most of her time. She'd always wondered why so many 19th Century women had maids to help them dress. Now she knew.

Ella Rose had given her two gowns, which looked like the sort she'd worn for non-working hours. They were made of patterned cotton, modestly styled and worn to faded softness. Both of them buttoned down the front, which would make it easy to nurse Ruby.

The blue gingham was the nicer of the two. Hoping for the best, she shook out the wrinkles and pulled it over her head. It settled into place over her newly corseted figure, fitting perfectly.

Emma worked the buttons through their holes. Then, stepping back, she tried to see as much as she could in the murky glass. The color was good on her, the v-shaped neckline showing the slightest hint of cleavage. She'd never make the cover of *Cosmo*, but she looked prettier than she'd expected. Experimenting, she finger-combed her hair back from her face and twisted it up on her head. It wasn't long enough to stay put, even with pins, but maybe in a few more months...

But where would she be by the time her hair was long enough to pin up? Her whole world could fall apart before then.

"Very nice!" J.D.'s voice startled her from the doorway. She dropped her hand, letting her hair fall. He stepped into the cabin, filling it, as always. "Now you look like a real woman," he said.

A warm flush stole up her neck and into her cheeks. She'd wanted him to say something like that, wanted him to look at her the way he was looking at her now. She felt as giddy as a teenager.

"The stew's about done," she said.

"Smells good." He peeled off his coat and hung it on the rack. "I was thinking, since you mentioned climbing the walls, it's a nice day, and you've never seen the town. Are you and Ruby feeling up for a ride after lunch? I could snowshoe down the trail and bring my horse up for you."

"I'd certainly like to see the sights of Glory Gulch. But all that way in the cold with Ruby? Is that wise?"

"The sun's out and the trip's a short one, fifteen or twenty minutes by horse. Bundle her up warm and she should be fine. My mother always said a little fresh air was good for babies."

"Let me think about it while we eat," Emma said, although she realized that she'd already made up her mind. The cabin walls had been closing in on her. As long as it wouldn't harm Ruby, an outing would do her a world of good.

The stew was tasty enough to make Emma forget her pity for the rabbit. This was 1872, after all. It wasn't as if one could run to the supermarket and buy a pound of chicken tenders on a foam tray. If J.D. returned from his next hunting foray with Bambi's mother slung over his shoulder, she would accept it as the necessity it was and be grateful for the meat.

She could only hope he didn't expect her to skin his hunting spoils.

After the meal J.D. strapped on his snowshoes, shouldered his rifle and set off to pick up his horse at the livery stable. In his absence, Emma washed the dishes and straightened the cabin. The Christmas tree was drying out, and she'd eaten all the peppermint sticks. It would need to be taken down in the next day or two. She would be sorry to see it go, Emma reflected. It had been a long time since she'd had a Christmas that meant anything to her. For years it had been a day to be endured, usually alone. But this Christmas had changed her whole life. She was a mother now, learning a whole new set of survival skills. And she'd met a man who would turn her world on edge in any century.

Where would she be next Christmas? Here, in Glory Gulch? On her own somewhere with her daughter, struggling to make a living in the 1870s? Or even back in Lander, living her old life?

There could be no such questions about J.D. If history played out as documented in scores of books, articles and photographs, he'd be dead and buried, the victim of a meaningless quarrel over a stupid card game.

Emma reached out and touched the tarnished marshal's badge that J.D. had pinned to the top of the Christmas tree. There had to be something she could do. But what? How could she change what already existed as history in the world she'd left behind?

Ruby had awakened and begun to cry. Emma scooped her up and sat down in the rocking chair to feed her. She nursed hungrily, sucking with jerky little hiccups. Maybe it was true what Emma had heard, that babies could sense anxiety in people close to them. At the very least, Ruby seemed to be an old soul, looking out at the world with a wisdom her mother sadly lacked. What a shame she couldn't talk.

By the time Emma had changed Ruby and done some primping—minimal, with no makeup, curlers or hairspray—J.D. had returned on horseback, ready to take her down the trail to the gulch.

"It's not too late to change your mind," he said.

"Oh, I haven't. It's just—"She held up the parka, which, despite her best efforts, at loosening the down, was still flat and smelled of damp feathers. By now it was probably mildewing inside.

"Oh." He frowned and nodded. "Don't worry, I have something that'll do." He strode to the chest, raised the lid and unfolded the heavy black dress coat she'd seen earlier. "Haven't got much use for this anymore. Until you get something better it's yours."

Emma tried it on. Since the coat had been made to fit J.D., it was long on her, with a hem that fell past her knees and sleeves that hung a good six inches past her fingertips. But sleeves could be rolled up. Better yet, the coat was big enough that she could button Ruby into it, next to her body, keeping her warm and safe.

As for fashion—but that wasn't even in the picture.

She gave him a grateful smile. "Thank you, this will do nicely."

"Then let's go."

Tucking extra diapers into the coat's pockets, Emma bundled Ruby into her blankets, with the pretty pink shawl on top. The cat watched from its spot on the hearth as they closed the door and stepped out into the clear afternoon sunlight.

They rode double on the sturdy brown horse, J.D. in front and Emma behind him. She sat astride, her skirt and petticoats bunched over the back of the saddle, her knees nesting behind his. Ruby was tucked securely between them, buttoned into the coat. Emma had never been much of a rider, and, since she could only hold on with her knees, she could easily imagine herself sliding off into a snow bank. But J.D. took the horse at an easy pace down the snow-packed trail.

For a winter day in Wyoming it was warm. Even so, puffs of white vapor formed with every breath. Frost made a filigree of the bare aspen branches, like Belgian lace against the blinding sky. To the north, the Wind River Mountains rose dazzling white, like the snowy spires of some mythic temple.

Emma added sunglasses to the list of things she missed. But had she ever breathed air this clean and clear, even in the mountains? And the stillness, broken only by bird calls, the crunch of snow and the sound of the plodding horse—even Ruby was quiet. Only now did Emma realize what a noisy century she'd left behind. Road traffic, planes and snowmobiles, clattering machinery, bustling people, public address systems, cell phones, elevator music. She'd gotten used to the constant racket around her, so used to it that she'd forgotten how to listen to Nature.

Not all progress was for the better.

By now they were seeing signs of the settlement. Here and there, snow covered fans of earth spread below the diggings of a mine. Sluice boxes stood empty next to the trickling creek. Emma remembered the research she'd done on Glory Gulch. The strike had played out not because there was no gold but because there wasn't enough water to wash the gold grains from the placer deposits where they lay. Some of the miners had gone to hard rock digging, but it was grueling work for scant profit. Most of the crude shacks along the trail were deserted and falling down. The place was already on its way to becoming the ghost town she'd visited in 2010.

The trail emerged onto an open slope, littered with stumps where the trees had been cut for buildings and mine timbers. J.D. stopped the horse in a wide spot where they could look down the gulch. The town, what there was of it, was scattered along both sides of the creek. Buildings had been erected helter-skelter so that from above, they looked drab-colored blocks, flung down by a careless child.

"Welcome to Glory Gulch." J.D.'s voice had taken on a weary tone. "On your far right, that building with the unfinished roof was supposed to be a stamp mill, to break up ore from the hard rock mines. The money ran out before the machines could be carted in, and there it sits. Below that, on the near side of the creek is what used to be the General Store. The owner moved away this past fall, before the winter set in. When the roads are clear, there's a Dutchman in South Pass City who brings supplies up in a wagon and sells them for a damned king's ransom. Unless we want to drive down and bring them back ourselves, that's all we've got. The empty lot next to the store was set aside for a school, but the town never got far enough along to bring in families."

Not every spot looked as bleak as J.D.'s description. Emma could see the livery stable with a half dozen horses in the corral. And there were other buildings, most of them small and square, that could be either homes or business. People—all men as far as she could tell—drifted up and down the street, crossing the creek by a series of makeshift plank bridges.

At the far end of the street was the largest building of all. Beneath its rusting metal slab roof, there appeared to be both a first and second floor. Foot traffic in out of the front door was heavier than anyplace else in the town. It looked familiar. A shiver crept up Emma's back as she realized why.

J.D. followed the direction of her gaze. "That's Mame's place with the long tin roof. Hotel, restaurant, bath house, saloon, brothel and meeting house, all rolled into one. You're looking at the Laughing Lady."

# CHAPTER ELEVEN

It was colder in town than at J.D.'s hillside cabin, most likely because the sun barely penetrated the depths of the gulch. Emma cradled Ruby beneath the black woolen coat as they rode into town. Men slogging along the snowy street grinned up at them and waved. Everyone would know J.D. of course. And Emma recognized townspeople who'd brought gifts to Ruby.

Up close, Glory Gulch was even more dilapidated than it had looked from a distance. Only the Laughing Lady, which boasted crimson railings and shutters, had any color to it. That appeared to be where they were headed.

"You're taking us to the saloon?" Emma whispered in J.D.'s ear. "A woman and a baby?"

"The Lady isn't just a saloon. It's where everybody in town gathers, whether they're drinking, gambling, sporting the girls or just want to get out of the cold. Mame welcomes anybody, as long as they behave. If there's a traveling preacher passing through, she's even been known to open the place up for a Sunday morning sermon." He guided the horse around a pile of frozen manure. "Besides, she and the girls will be right glad to see you. They were all excited when I told them you and Ruby would be stopping by."

"Oh. Fine, then." She was being prudish, Emma lectured herself. She wouldn't have hesitated to go into a bar in Lander, especially if they had good music. Maybe she wouldn't have brought Ruby with her, but this was a different time and place. And Ruby was only a baby. It wasn't as though the saloon was going to be a bad influence on her.

About then, Emma remembered Mame's offer of a bath. It would be bliss to soak in a tub of hot water and fragrant bubbles. But her doctor back in Lander had warned her not to take sit-down baths until she was fully healed from the birth. That bit of pleasure would have to wait a little longer.

As they drew up to the hitching rail, J.D. cocked one long leg over the saddle horn and slid to the ground. Looping the reins over the rail, he reached up to help Emma and down from the horse. Everyone on the street seemed to be watching them, and she suddenly felt self-conscious. Clasping Ruby with one arm, she clutched his shoulder with her free hand and slid down the horse's flank. She landed off balance, and might have fallen if his big hands hadn't steadied her. Feeling like an awkward cow, she let him take Ruby while she got her legs under her. His blue eyes smiled down at her.

"Every man here is jealous of me," he murmured. "You're a fine-looking woman, Miss Emma Carlyle, and I'm right proud to have you at my side. Now let's go in so I can show you and that little one off!"

Cradling Ruby in the crook of one arm, he offered her the other, like a courtier at a ball. Emma took it and walked beside him down the snow-slicked boardwalk with her head held high. This was the gallant side of J.D., the charming side of him that fluttered women's hearts and drew them into his bed and inspired legendary catfights. For a time she'd thought it was myth. No more. Walking beside him, Emma felt like a duchess.

Word of their arrival had preceded them. Mame herself flung open the doors of the Laughing Lady and stepped aside to welcome them in. "My stars and garters, look who's here!" she exclaimed. "Clear a table! Get some chairs, and the best bottle in the house!" Her bejeweled fingers snapped, and a white-aproned waiter flew to do her bidding. She was dressed in a satin gown that matched the green of her eyes. It clung to her ample figure, its draped skirt caught into an elegant bustle at the rear. The low-cut bodice threatened to spill her spectacular breasts into full view, but the fleshy expanse of her chest was filled in with ropes of pearls, garnets and peridots which, to Emma's unpracticed eye, looked real. Citrine earrings set in gold, as lavish as chandeliers in a ballroom, dangled from her earlobes, falling just short of her plump, bare shoulders. Her cheeks and lips were rouged, her eyes heavily kohled in the Hindu style. On any other woman the effect of so much costume, jewelry and makeup would have been clownish. But on Mame, everything came together with a certain panache that somehow seemed to suit her. The Laughing Lady was her castle and she was every inch its queen.

The castle itself was less opulent than its owner. Mame had done her best, but in a remote spot like Glory Gulch, only so much quality material could be brought in. The rest was a matter of making do. The polished mahogany bar bore some deep scratches, probably from having been hauled up the gulch by wagon. Its oiled surface contrasted with the rough log walls and the cheap pine tables and chairs, which looked to be in need of replacing. The glassware was expensive, as was the gilt frame surrounding the voluptuous painted nude who reclined above the bar. The rosy female was proportioned much like Emma herself. Maybe she'd come to the right century after all.

A dusty upright piano stood in the far corner of the room, closed and covered by a shawl. It looked as if it hadn't been played in a long time, which struck Emma as odd. According to the interview with Asa Smith, the photographer, the piano had been playing the night of J.D.'s murder, right up until the first shot was fired. Smith had even recalled the name of the tune. It had been Stephen Foster's *Beautiful Dreamer*.

"Here you are, your usual table, Mr. McNulty." The waiter had hustled the customers at the center table to another location, cleared away the glasses and wiped off the nicked wooden surface. According to Emma's research, this was where J.D. always sat, facing the door with his back to the piano, while he dined, drank or played cards. As J.D. helped her out of his coat and into her seat, Emma's eyes were drawn to the bare floor behind his chair. She knew exactly where to look. She'd visited this very spot in 2010 and seen the dark brown stain where his blood had soaked into the wood.

The floor was innocent of blood now. But Emma could not look at it without a sinking sensation in her stomach. It brought home the reality as nothing else could. In six weeks, J.D. would be shot dead at this table, in that chair—and the name of the saloon girl who held him as his life bled away be no more than a sob on the wind.

J.D. handed Ruby to Emma. Then he pulled out his chair and took his seat. Beyond him, at the bar, Petunia and Angel were drinking with the customers, most likely tea, which looked like whiskey in the glass. The time-honored practice kept the girls sober and saved the house money. There was no sign of Ella Rose.

Mame brought a bottle and two glasses over to the table and sat down in one of the empty chairs. "Don't you look lovely in that dress, dear? And let me see that little princess," she cooed, reaching for Ruby. "Goodness, but she's just taking it all in! Look at those big, bright eyes!"

Ruby lay in Mame's arms, gazing up at the glittering earrings. "Lucky for you she's not reaching for things yet," J.D. observed, pouring a half glass of whiskey. "She'd have those earbobs in a flash." He poised the bottle above Emma's glass and raised one questioning eyebrow.

Emma shook her head. After what alcohol had done to her mother she'd sworn off liquor, even in college. "I'll have what your girls are drinking, Mame," she said.

Mame beckoned the waiter. The drink he brought back on his silver tray did indeed prove to be tea. It was room temperature and not especially good, but then, that wasn't its purpose.

Mame leaned back in her chair, bouncing Ruby in the cradle of one crossed leg. Ruby blew a little bubble, still eying Mame's earrings. "So what do you think of our little town, Emma?" Mame asked.

"It strikes me as a refuge for brave souls."

"And a few cowards," J.D. chuckled at his own mysterious joke and raised his whiskey glass. Emma noticed for the first time that he wasn't armed. He'd taken the rifle down the trail but had evidently left it on the horse. Given J.D.'s reputation, there was little chance of it being stolen. He hadn't been armed when he was shot, either—or wouldn't be. Maybe if she could persuade him to wear a pistol in town, it might make a difference.

"Granted, there's not much going on tonight," Mame said. "But in the spring, when the road's open, things will liven up. Even when we get a midwinter thaw, it brings a few visitors—peddlers, gamblers and the like, up from South Pass City. The miners will have a little gold dust saved up, and there's always somebody coming around to relieve them of it."

*Yes*, Emma thought. *One of those thaws will come in February.*

*And one of your visitors will be a gambler named Pomeroy. He'll sit right here where I'm sitting. He'll have an ace in a holdout up his sleeve and a two-shot derringer in his vest. And there won't be a thing any of us can do about what happens next.*

"Are you all right, Emma?" Mame was gazing at her, looking concerned.

"Fine. Maybe a little too much rabbit stew, that's all." She glanced around for something to divert the conversation. "I see you have a piano. Do any of your employees play?"

Mame laughed wryly. "I wish! I paid a small fortune to have the thing carted up here. Then the man I was counting on to play it, a little rat named Eddie Bacon, got a better offer somewhere else, and off he went. The piano's been gathering dust ever since." She brightened, leaning toward Emma. "Say, you don't—"

"Oh, no!" Emma interrupted. "Maybe a little, but not really. I don't even read music!"

The absinthe eyes narrowed. "We don't have any music. That went away with Eddie the rat. But you do play, right?"

"Only by ear—and that, hardly at all," Emma hedged. There'd been a piano in the clubhouse of the trailer park where she'd grown up. When no one was around, she'd enjoyed sitting there alone, picking out tunes. She'd gotten pretty good at it, even figured out some basic chords on her own, just because they sounded right. But she hadn't played in years.

Mame pointed a bejeweled finger toward the piano. "Go."

When Emma still hesitated, J.D. joined in. "Give it a try. Nobody's going to think the worse of you for it. And you'll be doing something to repay the folks who've been good to you. People get downright hungry for music when they don't have it."

J.D.'s persuasion had pushed Emma's guilt buttons. She rose. "Just promise you'll stop me if you think I'm making a fool of myself. All right?"

"Fine." J.D. flashed her a dazzling grin.

Nerves crawling, Emma walked to the piano, slid away the dusty jacquard shawl and raised the cover off the keyboard. The sound of voices, the slap of cards and Petunia's laughter blended in her ears as she settled herself on the bench. Her corset pinched and her fingers felt as stiff as Popsicle sticks but it was too late to back out now.

The first tune that popped into her head was "Chopsticks," which she could play with the left hand accompaniment. With luck, nobody would pay her any attention. Taking a deep breath, she placed her trembling fingers on the keys and began to play.

The first few notes on the piano plunged the room into startled silence. The instrument had a tinny quality and was badly in need of tuning. But once she began getting used to it, Emma didn't mind. It sound exactly like what it was—a twangy piano in an old-time Western saloon.

She ended the third repetition of "Chopsticks" to a round of cheers. Feeling more confident, she launched into "Heart and Soul." Men were wandering in off the street, filling the saloon. Each selection she played was greeted with wild applause. Just as J.D. had said, they were hungry for music, even hers. She, who'd grown up with access to radio, TV, tapes and CD's, to say nothing of the new gadgetry for playing downloaded songs, could scarcely imagine such a hunger.

Emma tried to choose songs people would know, like "Camp Town Races," "Turkey in the Straw" and "Buffalo Gals." But even when she ran out of ideas and started playing tunes yet to be written, they were received with cheers. She fumbled her way through Hank Williams, Patsy Cline and Johnny Cash—the old songs she'd taught herself as a girl alone in the clubhouse while her mother was passed out at home. The people in the saloon probably thought she was some kind of musical genius. No matter that she was a fraud, Emma enjoyed the pleasure she was giving them. It was a pity she lacked the voice, and the self-confidence, to sing along.

It was Ruby who ended the program, howling to be fed. Emma left the piano to wild applause and returned to the table. J.D. was actually beaming. Angel and Petunia had taken the empty chairs and were passing Ruby back and forth between them. Mame saluted her from behind the bar. Ella Rose, looking rumpled, gave her a tired smile as she came down the stairs.

"You can feed her in my room," Angel said. "I won't be using it till later. Come on, I'll show you the way."

The stairway and hall were so dimly lit that Emma could barely see the floor. She followed the pale shape of Angel's yellow dress to a room at the far end of the hall. Angel paused to gesture toward the line of closed doors. "The first room, there, is special for the bath. The next three rooms are for the hotel—for the guests who wish to sleep." She glanced down at the floor as if what she'd said made her feel ashamed. "This room is mine. Those two across the hall are for Ella Rose and Petunia."

"Where does Mame live?"

"Up another stairway, toward the back. I have never seen her rooms but a woman who used to clean there told me she has amazing things. Many books and beautiful pictures on the wall. And little statues made out of stone, very old, older than Jesus the woman told me. Now that I will not believe. Nothing could be that old."

Angel drew a key out of her pocket and used it to open the door. The flickering lamp that dangled from a wall hook revealed a small and cluttered room, little more than a bed, a wash stand with a mirror, and a wardrobe spilling tattered, faded gowns and silk petticoats. There was no room for a chair, so Emma sat on the bed. Ruby was fussing impatiently, butting her head against Emma's shoulder. Emma's swollen breasts had begun to leak, trailing wetness down the front of her bodice. It was a relief to nurse and ease the pressure.

Murmuring an excuse, Angel left her and went back downstairs. Emma sat in the shadows thinking of the degradation that had taken place in that little room. Angel had said she didn't mind the work that kept her fed and sheltered. But her sad dark eyes told a different story. How could any woman be happy in such a life, where the most tender and intimate parts of her body were violated again and again for the price of a few dollars?

The girls were here of their own free will, she reminded herself. Despite Mame's setting aside part of their earnings, none of them had found the courage to leave and strike out on her own. Maybe it was because they had no other place to turn for acceptance and friendship. She imagined them looking in their mirrors by daylight, dread rising as they counted the age lines and gray hairs and wondered what was going to happen when they could no longer pretend to be young and pretty. What a desolate feeling that must be.

It was none of her concern, Emma told herself as she laid Ruby on the bed and replaced her wet diaper with the dry one she'd brought along. She had her own problems—more than enough to keep her occupied. But these so-called soiled doves were women with minds and hearts and the battered vestiges of pride. They had been kind to her. She couldn't help caring about them.

She returned to the saloon to find the girls tending to customers and J.D. seated at the table with Mame. He rose and walked around to hold out Emma's chair, then returned to his own place with a view of the door. "Mame's got a business proposition for you," he said. "One that might work out right well for you if you're interested."

"I want to hire you to play here—on Saturday nights, at least. More often if you want. I'll pay you the same hourly rate as I offered Eddie."

"No," Emma said.

"No? But why on earth not, dear? Everybody in town will be coming to hear you!"

"I don't mean I won't play. I'd be happy to. But I couldn't take money from you, Mame. Not after you've been so kind to me."

"I see." Mame toyed with the fake heart-shaped beauty mole on her cheek. "But there's got to be something in it for you. I know for a fact that you showed up on J.D.'s doorstep without a cent to your name. You'll be making money for me. It's only fair that you make a little yourself."

"How about this?" J.D. said. "Emma plays for tips, laundry and a weekly hot bath? Fair enough?"

Emma's eyes narrowed. "Since when did you become my business manager, J.D. McNulty?"

Mame chuckled. "You've got yourself a newfangled woman here, J.D. Actually those terms would be fine. And I can have one of the girls tend Ruby for you while you play. Something tells me they won't be doing much business while you're at the piano. Do we have a deal, Emma?"

Emma accepted the plump, bejeweled hand. "We have a deal."

\* \* \*

Emma's free arm clung to J.D.'s waist as the horse wound its way up the snowy trail. The afternoon had been almost warm while the sun was out. But now dusk had fallen and the air had taken on a hard chill. Inside the coat, Ruby snuggled against her. She'd been restless at first but had finally fallen into a light doze.

The flame-brushed sky above the western peaks deepened to violet, then to indigo as twilight closed around them. After delivering her and Ruby at the cabin, J.D. would have to ride the horse back to the livery stable. Then he would hike back up the mile-long trail on snowshoes. It would be long past dark by the time he arrived home again.

Emma had asked him earlier why he couldn't just leave the horse outside until morning. J.D. had pointed out that there was no shelter from the cold or from marauding wolves and cougars. It would be cruel misuse of a valued animal to leave it out in the winter night. "Of course we could always bring the horse into the cabin," he'd suggested. "It might mean we'd have to do some shoveling tomorrow..."

Only when Emma noticed the twinkle in his eyes had she realized he was teasing.

Now he was silent, his body alert beneath the sheepskin coat, which smelled of the oil he rubbed into the leather to keep it soft and waterproof. The stillness was broken only by the crunch of snow and the distant call of a hunting wolf. Emma shivered. Her arm tightened around him. If it came to it, she sensed, J.D. would protect her and Ruby with his life. But it wasn't their lives that were in danger.

"Tell me something," she ventured. "Tonight in the Laughing Lady, I noticed the way you sat, on the far side of the table with a view of the entrance."

"A lawman never sits with his back to the door. Not if he knows what's good for him. Old habits die hard. These days that's all it is, a habit."

"But you weren't wearing a gun. You left the rifle on the horse. Is there some kind of rule—?'

"No."

"What if a man were to draw on you? How would you protect yourself?"

"Try to talk him down. I'm good at talking."

"And if that didn't work?"

"Then I'd duck down and hope for the best." A long exhalation ripped out of him, like a sharp hook tearing through flesh. "You might as well know. After Laramie—after that farce with the Cleary gang—I became the man to beat. I lost count of the hot young guns that rode into town looking to shoot it out with J.D. McNulty. With most of them, I managed to bluff my way clear. Sometimes there was no way out.

"The last one I had to shoot barely looked old enough to shave. Looking down at that boy, lying there in the bloody dust, I made a vow. I promised myself and God that I would never take another human life. Then I sent for the undertaker and rode out of Laramie—for good."

J.D. cleared his throat. "There's another story for your damned thesis, Emma Carlyle. I hope your readers will find it entertaining."

Emma refused to be baited. "At least it explains what you're doing in a place like Glory Gulch. You're hiding, aren't you?"

He shrugged. "At least that's an honest way of putting it. Sooner or later somebody's going to track me down. When they do, maybe it'll be time to stop running and face the payback I deserve."

"No! You could change your name, go to California or Mexico and make a new start. Who'd know?"

"It's a small world, Emma. Smaller than even you can imagine. Word gets around. A man my size is hard to lose."

A sob of frustration escaped Emma's throat. She wanted to shake him. She wanted to grab him by the shoulders and scream the truth into the darkness. *There's a man coming—coming here to Glory Gulch! And he's going to kill you for no reason at all! You'll die senselessly, in a pool of your own blood, because you were too stubborn to leave town or even carry a weapon to defend yourself!*

But she knew he wouldn't believe her, no more than he'd believe she'd traveled here from the future. He'd dismiss her claims as crazy, and she'd lose what little credibility she'd gained with him.

Things were already falling into place, like the piano. She would likely be the one playing it herself. And even if she swore on her life never to play "Beautiful Dreamer," she might be compelled to follow the script that history had already written.

What if she tried to interfere with the shooting herself? She could refuse to play. She could steal the cards, divert the gambler, tie him up and keep in his room. She could even set fire to the Laughing Lady. But the conflagration could spread to the whole town taking homes and innocent lives. Fire wasn't an option. Was anything else?

She remembered the short story by Somerset Maugham, where a man glimpses the face of Death in the marketplace of Baghdad and flees to Samarra to escape—only to keep his appointment with Death in Samarra the next day. The moral of the tale seemed to be that fate is foreordained and escape is useless. But did that mean it was true?

As they rounded the last bend she could see the cabin, dark against the white snow. J.D. helped her and Ruby down from the horse and stoked the fire before leaving again. They'd enjoyed a light supper at the Laughing Lady so there'd be no need to cook again until morning.

The cat darted outside as they opened the door. Emma made a mental note to make sure it came in again. There were owls and foxes prowling the darkness. Even a clever cat would be in danger of becoming a meal.

A fresh wind had sprung up, spilling clouds over the western peaks. The air was chilly with a hint of moisture. J.D. collected his snowshoes and staff from the porch and tied them to the saddle, donned his gloves and felt Stetson and swung onto the horse.

"Be careful," Emma said. "If it starts to snow, you may want to stay in town."

"No need. I'll be back." When she continued to gaze at him with a worried look, he added, "I've survived this long without your fussing over me, woman. Now, leave it be."

Hurt by his shortness, Emma stood on the porch, watching him disappear into the twilight. The moist wind chilled her damp cheeks and blew her hair back from her face. Emma had lived in Wyoming all her life, and she knew the signs of a coming snowstorm. They were the same in the 19th Century as they were in the 21st. But then, why should she worry about J.D. tonight? There was no historical record of his dying in a blizzard. Destiny would keep him safe until that fateful poker game on the night of February 17th.

Ruby had begun to fuss. Emma turned back toward the doorway and went inside. As she closed the door, the cat streaked past her legs and made a beeline for the hearth. Outside, the first flakes of snow had begun to fall.

J.D. plodded upward through swirling clouds of snow. The weather was getting worse by the minute and he had a half mile of steep trail ahead. Maybe he should've taken Emma's advice and stayed in town. Mame would have been glad to put him up in one of her spare rooms. But his mother had always told him he had more stubbornness than common sense. Stubbornness had won out tonight when he'd snapped at Emma for fussing over him.

What a jackass he'd been. He owed Emma an apology. And when he made it back to the cabin, he'd swallow his pride and give her one.

It wasn't as if she'd been out of line. Far from it. Her advice had been smart and well meant. It was just that after so many years alone, he wasn't used to having someone care about him. It was a door he thought he'd closed forever, and now Emma had opened it. Her concern made him feel raw and exposed. J.D. didn't like it. And he didn't like having a woman tell him what to do.

It had started with her asking him why he didn't pack a pistol when he went to town. He should have told her to mind her own business. Instead, he'd ended up spilling his guts about that fool kid in Laramie and why he'd left. It was a story he'd never told anyone. Now, if she put it in her thesis, it would be out there for anybody to read, unless the whole damned thesis was another of her crazy stories.

He could not think about Emma Carlyle without confusion. Part of him wanted to grab her in his arms and kiss her until she simmered like molasses taffy in a big iron kettle. The other part of him, the scared spitless part, just wanted to be safe—safe from loss, from guilt and from all the other miserable baggage that came with caring about another person.

Emma and young Ruby had turned his quiet life into a bedlam.

He already dreaded the numbing bleakness that would come when they were gone.

A blast of wind sent J.D. staggering sideways. Blinding flakes peppered his face, coating whiskers, eyebrows and lashes with thick snow. He brushed it off with one half-frozen glove. The cold seemed to bite though his sheepskin coat, all the way to his bones.

Even with his face cleared of snow, J.D. could barely see. He was groping his way now, unsure of the trail beneath his snowshoes. Drifts whirled around him, trapping his every step. He could no longer feel his feet or his legs.

Surely the cabin couldn't be far. He'd been more than halfway home when the storm struck. But J.D. understood the dangers. He'd known too many folks who'd become disoriented in blizzards like this one. There was one man he'd discovered himself, on a ranch near Sheridan, frozen to death a dozen yards from his house, with his wife and children waiting inside.

He imagined Emma coming outside after the storm and finding his frozen body on the trail, the awful shock of it. He hoped she'd know that the cabin was hers, along with everything in it. She and Ruby were the closest thing he had to family.

But what in Sam Hill was he thinking? He'd been in scrapes a hundred times worse than this and made it through. He wasn't going to freeze. He was going to march up the damned trail, find the damned cabin and warm up his innards with a long drink of whiskey. And if Emma didn't like it, that was too bad!

The snow was getting deeper. He jammed his staff into a drift, feeling for the solid ground beneath. He was still probing when the snow at the trail's edge gave way. Cursing and flailing, J.D. tumbled down the slope and vanished into the savage white jaws of the storm.

# CHAPTER TWELVE

The mantel clock struck eleven as Emma finished feeding Ruby for the second time and tucked her back into her box. J.D. was overdue by more than two hours. She could only hope the man had come to his senses and decided to stay in town.

It was a reasonable assumption, and there was no need to worry, she told herself. After all, if J.D. had changed his plans to return home, there'd be no way to let her know. It wasn't as if he could just pick up a phone and dial her number.

Punching her pillow into shape, she climbed back into bed, curled on her side and pulled the quilt over her shoulder. Strange, how she missed the way his big, rangy body crowded the mattress, despite his efforts to give her room. She missed the light, easy way he snored, like a cat, alert even in sleep. She missed the warm, smoky odor of his body in the darkness and the way his presence always made her feel cozy and safe.

Now she lay awake, listening to the storm that battered the wall of the cabin. She hadn't slept all night. Given her knowledge of future events, she'd believed that J.D. would be safe in the storm. But what if she was wrong? What if her arrival had thrown events out of kilter? After all, if she hadn't been here, there'd have been no need to bring the horse up the trail, and no need for him to return it. In that other past—the past she hadn't been part of, he might not have gone to town at all.

But did that other past even exist? Right now the answer didn't matter. For Emma just one thing had become sure. J.D. McNulty was the stubbornest of men. He would slog through the blasted ice age rather than take a woman's advice and stay in town. He was out there in the darkness, and something was wrong. Her gut knew it. Her heart knew it.

Easing her bare feet to the floor, she laid a fresh log on the fire and sank into the rocker. The cat jumped from the hearth into her lap. Its claws worked the worn flannel fabric of her nightgown, sending prickles up her legs. She stroked its head, rousing a rusty purr as the clock struck the half hour.

Maybe this was a dream—the cabin, the cat, J.D., all of it. Maybe she would wake up in the hospital with nothing but an empty ache where Ruby had been. J.D. McNulty would be no more than a name on the cover of her thesis. She would graduate with her Master's degree and take up her teaching again in the fall. Wasn't that what she'd planned? Wasn't that what she'd wanted?

What if he was lost out there in the storm? What if he never made it back? Silently she prayed.

A feeble thump on the door roused her from a light doze. Emma sprang to her feet, sending the startled cat streaking under the bed. What she'd heard hadn't sounded like a knock. It had sounded more like a heavy animal falling against the planks.

Dared she open the door? Heart pounding, she found J.D.'s gun belt where it hung, slid the heavy Colt .45 out of its holster and thumbed back the hammer. With her free hand she slid back the bolt and opened the door.

A spectral figure, looking more like a tower of ice than a man, stumbled into the cabin.

"Oh, thank heaven!" Emma uncocked the pistol and clasped him in her arms. His face was a mask of snow. His clothes were rigid with ice. His hat was gone, his hair frozen to his head. "What happened?" Her frantic fingers worked off J.D.'s gloves. His hands were stiff with cold but thank heaven they didn't appear to be frostbitten. She rubbed them, blew on them, kissed them.

Getting the coat off him was like undressing a statue. He hadn't answered her question, but never mind. How could she expect him to speak when he was so cold? Under the oiled sheepskin, his shirt and the upper part of his long johns were dry, but the skin underneath was like ice. Emma heaped kindling on the fire and walked him to the rocking chair. His teeth had begun to chatter. He gestured downward, seemingly toward his feet. Yes, she needed to get his boots off. And she also needed to get some hot coffee down him. She checked the blackened pot and set it on the grate. The coffee had been sitting most of the day and would probably taste like battery acid, but at least it might jar his body awake. With the fire blazing, she went to work on his frozen bootlaces.

By the time she got J.D.'s boots off, he was talking a little. "Stepped off the damned trail. Thought I'd never make it back up. Hand me that jug, Emma girl. Twist the cork out if you don't mind."

Emma did as he asked. This was no time to argue or to bridle at his calling her "Emma girl." J.D. raised the jug. Snowmelt from his hair trickled down his face and throat as he drank. Emma had peeled off his socks and was rubbing the circulation back into his icy feet. Like his hands, they were long and narrow, almost elegant.

"That's more like it," he muttered, lowering the jug and setting it on the hearth. "When I was clawing my way back up that hill, the thought of a good stiff drink at the end of the trail was all that kept me going."

Emma's jaw dropped. She made a little sucking sound, as if she'd been gut punched. She'd prayed that he would come back— come back to *her*, not to that cursed jug. It was life with her mother all over again.

In cold silence, she snatched up the jug. Next to the bookshelf there was an open knothole in the floor. It had been stuffed with an old sock to keep out cold and vermin. Ripping out the sock, Emma tilted the jug and began pouring the rotgut whiskey down the hole.

"What do you think you're doing?" His voice was a croak.

"What does it look like I'm doing?"

"Cuss you, woman, that's not your property! You've got no right—" He strained against the chair, then sank back in helpless rage, too weak to get up. He watched with murder in his eyes as she poured the last of the whiskey through the floor.

"Why in hells name—?" He paused, groaned and shook his head as if the light had just dawned. "It was what I said about the whiskey getting me up that hill, wasn't it?"

"At least I don't have to draw you a picture." She set the jug, now empty, back on the hearth and poured him a mug of steaming black coffee. He accepted it, glaring at her from beneath his dripping eyebrows as she went for a towel to dry his head.

"What if I told you that the whole time I was crawling back up to that trail, all I could see in front of me was the vision your beautiful blue or brown or whatever the hell color they are eyes, and that they guided me home and saved my life?"

"I'd say that was a crock of bullshit."

"And you'd be right. So what's your problem, lady?"

Emma rubbed the springiness back into his hair, fighting the urge to twist his head and snap his neck commando style. "Nothing," she muttered. But no, that wasn't true. If she didn't speak her mind now, the anger would chew on her until she did.

She hesitated, groping for the right words. "It's just that I expected so much of you, JD. While I was working on my thesis, you were my hero. I thought of you as brave and gallant, even romantic. Then what happened? I met you, and you turned out to be this grumpy, smelly, foul-mouthed, chauvinistic, whiskey swilling wreck! Can you blame me for being upset?"

The towel had dropped from her hand. In the silence she could hear the hiss of his breath between his chattering teeth. He was dangerously chilled, Emma reminded herself. What he needed was warming up, not chewing out. Pouring the whiskey down that knothole had been a foolish impulse. Before the night was over, she might wish she hadn't done it.

His glacial eyes drilled into her. Now she'd done it, Emma thought. As soon as the weather cleared J.D. would send her and Ruby packing.

"I apologize for not meeting your romantic expectations," he growled. "As for the rest, I'll plead guilty to being a grumpy, foul-mouthed, chauvinistic, whiskey-swilling wreck. But smelly? Now that's a low blow, Emma Carlyle! Nobody ever called me smelly in my entire life! Now make yourself useful and help me out of these britches before I turn into a damned icicle!"

Emma counted her blessings and went to work.

The coat had protected J.D.'s upper body. But his blue jeans were frozen to his legs. They'd have to come off, and the long johns with them, before she could get him into bed and get him warm.

"It would be easier if you'd stand up," she said.

He dragged himself to his feet, one hand gripping the mantel for support. "I can make it this far, but I don't think I can bend over. You'll have to do the job for me, Emma girl. Sorry about your sensibilities. If the sight of a man bothers you, just pretend you're skinning a rabbit."

"Shut up and hold still." Emma ducked her burning face and began undoing the buttons of his thick flannel shirt. A rabbit indeed! Undressing J.D. would be more like skinning a grizzly bear!

She got the shirt and the top part of his long johns unbuttoned and peeled them down off his shoulders. His upper body was all muscle and sinew, the chest and shoulders broad, the skin dusted with a sheen of crisp, dark hair. He was as pale and cold as a corpse. A lesser human would have fallen to the storm and died of hypothermia, she realized. Only J.D.'s immense physical strength and will to live had kept him moving.

Her eyes found the ugly white-scarred pit where the rifle ball had buried itself in his side. Now she saw that there were other scars, white nicks and gashes from years of dangerous living. How many more scars were there on the inside? Emma wondered as she fumbled with the cold steel belt buckle. Her thesis research had barely skimmed the surface of the real J.D. McNulty. The man was as intelligent, profane, complex and tormented as a character in a James Joyce novel. Understanding him would be the quest of a lifetime.

And J.D.'s lifetime was growing perilously short.

His leather belt was stiff with cold. Emma managed to work the buckle open, only to be confronted with the frozen fastenings of his jeans. Her fingers had grown so numb she could no longer feel the buttonholes. She dropped to her knees on the rug to get a closer view of the task. Even then it was awkward. She tugged at the stubborn denim, her frustration growing by the second.

Little by little she became aware of a light pressure on the top of her head. J.D.'s hand was resting on her hair, his fingers tangling in her rumpled curls. The contact brought a freshet of hot tears to her eyes. They overflowed, spilling down her cheeks.

"It's all right, girl," he murmured. "These hands have had a lot more practice than yours. Move aside."

Emma sank back onto her heels, the hem of her nightgown pooling around her. His hands were stiff with cold, almost unusable, but he managed the buttons with more skill than she had. She rose to her feet as the top of his jeans fell open. Her crouched position had constricted the blood in her legs. The head rush sent her stumbling against him. He reached out to steady her, his hands icy cold through the worn fabric. Only then did he see the tears.

"Oh, lord, girl, don't cry." He gathered her against his chilled body. "I'm sorry. I can be a real son of a bitch when the mood strikes me. I know I put you through a bad time."

Emma's arms slid around him. He was shivering. She molded her body to his, kneading his back in an effort to warm him.

"Oh, damn it, Emma—" His knuckles caught the edge of her jaw, raising her face to his. His lips were raw and hungry. She fell into his kiss, flinging her soul wide open, holding nothing back. His tongue was cold in her warm mouth. He tasted of snow and whiskey and the foul black coffee she'd given him to drink. She couldn't get enough of tasting him, feeling him.

Her hands pushed downward, peeling away his frozen pants and long johns. His buttocks were like solid lumps of ice. "We've got to get you...warm," she gasped against his lips.

"I'm getting warm already."

"You need to be in bed."

"Sounds like the best idea you've had all night." The half-frozen garments slid down his legs to pool in a sodden ring around his ankles, leaving J.D. as naked as the day he was born. Skinning a rabbit, indeed! Right now that was the furthest thing from Emma's mind.

But he was still cold. With only her nightgown separating his flesh from hers, she could feel him shivering. Her hands could feel the goose bumps on his skin. "I can get you a quilt," she offered, "or some clean underwear."

His response was a rough laugh. "The bed will do fine, Emma. As long as you're in it."

Reeling across the cabin, he crawled between the sheets and reached out, tugging at her hand to pull her down beside him. Her eyes widened.

"But I'm not—"

"Come here, Emma." He drew her down into the bed and pulled the covers over them both. "Don't worry. I know you're not healed from the baby, and I swear to God I'd never hurt you that way. Right now all I want is to get warm. And believe me, until I do, you're in no danger whatsoever. Now, be a good girl and turn over. There you go."

He guided her onto her side and curled behind her, fitting her buttocks to his groin and his knees behind hers so that they lay like spoons. His body was as cold as marble, but at least the shivering had stopped. He sighed and draped his arm over the top of her, gently cradling one breast in his big palm. "You have the loveliest tits on God's green earth, Emma Carlyle," he murmured, "and many's the time I almost told you so."

"You're incorrigible," she whispered, but J.D. had already drifted into exhausted slumber.

When Emma next opened her eyes, the storm had passed. A thin crescent moon shone through the windowpane, casting a phantom square of light on the far wall. J.D. lay spooned against her, his sleeping body warm against her back. He was snoring lightly, his breathing deep and even. She yawned and nestled closer.

Her eyes shot wide open. The stallion-sized shaft jutting against her rump had *not* been there when they'd gone to sleep.

Hot faced, she lay there, wondering if she should move away from him. Propriety dictated yes. But the fire was already sizzling through her veins, like a trail of lit gunpowder about to reach the keg. Stuff propriety! J.D. McNulty was plastered against her with a hard-on to match the Washington Monument, and she wasn't going anywhere.

What a rotten time to be out of commission!

"Is it too early to say good morning?" His husky whisper curled in her ear like a wisp of smoke.

"I take it you've warmed up," she whispered back, not wanting to wake Ruby.

"So have you," he chuckled, sliding his hand to brush her breast through the soft flannel. His fingers toyed with the buttons in front, undoing them with the skill of a man who'd clearly had a lot of practice. She went molten as his hand closed gently over her bare flesh, his thumb brushing her nipple. "Lord, Emma, you can't know how much I've wanted to do this..."

She groaned. "J.D., you know I'm not ready to—"

"Hush." Leaning over, he brushed a kiss across her mouth. "I know you're not. Trust me, sweet girl."

He turned her toward him, the kiss deepening as he pulled the nightgown off her shoulders and worked it down past her hips. His mouth followed his hands, grazing her throat, nibbling along her collarbone. With a moan he pushed himself onto his elbows and buried his face between her breasts. She felt the bristly roughness of his unshaven beard, the muffled heat of his breath.

To her embarrassment, she realized her milk had begun to flow. She fumbled for her nightgown to blot it away.

"It's all right," he whispered. "Just let it be." His mouth moved downward, leaving a trail of kisses along her sternum and down to her slack belly. Emma would have given anything to be taut and slim, like an airbrushed supermodel or the heroine in a romance novel. But he didn't seem to mind. He pressed his face into her soft flesh, tasting her with his tongue. "I'm sorry to be so out of shape," she murmured. "I want to be beautiful for you..."

"You are beautiful, Emma. So beautiful with that soft, ripe belly. Think about what that belly's done and what it's been through. Be proud of it."

She arched against him, her hands tangling in his hair. Her body had become a throbbing well of need. She ached to feel him inside her, filling her, thrusting deep and hard. But he was so huge, and she was still sore from the baby. J.D. had told her to trust him, and she did. But could she trust herself?

He shifted in the bed, moving up beside her again, rolling onto his side and pulling her with him, so that they lay face to face. Once more he kissed her mouth, his hands sliding down her back to cup her buttocks and pull her in against his swollen cock. Emma moaned and ground her hips against him, wanting him so desperately that she was almost sobbing. His hand moved to her thighs, parting them to find the hot, wet folds and the distended nub at their center. His fingers stroked her lightly, gently through the slickness. She exploded as soon as he touched her, writhing and bucking against his hand, wanting more...more...

"Don't be afraid," He pressed in against her, slipping his immense cock forward to lie between her thighs. Understanding, she lowered her leg to cradle his shaft against her sensitive flesh.

Then he began to move—slowly at first, rubbing along her opening, triggering sensations so exquisite that it was all she could do to keep from crying out and waking the baby. His hands cupped her buttocks, clasping her to him. She met his thrusts, pushing wildly. Her hands clawed his bare back as wave after wave crashed through her body. His breath rasped in her ear, as he drove between her legs, harder and faster, sending her into a dizzying upward spiral. As a huge climax swept over her he moaned and released himself, spilling the warm slickness of his seed down the backs of her thighs. She held him as his breathing slowed, kissing his hair, his shoulders.

"Oh..."she whispered, falling onto her back. "That was...amazing."

He rose on one elbow. His eyes twinkled down at her in the darkness. "Think how much fun it'll be when we can do it for real."

The necessary bumping around, wiping up and resettling had awakened Ruby. J.D. lay back on the pillows as Emma, dressed in her nightgown once more, scooped her daughter up from her box and uncovered her breast.

Was there anything sweeter than lying here in the warm darkness watching the woman you'd just made love to nurse her baby? J.D. sighed with contentment. The only way it might be better would be if Ruby were his own child. But then, she was the next best thing. He had brought her into the world. His hands had been the first to hold her—by anybody's definition that ought to be good enough.

In the peace of the warm, quiet night, he allowed himself to dream. A little girl needed brothers and sisters. He imagined giving her a house full of them as he filled Emma's lovely white belly again and again. He imagined all of them together, growing up in a big, noisy, happy family, the kind of family he'd hoped for when he married his Maggie after the war. Now, with Emma, that hope almost seemed within reach again.

*Almost.*

J.D. knew better than to question the power of that word. For him, it carried the same meaning as *never*.

He had to make sure she understood that.

J.D. gazed up at Emma where she lay against the pillows with Ruby at her breast. A shaft of moonlight fell on her rumpled hair, casting a Madonna-like halo around her heart-shaped face. He filled his eyes with the sight of her. Lord, but she was beautiful. More than beautiful. She was wise and warm and funny and totally without guile.

Even while she was pouring his whiskey down that knothole, he'd been entranced by her innocence. It was probably the only thing that had kept him from breaking her pretty neck. But never mind. He could always buy more whiskey. But he could never find another woman like Emma...which is what made things so damnably difficult.

"What are you thinking?" She was gazing down at him, her breasts exposed to the moonlight.

"Naughty, wicked thoughts. Man thoughts."

"You can tell me."

"I'd rather show you."

She gave him a wink as she lifted the baby to her shoulder. "You nearly froze to death tonight. You'd better save your strength for later. Something tells me you're going to need it."

"I hope so." The thought of having her again was already making him hungry for the next time. This couldn't wait, he told himself. The longer he delayed telling her the truth, the harder it would be.

He waited until she'd settled Ruby in her box and wriggled back down into the bed beside him. Then he propped himself on one elbow, cleared his throat and prepared himself to say what needed to be said.

"You're a wonderful woman, Emma. In fact, you're everything a man like me could ask for. Making love with you was like tumbling into heaven. But what we have here, you and me and the little one—it can't be for keeps."

"Oh?" Her tone was cautiously neutral.

"A lawman like me makes a lot of enemies over the years, and there's no telling when one of them, maybe a whole gang of them, will show up looking for trouble. Even in a godforsaken spot like this, they could track me down, or even come across me by accident. I'll likely spend the rest of my days moving from place to place, trying to stay one step ahead of them. Do you understand what I'm saying?"

She nodded, her eyes large and luminous in the darkness. "I do, and I was expecting it. When it comes time to move on, you can't be burdened with a woman and child. Right?"

"You and Ruby could never be a burden to me, Emma. If I thought there was a way for us, I'd be on my knees to you right now. But there's no way. A fine woman like you deserves a better life than what I could offer. A fine home, a respectable place in society, money, safety, all the things I can't give you—"

"Oh, for heavens sake, J.D., stop making a speech, especially one that sounds like you've already made it to a dozen women! Just because we had a good time in bed doesn't mean I'm expecting you to propose!"

He stared at her, startled and bemused. She had him. He *had* delivered similar speeches a number of times before, usually to the accompaniment of tears, wails and flying objects.

"Well, that's refreshing at least."

"I'm a modern woman. I have a good education and I'm not afraid of hard work. It may take a little time, but Ruby and I will be fine. So stop patronizing me. I'm a big girl. When the time comes, I can deal with reality."

He cleared the tightness from his throat. "There's something else you need to know. You and little Ruby are the closest thing to family I've got right now. If anything happens to me, f I have to leave, or something worse, the cabin and everything in it is yours. You'll find a few bags of gold dust under the floor. Not much, but enough to help you make a new start somewhere."

"J.D.—"

"No, listen. I haven't had a chance to draw up papers. But Mame knows. I told her tonight when I brought the horse back to town. She'll see that it's taken care of." He leaned over and brushed her sweet, ripe lips with his. "Now, what do you say we get some sleep while we can? It'll be morning all too soon."

*All too soon.*
Emma lay beside him in the darkness, listening to the deep sound of his breathing. In a few hours the darkness would begin to fade. The birds would awaken to song. J.D. would stir beside her and get up to start his day. One more day of the time that remained.

Did he sense what was going to happen? Surely he did. His generous provision for her and Ruby wasn't the act of a man who expected to live a long time. J.D. was a man in touch with his instincts. Those instincts had seen him through a lifetime of danger. It could well be they were telling him the end was near.

It crossed her mind that he might be hiding some grave illness. But that couldn't be true. J.D. was as strong as a bull. No sick man could survive a long fall, climb out of a canyon in a raging blizzard and make love to a woman, all in the space of a few hours. He had lived a violent life. It was only natural that he'd expect a violent death.

Should she tell him what she knew? Would it make any difference?

Emma curled against his side, matching the pace of her breathing to his. She had time, about five weeks by her reckoning, to make a decision. Meanwhile, she would do the only thing that remained to her. She would love him with all her heart, body and soul, holding nothing back. If her love could save him, she would thank heaven for the miracle.

If it couldn't... A single tear pooled along the side of Emma's nose. If J.D.'s fate was cast in stone, she would have to accept the inevitable. But when he died, a vital part of her would die with him.

She'd lain awake most of the night. Now, at last, she dozed off. Dreams stirred and awakened in her mind. She was back in Lander, grocery shopping at the Wal-Mart Super Center on Main Street. She'd left Ruby on the cart in her baby seat while she reached for something on a high shelf. When she turned around, the cart and Ruby were gone. Frantic, she raced up and down the aisles wrecking displays in her haste. Cans and boxes crashed to the floor as she ran, screaming her daughter's name. From near the front of the store, she heard two gunshots. She plunged toward the sound, knocking shoppers and carts out of the way. A few yards from the Express Checkout register, she found J.D. sprawled on the linoleum. Blood streamed from one bullet wound in his shoulder and another in his chest, right where his heart would be. People were rushing from all directions. Someone was screaming for an ambulance. Ruby was nowhere to be found.

Emma's eyes flew open. She stared up into the darkness as her panic ebbed. She'd been dreaming; that was all. Ruby was sleeping peacefully in her box. J.D. was snoring softly beside her. For now, her little world was safe.

But for how long?

How long before the nightmare became reality?

For the rest of the night she lay pressed against J.D.'s warmth, afraid to close her eyes again.

# CHAPTER THIRTEEN

The corner where the Christmas tree had stood was empty now. The young pine had stayed green for nearly three weeks. Then its needles had turned brown and begun to drop. J.D. had declared it a fire danger and hauled it outside to be broken up for kindling. Emma had suppressed a sigh at its passing. One more good memory gone.

The origami figures weren't worth saving, and the peppermint sticks were no more. That left the star, which J.D. had unpinned from the tree and placed in Emma's hand. "For Ruby, as a keepsake," he'd said.

Emma had tucked the marshal's badge under the blankets in Ruby's box for safekeeping. For J.D., the star was a reminder of a past he wanted to forget. For Ruby it would be a memento of her birthday and the man who'd brought her into the world. Maybe someday she'd pin it to the top of her own Christmas tree, in memory.

The days were flying past. Emma had sketched a crude calendar in pencil on a scrap of wrapping paper. She kept it tucked between the pages of *Great Expectations* and only marked it when J.D. was out of the cabin. With every "X" she made over a date, her anguish deepened.

In her mind she'd played out dozens of scenarios that might save J.D. —knocking him out and tying him up, stealing his pistol and shooting the gambler herself, even leaping in front of him at the critical moment. Any one of those wild schemes might work. But it came down to the question of changing what was fated to happen. How could she save the man she loved from a senseless death when the date, the circumstances and that ghastly photograph were all a part of recorded history?

The answer to that question lay beyond Emma's powers of reason. She only knew she couldn't let it stop her.

Today was Tuesday, the 23rd of January. The day was clear and chilly, the snow diamond bright in the icy blaze of the sun. J.D. had taken the rifle and gone out early for some hunting. Emma had long since abandoned her soft spot for Bambi. If J.D. could bag a deer they'd have fresh meat for a couple of weeks, as well as a stash of jerky, which she loved.

In his absence, she'd decided to give the cabin a midwinter cleaning. Heating some water, she scrubbed down the kitchen. Then she found an old broom and began to sweep the floor. She was shaking a rug off the porch when she spotted a rider coming around the last bend in the trail.

Shading her eyes against the glare, she recognized Mame's stocky figure and drooping cloak. She was riding J.D.'s brown horse, which he'd invited her to use anytime she came up to the cabin. Emma gave her a welcoming wave and hurried inside to put on some water for tea. Mame came less frequently now that Emma was strong enough to take care of herself and Ruby. But her visits were always a treat.

Emma hurried outside to hold the reins and take the carpet bag while Mame climbed out of the saddle. She descended precariously, landing on the packed snow with a little grunt.

"I've got your gown in here," she said, reclaiming the carpet bag. "Ella Rose made it to her own measurements. You'll want to try it on before you wear it Saturday night. But first I want to see my little darling!"

She bustled into the cabin, dropped the carpet bag on the bed and swept Ruby out of the cartridge box. "There's my little love! My stars, but she's growing!"

Ruby was thriving on Emma's milk. Over the past month she'd blossomed into a plump, rosy, adorable little girl. Mame cuddled her against her pillowy breasts, crooning and murmuring baby talk. Ruby gazed up at her with wondering blue eyes. Wanting its share of attention, the cat jumped down from the mantel to rub against Mame's skirts.

"Open my bag and look inside," Mame said. "Ella Rose has been busy."

Emma reached into the carpet bag to find two baby-sized gowns, one muslin and one calico. Both were cut long with drawstrings at the bottom. Delighted, she held one, then the other up to the baby. "Look at that, Ruby! Your first real outfits! Something tells me I'm going to have to learn to sew!"

"All in good time, dear. Now let's try on the gown. Then we can have some tea and visit."

While Mame bounced Ruby on her lap, Emma brewed the tea, then unbuttoned her calico house dress and pulled it off over her head. "My, but you're looking fit," Mame commented. "Who would believe you'd just had a baby?"

The compliment pleased Emma. On this 19th Century regimen of active days and no junk food, she was actually losing weight. Her bones had sharpened, her flabby stomach was melting away and the corset no longer cut off her breath.

Mame laid Ruby on the bed next to the cat. Then she took a paper-wrapped bundle out of her carpet bag and untied the strings. She'd made up her mind weeks earlier that Emma should have a fancy gown to wear for her weekly piano concerts at the Laughing Lady. Emma had gone along with the plan to please her, but even she had been caught up in the excitement. Ella Rose, a gifted seamstress who made gowns for herself and the other girls, had been busy stitching it out of a spare bolt of satin. This would be the first time Emma had seen it.

"Oh!" Emma gasped as the soft, copper-colored fabric tumbled free of the paper. "Oh, Mame, it's beautiful! So elegant!"

"Try it on. We want it to fit."

Emma slipped the gown carefully over her head. It glided over her corseted figure. It was elegant in its simplicity, with hand-stitched tucks and smocking , drawn up to a modest bustle in back and cut in a wide v in front to display Emma's creamy shoulders.

Squinting nearsightedly, Mame helped her with the fastenings. "It's perfect!" she pronounced. "And the color is gorgeous with your hair and eyes. J.D. is going to bust his buttons when he sees you Saturday night! I only wish we had a full-length mirror so you could see yourself. That will have to wait."

Emma did a slow pirouette. "I've never had such a beautiful dress! I feel like Cinderella! And you're my fairy godmother, Mame! You and Ella Rose! Help me think of something nice to do for her!"

"Just the pleasure of seeing you will be enough. That and hearing your music."

"She does beautiful work. She should be a seamstress. Maybe when she leaves the business—"

"That's what I've told her. I've even offered to advance her a loan for a little dress shop in Cheyenne. I'll be shutting the Lady down this spring. All three of the girls will need a place to go. Angel's got a man who wants her to marry him. He's not rich or handsome, but he'll be good to her. And Petunia?" Mame shrugged. "She's talking about Virginia City. I expect she'll end up like me, with a place of her own."

"And what about you, Mame? Will you be all right?"

"Oh, I'll be fine. Maybe I'll go someplace warm, like Arizona. I've got a knee that troubles me in cold weather, and it's cold most of the time here."

"But the town will miss you, Mame. The Lady's the only place where friends can get together." Emma undid the buttons, slipped off the dress and folded it carefully.

"The town's dying. I reckon everybody will be moving on once the roads are dry and the grass is green. Change is the way of the world, dearie."

"And what can you do if you don't want things to change?" Emma asked impulsively.

Mame had picked up Ruby again. She sat in the rocker, watching with her strange, painted eyes as Emma pulled on her calico dress and retied her apron. "So, it's J.D., is it?"

"J.D., Ruby, this cabin. Everything I want is right here, right now."

"But surely, when J.D. moves on, he'll take you and the baby with him."

Emma shook her head, afraid to tell even Mame the whole truth. "He says it's too dangerous for a woman and child. And I'm guessing that having us along would be more dangerous for him as well. He's made it quite clear that when the time comes for him to go, he'll go alone."

"He told me about wanting to leave you the cabin and the gold."

Emma poured tea into two mugs and gave the best one to Mame. After putting Ruby back in her bed, she took her own tea and sank onto the hearth. "I'm afraid for him, Mame. Something's going to happen. I can feel it, and I think J.D. can feel it, too. What can I do to protect him?"

"A man like J.D.?" Mame blew lightly on her tea, then shook her head. "You can't protect him. No more than you can protect a wild animal. He wouldn't stand for it."

"But if I knew what was going to happen—and if I knew when and how. Could I stop it?" Emma was skating dangerously close to the truth. Maybe too close. The last thing she wanted was for Mame to think she was delusional.

Mame lowered her mug. "But how on earth could you know such a thing? Are you aware of some plot against J.D.?"

"I wish I were. Then I could just tell him about it. But no, this is more like a premonition. " Emma groped for a better approach. "What if I asked you not to open the saloon on one Saturday night next month? Would you do as I asked?"

"Maybe. But only if you could give me a solid reason."

"I can't. Not one that you'd believe."

"What I'd believe might surprise you. At least I promise to keep an open mind."

*Would you believe it if I told you I came here from the future?* Emma's mind spoke, but the words refused to come. Had she become so immersed in the past that she'd stopped believing her own story? That world she'd come from, with all its stress and clamor, was becoming more remote, more dreamlike with each passing day.

"Emma, are you all right?" Mame asked. "I've known women to get a bit strange after the birth of a child."

"I'm fine. It's just that—"

"Hello in there!" J.D.'s shout rang across the yard. "Did anybody order roast venison for dinner?"

Evidently the hunt had been successful. Emma threw on her parka and followed Mame outside to where J.D. was dragging the carcass of a well-fed yearling buck over the snow. His face wore a triumphant grin. "Found him just over that low ridge and dropped him with the first shot. There should be enough meat on this boy to keep us in venison stew for a month!"

His words twisted in Emma's gut. If history played out as written, the meat would last longer than J.D.'s life.

Overcome by despair, she turned away. Only after she'd composed herself did Emma turn around again. J.D. was occupied with the deer and had noticed nothing. But Mame was watching her with a puzzled, yet knowing expression on her painted face.

It was Saturday night in Glory Gulch, and the Laughing Lady was filling with customers. J.D. sat at his customary table, shuffling the deck of cards in his hands. Not that he planned to play them. Tonight he was here for Emma.

She and Mame had been downright secretive about that gown she planned to wear. Since the dress was stored in a closet at the Laughing Lady, Emma had worn her plain blue gingham for the ride down the trail. Mame had insisted on her coming early for her bath, so the girls could do her hair and add a few touches of makeup and jewelry.

J.D. glanced at his pocket watch. He loved the soft, natural look of Emma in her hand-me-down cottons with her breasts straining the frayed seams and her rumpled hair falling around her face. But the idea of seeing her all dolled up in satin and rouge intrigued him. He looked forward to the next hour—and to a night of loving her in the cozy warmth of their bed.

They still made love in the restricted style he'd shown her that first night—although, between them, they'd come up with some delicious variations. He was getting anxious to have her in the good old-fashioned way, with his cock buried to the hilt inside that hot, wet, voluptuous body of hers. But J.D. was determined not to rush her. When she was fully healed, Emma would let him know.

Leaning back in his chair, he glanced around the main salon of the Laughing Lady. Chairs were crammed around the tables, with extra seats lined up along the back wall. Every mother's son in Glory Gulch was here, even the Chinese brothers who did the laundry. Even J.D.'s own table was full.

Petunia was tending bar and Ella Rose was waiting tables. J.D. spotted Angel at a corner table with Ruby in her arms. A husky miner with pale eyes and a homely, honest face sat beside her, one hand resting possessively on her shoulder. J.D. had learned they were going to be wed. In light of that fact, Angel was no longer working upstairs.

There was no sign of Mame. She was probably helping Emma dress. J.D. was glad the two women had become friends. For all her strange looks and tarnished profession, Mame had a heart as good as the earth itself. As for Emma, he was still trying to corral his feelings for her. Love was something he'd given up on years ago. But with Emma and little Ruby sharing the cabin, he was as close to being happy as he'd been in years. For the first time in recent memory he looked forward to waking up each morning, knowing that when he opened his eyes he would see her sweet, sleepy face next to his on the pillow. It was a face he wouldn't mind waking up to every morning of his life—if only he could promise her the peace and security a good woman deserved.

He was grateful, as well, that her mind had cleared. She was no longer spouting gibberish about invisible libraries and machines that could take pictures of unborn babies. That bump on her head had rattled her brain something fierce. But now that it had healed, she appeared normal in every respect—better than normal in one, he mused, thinking of their nights together. There were still things he couldn't explain, like those ungodly clothes she'd been wearing the night she showed up at his door. But as long as she was all right, and they had what they had, maybe that didn't matter.

A hush had fallen over the room. As J.D. swung his chair around to face the piano, he saw Mame walk in from the back, followed by Emma. His breath caught in his throat. Emma had always been a beautiful woman, but tonight she looked like a queen in a satin gown that flowed over her ample curves like liquid copper. Mame's girls had pinned up her taffy-colored hair and added a fall of fake ringlets down the back. They'd kept her makeup subtle, adding just enough color to enhance her features. Her throat was bare but a pair of splendid carnelian earbobs dangled almost to her shoulders.

His Emma was a goddess tonight. Every man who looked at her would be drooling down the front of his shirt. But only he knew the woman beneath the trappings—knew her in every sense of the word. J.D. beamed with masculine pride.

Arranging her skirts, she sat down at the piano. The first half dozen tunes she played were familiar favorites. Then she began taking requests, a practice her audience had come to relish. She played "Amazing Grace," followed by "Golden Slippers" and a newly popular song, "Little Brown Jug."

"Play 'Beautiful Dreamer!'" a voice called from the back of the room.

J.D. saw her body stiffen. Her fingers froze in midair.

"'Beautiful Dreamer!'" Another call came from a miner at the bar.

Still Emma hesitated. Only when a third voice took up the call did her fingers drop to the keyboard. She took a deep breath. A shudder passed through her body. Her fingers stumbled through the first notes of the haunting Stephen Foster song, then eased into the melody like a stream breaking through spring ice. The music flowed through the room, opening doors to poignant memories. J.D. had never heard her play with more emotion.

When she finished there was a moment of silence. Then a burst of applause swept through the saloon. Emma sagged on the bench. When she turned toward J.D. he saw that her face had gone pale beneath her rouge.

Alarmed, he rose and strode to the piano. "Emma, are you all right?" he asked in a low voice.

She nodded. "Fine. Just this blamed corset." she muttered.

"Show's over, folks!" J.D. announced to the crowd. Then, as the room filled with grateful applause, he gave her his arm and escorted her into the back hallway.

"What is it?" he demanded as soon as they were alone. "I was afraid you were going to faint out there."

The color was returning to her face. "I'm all right. I can go even back and play some more if they want me to."

"You're through for the night. Let's get you out of that corset and get you home to bed."

"Are you giving me orders, J.D.?" Her voice flung a challenge but her hand quivered against his arm.

"Yes, damn it, I am. Now, where's the dressing room?"

Mame had bustled in from the bar. "Are you all right dear?"

"Yes, really. Just need this corset loosened a little."

"We'll take care of that." Mame's eyes flashed toward, J.D. "Run along now. We'll be fine."

J.D. watched the two women disappear through a side door. Something was wrong; he could feel it in his bones. Emma had been fine until she played that song. Clearly it meant something to her. His first guess might have been a lost love or some other tragedy. But J.D., who prided himself on his ability to read people, sensed that the emotion on her white face hadn't been grief or regret.

It had been stark fear.

They left town earlier than usual, riding double on J.D.'s patient brown horse. After his ordeal in the storm, J.D. had hired a youth to follow them home on a mule. The young man would lead the horse back to town, saving J.D. the long uphill walk in the dark. So far the arrangement had worked out well—so well that Emma was sorry they hadn't thought of it sooner.

The night sky was diamond clear, the waning moon two nights past fullness. Snow crunched a lulling cadence beneath the horse's hooves. The air was so cold that breath emerged in clouds of white vapor. The silent trees were coated with frost. On such a frigid night, it was hard to believe that a midwinter thaw was just around the corner.

Maybe the thaw wouldn't come. Maybe the winter weather would hold, keeping them safely snowbound until spring. But that, Emma knew, was wishful thinking. The thaw would come. The road would open. And in three weeks J.D. was destined to die.

The boy on the mule was lagging well behind the horse. On most nights, Emma would have welcomed the privacy. But tonight she sensed that J.D. was preparing to grill her about tonight's strange behavior. His questions would demand answers.

She'd long since grown sick of lies and evasions. But how could she tell him what she'd realized tonight—that *she* had been, or would be, at the piano, playing "Beautiful Dreamer" when the fatal bullet entered his heart?

The implications of her discovery were staggering. Had she been living in the past all along? Had her whole existence in the 21st Century—her childhood, her teaching career, her unplanned pregnancy and her thesis—been nothing but a long, involved dream, a dream from which she'd awakened the night she'd found J.D.'s cabin?

If she hadn't come from the future, who was she? How had she come by the knowledge that J.D. was going to die?

Heaven help her, she was starting to question her own sanity.

Ruby stirred against her, whimpered and settled back into sleep. Emma bent over her, filling her senses with the sweet baby smell. Her daughter was the one solid reality her life. No matter which century her daughter had come from and who had fathered her, Ruby was flesh of her flesh. As long as they had each other, they would never be truly lost.

"Are you all right?" J.D. asked. "It's not like you to be so quiet."

Emma's arm tightened around his waist. "I'll be fine," she said. "Don't worry."

"It was the song, wasn't it?"

"The song?" She feigned innocence.

"'Beautiful Dreamer.' Something about it frightened you. When you turned away from the piano you looked like you'd seen the devil himself. What was it, Emma? I want the truth."

"Is that why you're using your marshal's voice?"

"Damn it, woman, don't you know I care about you? If something's wrong, I want to help."

"There's nothing you can do. Nothing I can do, either. So there's no point in my telling you, is there?"

He muttered under his breath. "Blast it, Emma, I don't like my woman keeping secrets from me!"

His words rankled her. "So I'm your woman, am I? Then what about you, J.D. McNulty? You hoard your precious secrets as if they were diamonds! You've been good to me. You've been generous with your food and your bed, but when it comes to sharing what really makes you tick, you're as miserly as Ebenezer Scrooge!"

"Why should I tell you anything?" he growled. "You're just going to write it down in that damned thesis of yours for all creation to read!"

"My thesis doesn't exist, J.D. Not in this world!"

"You're saying you made the whole thing up?"

Emma shook her head. This discussion was getting off track and out of control. "It's too complicated to explain right now. All I meant to say was that when a man and woman are sleeping together, there should be an emotional connection as well as a physical connection."

"Horsefeathers! Two people can have one helluva good time without even knowing each other's names! I happen to know that for a fact Miss Emma Carlyle!"

"I've no doubt you do," Emma muttered.

"So what are you whining about?"

"I'm not whining. And this discussion is over."

"Fine with me." He sat rigid in the saddle as the horse rounded the last bend in the trail. Emma slumped behind him, struggling to regroup her thoughts. At least she'd sidetracked his questions about the song. Aside from that, it was all she could do to keep from pummeling his back in frustration.

J.D. had said she was his woman. But he'd said it as if she were a possession, like his horse or his rifle. And the point she'd tried to make about emotional intimacy had been completely lost on him. Maybe such impractical notions didn't exist in this century. Either that or J.D. McNulty was the most thick-headed, insensitive male who ever strode the face of the earth.

By the time they reached the cabin, the mule and its rider had caught up with them. J.D. helped Emma dismount and paid the lad to take the horse back to town. Ruby was awake and fussing. Emma changed her diaper while J.D. lit a lamp, stoked the fire and made sure the cat was safely in. Then she sat down in the rocker and put the baby to her breast.

The awkward stillness was broken by the hiss of burning sapwood and the hungry little grunts of Ruby nursing. Emma kept her eyes on the baby while J.D. puttered in the kitchen, preparing the sourdough for tomorrow's biscuits. The tension between them was heavy and cold. She'd pushed him too far. He'd pushed right back. Now they were at an impasse.

J.D. stole furtive glances at Emma as he worked. She looked beautiful, there in the rocker with the baby at her naked breast; even more beautiful then she'd looked at the piano tonight, wearing that spectacular gown. But she was still angry. The tight set of her mouth left no room for doubt of that.

With an ordinary woman, a few kisses and pretty words might

set things right. But his Emma was anything but ordinary. She had depths that even he couldn't penetrate.

J.D. had played dumb on the ride home. But he understood what she wanted. Emma was asking for something he hadn't given any woman since Maggie. She was asking for his soul.

He added flour and a little sugar to the sourdough and set the bowl on a high shelf where the warm air would help the yeast bubble. Emma had evaded his question about the song. She had secrets of her own, and he wasn't going to pry them out of her without paying the price. But maybe it was time. Before he could protect her, he needed to find out what she was hiding.

In the hospital tent at Gettysburg, when the doctor had removed the rifle ball from his side, J.D. had endured the agony without anesthesia. He recalled that feeling now as he took a seat on the hearth, facing the rocker.

This was going to hurt like hell

He needed a drink.

He fought the temptation as Emma rose to put the baby to bed. She brushed past him coldly, avoiding his eyes. The devil with it— he hooked a finger through the handle of the jug, twisted out the stopper and raised it to his lips.

Emma lowered Ruby into her box and tucked the blankets around her. Her buttons were still undone in front. No matter, she'd be getting ready for bed in a few minutes. The evening in town and the spat with J.D. on the way home had left her drained. All she wanted to do was sleep.

She turned around just in time to see J.D. raise the jug and take a leisurely swallow of whiskey.

Already raw, she lashed out at him. "Do you have to drink now? You know how much it annoys me! Sometimes I think you do it just to show me you can!"

"So it annoys you, does it?" He jammed in the stopper and set the thick ceramic jug back on the hearth with a thud. His eyes narrowed dangerously. "Maybe I need to remind you whose cabin this is."

"You sound like my mother!" Emma snapped. "She claimed she had the right to drink whenever and wherever she wanted. She didn't care how much it hurt people who loved her, and neither do you! Go ahead, then. Exercise your precious right! Empty the whole blasted jug if you want to! I'm going to bed!"

She spun away, but he lunged for her and caught her arm. "Sit down," he growled, steering her toward the rocker. "You want to talk about my drinking? Fine, we'll talk about it. First of all, Emma Carlyle, you've never really seen me drink. Oh, you've seen me take a swallow or two. But you've never seen me drink myself into a stinking stupor. You've never seen me passed out on a crap heap in some back alley, so far gone that I didn't care if I lived or died. I haven't done that in years. But I've been there. Sit down, lady, and I'll tell you the whole story."

Quivering, Emma lowered herself to the rocker and clasped her white-knuckled hands in her lap. J.D. had never talked to her this way before. He had never *looked* at her this way.

He sat down on the hearth, facing her. "I started drinking after Gettysburg," he said. "First it was because of the wound. There was a lot of pain and I needed something. I chose alcohol over morphine because I judged it to be the lesser evil. But even after the worst was over, I kept on with it. Whiskey became my crutch. It helped me forget what I'd seen on the battlefield—men dropping around me, friends blown apart by shells, the stench of guts, the Rebel boy who died on the end of my bayonet—Lord he couldn't have been more than sixteen, and he bawled for his mother before I finished him. By all odds I should've died that day. There've been plenty of times when I wished I had."

Emma's free hand reached out to stroke J.D.'s shoulder, then stopped. She wasn't going to coddle him. "A lot of men who fought in the war had to deal with wounds and bad memories," she said. "That didn't mean they crawled into a bottle when they got home."

"Don't you think I've told myself that? Don't you think I've wished myself in hell a thousand times for what happened?"

She saw the torment etched on his face. Unvoiced questions froze in her throat.

"You wanted the truth. Fine, I'll give it to you. And when I'm done you won't want anything more to do with me.

"Before the war, I was promised to a girl I'd known all my life. Maggie was her name, and she was as pretty as a little spring violet. When I came home, she was waiting for me. She had a loving heart, and she loved me with every blessed beat of it. She didn't care that I was a broken man. All she wanted to do was get married and start a family. So we did.

"For a while I thought that Maggie's love, and the baby that was coming, would be enough to save me. But the nightmares about the war didn't stop. I'd wake up in the night sweating and cursing, scaring the poor girl to death. Some of my friends had come home from the war with their own nightmares. We started talking together, then drinking together, staying out till all hours. Before I knew it, I was out of control.

"One night I came home late, so damned drunk I could barely stay in the saddle. I staggered into the house and found Maggie on the floor. I'd left her alone, and she'd started her labor early. We lived out of town with no near neighbors, and she was too far along for me to leave her and get help."

Emma's hands twisted the fabric of her skirt as she imagined the scene—J.D. staggering in through the door, finding his pretty little wife in agony. A memory like that would be enough to destroy a man. And it very nearly had.

"She was too small to have the baby, and I was too drunk to save either of them," he said. "All I could do was hold her while she died. Somebody came by the next day and found me with her still in my arms. I don't remember it all, but they said I was howling like a dog."

He stared into the fire, which had grown to a crackling blaze. Emma sensed that if he could he would simply fall into the flames and burn like a soul in hell, the way his soul had been burning for years.

"J.D.—" She wanted to reach out to him but her hand wouldn't move. He shook his head, rose and walked away from her.

"I sobered up long enough for the funeral. Then I went on a bender that lasted Lord knows how long. At some point, I crawled into a boxcar and woke up on a pile of garbage behind some cheap Cheyenne saloon, with two black eyes and a broken nose that I couldn't even remember how I'd come by. Cleaned myself up and reasoned that as long as I was going to hell, I might as well do something useful along the way."

He turned to face, Emma, looming above her. "Since you've

done your homework, you know the rest of the story. I don't give a damn what you do with what I've told you. For all I care you can write it up in a dime novel and earn yourself a few dollars. It doesn't matter."

He picked up the whiskey jug, twisted out the cork, stared down into the hole as if he wanted to vanish into it, then replaced the stopper and set the jug back onto the hearth. "I know you won't want to stay after this, Emma. Soon as the road thaws out, I'll take you to South Pass City," he said. "If you want to stay, you can get work there—I'll introduce you to Esther Morris if she's still around. Maybe that Tilly friend you mentioned can help you out as well. Or if you'd rather move on, you can get a ride to the railroad depot in Green River. I'll give you enough gold to take you wherever you need to go. Until then, I'm afraid you'll just have to put up with me."

"J.D.—" She rose from the rocker, but he turned away from her. Catching him from behind, she flung her arms around him, binding him tightly to her, as if defying anything on earth to separate them.

"Come with me!" she said. "We can leave as soon as the road thaws. We can start over somewhere else, change our names if need be. Just don't make me leave you, J.D."

"Now why the hell would you say that?"

"Because I'm your woman!" Her arms tightened around him. Her voice rasped with desperation. "I'm your woman! You said it yourself! And I don't care about the past, only about now!"

For a long moment he was silent. "Drop your arms, Emma," he said at last. "Let go of me."

Sick with despair, Emma released him and stepped away.

J.D. turned around, seized her shoulders and crushed her against him.

# CHAPTER FOURTEEN

This time there could be no holding back. Emma knew it, and she sensed that J.D. knew it, too. His kiss was rough and hungry, tasting of the whiskey he'd drunk. Her mouth opened to the thrust of his tongue. She wanted to feel him in every part of her.

His big, callused hands peeled her gown and chemise off her shoulders, baring her breasts above the corset. He buried his face in the damp hollow between them, his fingers fumbling to loosen her laces in back. "Damnation, but I want you, girl," he muttered against her skin. "We've waited long enough...too long..."

Emma's head fell back as he nuzzled her breasts. Her pulse was racing like a wild horse, out of control. Yes, they'd waited long enough. She wanted him where he belonged, thrusting deep into her hot, wet center. She wanted to feel the spurt of his seed inside her, to keep that part of him and make it her own.

Her fingers clawed at his buttons, pulling his shirt and long johns open. He peeled off her corset and shoved her underclothes downward, letting them drop around her ankles. His hands ranged over her bare skin, cupping her buttocks to pull her against his jutting erection. She pressed into his shaft, her hips writhing with need. A groan rose in his throat.

"Into that bed, lady," he growled. "Now."

There was an awkward moment of teetering bodies and thumping boots. Emma reached back to turn down the covers. They sank onto the sheets in a desperate tangle of arms and legs. "Yes," she murmured, making sure he understood. "I'm ready. And I want you, all of you."

He laughed roughly. "Well, bless you, Miss Carlyle, it's about time."

Shifting in the bed, he eased her onto her back. His mouth trailed downward, skimming her throat, brushing her nipples, searing a path down her sternum to belly. Her hands raked his hair as he moved lower, finding his way through the tangled nest of curls. J.D. had never done this to her before. No one had. When his tongue touched her small, exquisitely sensitive shaft, her body exploded with sensation. She gasped, then moaned, pushing upward against him.

"So you like that, do you?" he teased.

"Don't....talk," she muttered, her hands working his hair. "Just... oh! Oh...!" Starbursts of ecstasy rocked through her veins, peaking again and again until she had to beg for mercy. "No more," she whimpered. "Take me. Take me now, please..."

Shifting upward, he lay poised above her, braced on his elbows with his eyes looking down into hers. Emma's lips moved as she groped for words that wouldn't come. Her moisture-slicked thighs opened to welcome him.

"You're my woman, Emma," he whispered. "Whatever happens, never forget that."

He entered her in one long push, going deep. Emma's newly healed flesh stretched and tightened around him. Her breath sucked inward, then released in a long sigh as he began to move, easing deeper yet inside her. "Welcome home," she whispered.

J.D. did not reply. He was lost in her, as she was in him. Her legs curled upward to wrap his hips, binding him to her as she met each thrust. Her hands clutched his shoulders. Her hips arched beneath him, rising and falling with his rhythm. Her head fell back. Her breath came in sobs as they crested together in a shuddering climax. His body jerked inside her. Then, with a long sigh of satisfaction, he sank into her arms.

They lay in the dark peace of the cabin, their bodies lit by the red glow of a fire that had burned to embers. Emma rested with her eyes closed, his head cradled between breasts. If only she could freeze time in this one perfect moment—the two of them warm and close and deliciously spent, Ruby sleeping sweetly in her cartridge box. Everything she wanted was right here, within reach.

But as Robert Frost would say in the poem he had yet to write, nothing gold could stay. The changes were already in motion— changes that would shatter her precious little world forever.

J.D. had bared his soul to her. She owed him as much. No more lies, no more evasions. She would have to tell him everything and convince him of the truth. It was her one best hope of saving his life.

Sleep was dragging her down. J.D. was drifting off, too. Surely the matter could wait until morning when they were both more alert. Emma sighed drowsily, then forced her eyes open. No, it couldn't wait. Anything could happen tomorrow. She needed to tell him now.

"J.D." Her lips brushed his hairline. He grunted and stirred.

"If it's more of the same you're wanting, lady, that might take a bit of time. I'm not as young as I used to be."

"I wish that was all I wanted." She inched lower in the bed so that her face was on a level with his. "We need to talk. Or to put it more accurately, I need to talk and you need to listen."

J.D.'s only response was a sleepy grumble, but something had come awake in him. Emma could feel the tightening of his muscles where he lay against her.

"Are you listening?"

He nuzzled her shoulder. "I am."

"Then hear me out, J.D. And don't tell me to stop talking gibberish. You may not believe me, but what I'm about to tell you is the truth. I swear to God."

"This sounds serious." He was wide awake now, his eyes probing hers in the dim firelight.

"It is. And it's a matter of life and death."

She told him the story then—her pregnancy, her thesis, the meeting with Tilly Farson, the storm that drove her onto the mountain road and her tumble down the snowy slope. "I can't explain what happened to me. I only know that when I woke up, there was no sign of my car. Even after I found this place and met you, I couldn't believe I'd traveled into the past. I thought I'd stumbled into some kind of staged production, or that I was hallucinating."

His dark brows met above the bridge of his nose. Aside from that, his face was expressionless.

Praying that he'd believe her, Emma plunged ahead. "I've stopped asking myself how it all happened. The more important question is *why?* Why here? Why now?" She was talking too fast, her heart pounding. "I've spent months doing research about you. I've read everything I could find, newspapers, journals, letters." She hesitated.

"Say it, Emma. You think you know when I'm going to die."

His directness stunned her.

"I *do* know," she whispered. "I've known all along."

"Will it be soon?" His voice was flat, emotionless.

"Very soon. Less than three weeks, unless we can think of a way to save you."

"Tell me how it's going to happen."

Emma told him everything she knew—the date and time and place. The thaw. The gambler. The fateful poker game with "Beautiful Dreamer" playing in the background. The two shots.

"You're sure about this?" His question was as calmly spoken as if she'd just told him they were low on coffee.

"I've seen a photograph," she said. "You're lying in your coffin, wearing the black suit that's in the bottom of your chest, the one with the odd button. And you're buried in South Pass City. I've seen the marker, and the date—February 17, 1872."

J.D. had shifted onto his back. He lay there staring up into the dark rafters. "February 17, 1872." He repeated the date slowly, as if tasting each syllable. "It has a nice ring to it. I'd guess it's as good a time as any."

"No!" Emma sat up and seized his shoulders, gripping so intensely that her fingers dug into his flesh. "We don't have to let this happen, J.D.! We can stop it—or at least we can try!"

"How?"

"Any number of ways! You could stay home from the saloon that night. You could wear your pistol and beat the gambler to the draw, or just avoid the argument with him. Better yet, we could leave Glory Gulch as soon as the road clears. We could go to South Pass City, or someplace far away, where nobody knows you. We could—"

"Hush, Emma." He laid a finger on her lips. "There's no reason to get so worked up."

"No reason! You're going to be killed, J.D.! All because of a senseless argument over a poker game! If you don't do anything to stop it, I'll lose you forever! I know it sounds crazy, but you've got to believe me!"

He pulled her head down and kissed her gently. "You've given me plenty to think about, I'll say that much. But you can't tell me what to do. Any decision will have to be mine. Now go to sleep, love. We'll talk about it in the morning."

"J.D.!" Her frustration surged. He was dismissing her as if she were a pestering child.

"I mean it, Emma. There's time. We'll talk about this tomorrow, when we're not so tired. Now let's both get some rest."

Emma flopped onto her side, deliberately turning her back on him. J.D. had spoken to her as if he were trying to calm a case of hysteria. Maybe he thought that if he waited long enough, she'd come to her senses and forget this craziness. Isn't that what any reasonable person would think?

Biting back a sob, she closed her eyes. J.D. was right about one thing. They had time. Not much time, but more than tonight. Tomorrow when the sun was up and they weren't sated with loving she would try again. Maybe by then he'd be ready to take her seriously.

For all her anxiety, Emma was exhausted. She sank into sleep within minutes. Dreams flitted through her unconscious mind. "Beautiful Dreamer," cranking out like the notes of an old-time hurdy-gurdy, faster and faster. Bullets striking flesh. Crimson blood soaking into the plank floor.

Her eyelids jerked open. The cabin was dark, the fire burned down to faintly glowing coals. She reached across the bed, fumbling for J.D.'s reassuring bulk.

J.D.'s side of the bed was empty.

She lay still for a moment. Maybe he'd gone out to the privy. He'd likely be back soon, shivering and cursing the cold, needing her to warm him. But no—when she felt the sheets again, all traces of warmth were gone.

Rising to her knees, she peered through the small window above the bed. In the shadows of the front porch she could make out the glowing tip of J.D.'s cheroot. Heaven knows how long he'd been out there. Maybe she should make him some hot coffee and take it outside. But J.D. would see that as an excuse for her to badger him. If he was out on the porch in the middle of the night, it was because he wanted to be alone. The least she could do was respect that wish.

Ruby had awakened and started to fuss, butting her head against the end of the box. She was already outgrowing her makeshift bed. Soon J.D. would need to find her something bigger.

*Soon.* Cold chills slammed through Emma's body. There would be no "soon," Emma reminded herself. There would be no more holding him in the night, no more waking up to the warm, smoky male aroma her senses had come to crave. No more sourdough flapjacks for breakfast or the smell of jerky drying in the smokehouse. There would be no more snuggling by the fire on cold nights or watching as those huge hands cradled Ruby, rocking and soothing her when she cried. J.D. had even mastered Ruby's favorite lullaby, "I Can't Get No Satisfaction," which he sang in an off-key Papa Bear voice that always gave Emma the giggles.

What in heaven's name were they going to do without him?

Surely J.D. would come to his senses! Surely he'd help her find a way to avert this senseless tragedy.

If only she could believe that.

Scooping Ruby up in her arms, Emma wriggled back under the covers and opened her nightgown. The tug of that hungry little mouth flowed through her body, triggering a flood of emotion. They'd become a family, she and J.D. and the baby. How could she stand to lose him now—this big, gruff, maddening, wonderful man? What would Ruby miss, growing up without him?

Silently she prayed. *Please let him believe me. Please let him be willing to fight for us, for our future...*

J.D. tossed the glowing stub of the cheroot out into the darkness. The red dot soared in a burning arc, landed in a snow bank and went out.

Life was the same way, he thought. You lived, you burned out and you were done. And he'd felt himself burning out for a very long time. These past weeks with Emma and little Ruby had been a taste of sweetness, a reminder of what it was like to be happy. But J.D. had long since learned that happiness was as fleeting as a sunset, or a comet blazing its path across the sky. Happiness ended. And then fate collected whatever price was due.

He settled his buttocks on the edge of the porch. The rough-sawn planks were cold and sharp against his bones. The sky overhead was a glory of stars. J.D.'s eyes traced the Milky Way, arching across the sky like a pathway to heaven, where worthier souls than his could traipse upward to eternal glory.

Was Emma right about his coming death? He had no doubt that she believed everything she'd told him. He'd recognized the ring of absolute conviction in her voice. But that didn't mean it was true.

When he was a boy, J.D. remembered, an itinerant preacher had arrived in town claiming that the second coming of Jesus was at hand. He'd used a combination of scripture and mumbo jumbo to come up with an exact date. The man had been convincing enough to win over a fair-sized congregation. When the day came, they'd all climbed a nearby hilltop to wait. Nothing had happened, of course. When his followers realized the man was as crazy as a bedbug, they'd run him out of town.

Was Emma crazy?

The very thought made him shudder. Emma Carlyle was sweet and loving and damned sexy. She was also intelligent, well spoken and a fine mother. Since her recovery from that bump on the head, she'd been the soul of common sense. But either she'd had a relapse or she'd really done the impossible—traveled back in time from the future.

So what if he assumed she was telling the truth? What if she knew when and how he was going to die?

Would it make any difference?

Everybody cashed in sooner or later. Death took some people by surprise. Condemned criminals, on the other hand, knew exactly when the fatal moment would come. J.D. had attended enough hangings to know that some men met death with dignity. Others bawled like babies and peed their pants in fear. He had no doubt about which way he wanted to meet his own end.

Emma wanted him to run—to leave town or stay home on the night she expected the tragedy to happen. She wanted him to back down from the confrontation with the cheating gambler. But J.D. had faced death more times than he cared to remember. The fear was there, but so was the peace. His death would bring a measure of justice for Maggie's suffering and for the loss of their innocent child. It might even atone for the young lives he'd taken in his bloodstained years as a soldier and lawman.

Run? No, running wasn't in him. Neither was killing or backing down. If Emma was suffering from a fevered imagination, then he had nothing to worry about. If she was right about what was going to happen, then he would place himself in the hand of fate. Whether he lived or died would be determined by a higher power than his own.

The cat had followed him out onto the porch. Now it crouched next to him, its bony elbows jutting like wings. J.D. stroked its thick winter coat, eliciting a rusty purr. He would miss small pleasures like this after he was dead. Sitting on the step, gazing at the stars with a beast who'd chosen to be at his side. He would miss the crackling sound of a morning fire and the sight of Emma's sweet face as she opened her eyes for the day. He would miss Ruby's small, warm weight in his arms, miss the milky baby smell of her and the hidden wisdom in her dark blue eyes.

So many little things would be left behind, more than he could count. He would miss the crunch of snow under his boots, the sight of the first spring wildflowers and the glory of autumn leaves. He would miss the nights with Emma's lovely, ripe body molded to his, the silky moistness of her flesh, her little cry as their lovemaking carried her over the brink. He would miss her golden laughter. He would miss the spirited arguments that ended, often as not, with the two of them falling into bed.

Damn it, he didn't want to die!

But would it be any better to end his life as a bitter, lonely old man who never stopped looking over his shoulder?

J.D. rose wearily to his feet. The past few weeks had been among the happiest he'd ever known. But the danger would return. It always did. If he stayed here, or took Emma with him, she and little Ruby would be caught up in his nightmare. He couldn't let that happen; and much as he wished it, he couldn't change the one constant reality in his life.

As long as he lived, there would be some damned fool out to get J.D. McNulty. That reality would end only when he was dead.

Maybe it was time to end the chase once and for all.

* * *

When Emma opened her eyes it was morning. J.D. was up, dressed and making coffee. His side of the bed was so cold that she wondered if he'd slept in it at all. If he'd crawled in beside her, she'd been too far gone to notice.

"Good morning, sleepyhead." His eyes were bloodshot, his cheeks and chin unshaven. He looked as if he'd been awake all night.

Emma sat up and yawned. "Didn't you sleep?"

"Would you sleep if somebody had told you what I heard last night?"

"Then you believe me!"

"I didn't say that." He poured coffee and passed it to her with a rag wrapped around the tin cup to protect her hands. J.D.'s tarry black brew had begun to grow on Emma. She sipped it slowly, letting it ease her into wakefulness.

"Then, what?" she demanded.

He turned away to stir the sourdough. "I've done a lot of thinking over the past few hours, Emma."

"And?"

His sharp glance warned her to be patient. "I know what you want me to do. And I've decided not to do it."

She stared at him in horror.

"Hear me out," he said. "The way I see it, there are three possibilities. One, you were lying to me last night. Two, your brain's slipped a cog. Three, what you're telling me, crazy as it sounds, is God's own truth."

"J.D.—"

"Listen, woman!" His scowl would have dropped Wyatt Earp in his tracks. "I've ruled out the possibility that you're lying. Whatever you've told me, I know it's what you believe. But as for the rest, if your mind's playing tricks, there's no need for me to do anything."

Emma lurched to her feet, spilling coffee on her nightgown. "My mind isn't playing tricks, J.D.! How would I know so much about you if I hadn't come from the future? You've got to believe me!"

Her voice woke Ruby, who began to howl. Not only was she hungry, but she needed changing in the worst way. While Emma wiped, washed and greased her plump little bottom, J.D. went about preparing breakfast. What was wrong with the man? How could he be so calm when she was frantic?

With her daughter changed and clamoring to be fed, Emma rearranged the pillows, slid back under the quilt and opened the front of her nightgown. Ruby seized the nipple and sucked like a starving piglet, gulping noisily as she swallowed. Emma leaned back against the pillows, aware that J.D. was watching her. He looked worried. Not that she could blame him. With her sleep-swollen eyes, tangled hair and coffee-stained nightgown she looked like the stereotype of a mentally deranged woman.

Somehow she had to convince him she wasn't crazy.

"Go get my green parka," she said, nodding toward the hook where it hung. "Take a close look at it. Tell me if you've ever seen anything like it."

By the time she'd finished speaking, J.D. had the parka in his hands. He hooked the ends of the zipper, as he'd learned to do, and slid the tab up and down.

"I was wearing that the night I came here," she reminded him. "You'd never seen a zipper before. You didn't know how to get it open."

"True," he said. "But that doesn't mean it came from the future. It could've been some newfangled invention from back East, something we hadn't seen in these parts."

He inspected the flattened coat, inside and out. Emma sighed. His logic was dead-on. There could be any number of new inventions that people on the frontier hadn't seen. "Look at this," he muttered, finding the label in a side seam. "Made in the Philippines. So your zipper's some kind of foreign contraption. Where did you get this coat?"

"At the Wal-Mart, in Lander. And don't ask me to explain. You wouldn't believe me if I did."

He reached into one of the pockets. "Can't say much for their workmanship," he muttered. "And not much for your mending skills either. You've got a good-sized hole in the pocket of—what's this?" He had thrust his fingers down through the hole and into the lining of the coat. When he pulled his hand out, he was gripping a shiny copper-hued coin.

Emma's pulse rate exploded. She wanted to shout, but she spoke softly to keep from startling Ruby. "It's a penny! The ones you use have an Indian head on them! Look at that one!"

J.D. walked over to the window and held the penny up to the light. "Well, I'll be damned. It looks like old Honest Abe himself. And the other side looks like some kind of building. When did they start making pennies like this one?"

"Look at it, J.D.!" Emma fought the urge to leap out of bed and shake him. "Look at the date!"

He squinted , slanting the face of the coin toward the light. "I can just make it out. It looks like two, zero, zero...Oh, my God!" He lowered his arm and turned back toward her. His face was the color of alkali dust.

"You see, I'm not crazy after all," Emma said gently.

He lowered his lanky body to the hearth and sat there staring at the floor. Emma finished feeding Ruby and put her back in her box. Then she slipped out of bed, padded across the floor to where J.D. sat, and laid her hand on his shoulder.

He flinched at her touch. "Who are you?" he rasped. "*What* are you?"

Stunned and hurt, she backed away a step. "I'm exactly who I say I am—an ordinary woman. It wasn't my idea to show up here. I don't even know how it happened. But I can't help thinking I was sent for a purpose—to save your life."

He groaned softly, drew her back toward him and buried his face against her belly. Her fingers twined themselves in his thick hair, holding him close.

"Let it go, Emma," he muttered, the words half muffled by her nightgown. "My life isn't worth saving. Besides if it's as you say, that the story's already been written up in books, and the picture's been published, how can we change it? If I run away and save myself, will those letters on the pages change? Will the photograph cease to exist? What makes you think we can rewrite history?"

"I've asked myself the same question, and I don't know the answer." Emma blinked back tears. "I don't know if history can be changed before it happens. But we have to try. I love you, J.D. I need you. Ruby needs a father. I can't stand the thought of losing you."

He drew her down beside him, cradling her head against the

hollow of his shoulder. "Listen to me, Emma. You and Ruby have made me happier than any cussing, drinking, washed-up gunslinger has a right to be. But don't you see that you'd lose me anyway? When I told you I'd be moving on, I meant it. I can't risk you and your baby to the danger that follows me every place I go. If I thought I could keep you safe, I'd get down on my knees right now and ask you to marry me. But I can't offer you a life. I can't even promise you tomorrow."

She flung her arms around him, clinging fiercely. "That doesn't mean you have to die!"

"We all leave this tired old earth sooner or later." He brushed his lips along her hairline. "If it's my turn, I'm ready to accept fate and die like a man."

"No!" She clasped him with all her strength, as if her arms could hold him to life, to her. "You have to fight it, J.D., whatever it takes! If you won't do it for yourself, do it for me, and for Ruby."

"No, Emma." He eased her away from him, holding her at arms' length. "I told you it would be my decision. I've made it, and it's final." His gazed softened. "But it doesn't mean you need to be there."

"Yes it does! I'm the one who'll be playing the damned piano!"

She tore herself away from him and plunged outside, onto the porch. The cold morning air hit her like a shotgun blast. Her skin shrank into goose bumps beneath the thin, damp nightgown. Forcing herself to stand the shock, she gazed out at the blinding landscape of snow and sky.

A raven, the traditional symbol of death, squawked at her from the branch of a scraggly lodgepole pine. Its raucous call mocked Emma's presence, as if the huge black bird sensed what was going to happen, as if it were waiting.

Emma picked up a stick of kindling from the pile next to the door. With all her strength, she flung it toward the bird. "You can't have him!" she said. "I won't let you!"

The stick missed the pine tree by yards. Undisturbed, the raven squawked at her again, bobbing its massive head in avian laughter.

Emma swallowed the bitter lump in her throat. J.D. was as stubborn as any man on the face of the earth. He was resigned to his death and would not be moved. If there was any way under heaven to save him, it would be up to her to find it.

But what could she do if he wouldn't cooperate? How could she stand against fate, history and J.D. McNulty when she didn't even know where to begin?

Shivering, she turned back toward the door.

# CHAPTER FIFTEEN

On the night of February 11, a warm, dry Chinook wind swept down the eastern slope of the Rocky Mountains. Like a lost child of springtime, it sighed through the canyons. Icicles began to drip. Frozen layers of snow thinned, crumbled and slid crashing down the slopes. Tree branches, sagging under the winter weight, showered moisture as they sprang free. Mountain streams gurgled with fresh snowmelt.

Emma heard the wind as she nestled beside J.D. in the darkness. She lay wide eyed, listening as it whistled under the eaves and turned the snow on the cabin roof to drizzling slush. There could be no mistake. The midwinter thaw had arrived.

She eased into J.D.'s warmth, fitting her curves against his sinewy body. He made a muzzy little sound and pulled her closer. His erection jutted against her hip.

With a welcoming sigh, she turned over, into his arms. His hands slid her nightgown up past her ribs to expose her milk-swollen breasts to his touch. She moaned and opened her legs as he stroked her. No more preliminaries were needed. They were warm and sleepy and deliciously aroused. He mounted her and entered in one long, deep thrust. Her legs wrapped around him, drawing him deeper still as they lost themselves in slow, languorous loving.

Their lives, of late, had become bittersweet. J.D. was tender and thoughtful and had even cut back on the whiskey. Their nights were a feast of sensual, desperate lovemaking, with a hunger for each other that never went away. But the tension was there, too. J.D. had not budged in his determination to play out the final scenario of his life. For the sake of their time together, Emma had stopped harping on the matter. But it was there. Even when they made love, it was there.

The Chinook blew all night and into the next day. By first light the snow was gone. They awoke to bare earth, flattened brush, soggy brown leaves and water dripping off the roof of the cabin. Thick gray mud clung to their boots whenever they went outside. J.D. had to shovel lime down the privy to douse the rank aroma.

Chickadees and juncos flocked among the bare trees, twittering over seeds laid bare by the thaw. J.D. took the shotgun out and brought back two grouse, which Emma plucked and roasted on a spit over the fire. She was becoming adept at frontier-style cooking, which pleased J.D. to no end.

Under different conditions, the thaw would have been a happy event. But Emma could only think of the open road and the gambler named Virgil Pomeroy, who would be on his way to Glory Gulch, along with the man whose camera would record the image of J.D. in his coffin.

By the second day the mud was dry enough to walk on without sinking. Emma suggested an outing—one she'd begun thinking about long before the thaw. "I'd like to walk up the road and find the spot where my car went off," she said. "Maybe seeing it will help me figure out what happened."

J.D. was more than agreeable to the idea. "I wouldn't mind seeing it for myself," he said. "You're not the only one who needs to understand how you got here."

After lunch, when the sun was at its warmest, Emma bundled Ruby into her blankets. J.D. shouldered his rifle and latched the door behind them. The sky was a cloudless blue, the wet leaves slippery under their boots. Birds flitted from tree to tree, their calls ringing on the sunlit air.

Emma hadn't walked this route since the night of the blizzard, when she'd stumbled up the slope and found her way to J.D.'s cabin. Now everything was different. It was daytime. The snow was gone, and she was no longer alone.

Was there any hope that her idea would work?

The plan had flashed into her mind weeks ago, when it was still cold and snowy. What if she'd passed through some kind of invisible gate to travel into the 1800s? What if that gate still existed, near the spot where she'd fallen down the slope? If she could find it again, it might be possible to travel back to the 21st Century, and to take J.D. and Ruby with her. J.D. would be out of danger then, and free to explore a fascinating new world.

It was a farfetched notion, straight out of a sci-fi television show. But if there was one chance in a million that it could save J.D.'s life, Emma knew she had to try it. There was only one danger—that she could be transported back to 2010 alone. She would have to keep a tight hold on them to make sure that didn't happen.

"Is this the way you came?" J.D. walked beside her, slowing his steps so she could keep up.

"I'm not sure. With the darkness and the snowfall, it's hard to remember. All I know is that I stayed on the road until I saw your light. Then I made my way across the slope, through the trees toward the cabin."

"I know where that would be. It's the only place where you can see the cabin from the road. We'll cut over from here, then follow the road around the hill. Maybe you'll see something you recognize."

That wasn't likely, Emma thought. The thaw had changed the landscape so much that nothing looked familiar. But she couldn't give up hope yet. Maybe a little of the magic that had brought her here would be lingering around the place where she'd fallen. She could only hope for the best.

The terrain was rough and hilly. Emma could scarcely believe she'd crossed it in a blinding blizzard, just hours before giving birth. Ruby was growing heavy in her arms. What a shame nobody had invented the jogging stroller.

"Here, I'll take her." J.D. shifted the rifle to his back and scooped Ruby into his arms. She cooed and made little burbling sounds as he settled her against him. He was clearly her favorite person, except, maybe, when she was hungry.

By the time they reached the road, Emma was out of breath. Her heart sank as she gazed at the fresh ruts and hoof prints along its muddy surface. Wagons and horses had already passed this way, both going and coming. Virgil Pomeroy could already be in Glory Gulch, settled in one of Mame's spare rooms. Maybe he was enjoying a whiskey at the bar or flirting with one of the girls to pass time while he waited for the nightly poker game to begin. J.D. hadn't planned to be in town tonight. But he would be there on Saturday to escort Emma and enjoy a game or two while she played the piano.

What if she refused to play? What if she feigned sickness and insisted on staying home? Would it make any difference—enough difference to stop the awful chain of events that would end in J.D.'s death?

These and other thoughts churned in Emma's mind as she followed J.D. along the grassy roadside. They had so little time left—days, hours. What was she going to do?

They'd been walking for fifteen or twenty minutes when she saw it, a spot where the road had been cut into the curving hillside leaving an edge that seemed to drop off into empty space. Hair prickled on the back of Emma's neck. "This is the place," she said. "It has to be."

Moving out ahead, she stood on the crumbling edge and stared down the rock-strewn slope. Its pitch was much as she remembered—steep enough to cause her fall, but not so steep that she couldn't have climbed back up. The rocks had likely been covered by snow—a good thing. Otherwise she might have been badly hurt.

The slope ended in a small gully. At its bottom was a Volkswagen-sized boulder. During the storm the monolith might have been hidden by drifting snow. But that didn't mean she couldn't have struck her head on it.

"This was where my car slid off the road. This is where I fell. I'm sure of it." She glanced back at J.D. "I'd like to go down there and have a closer look at that rock. Would you mind coming with me?"

J.D. scowled. "You're sure? It's a long way down and a hard climb back up."

"I know. But whatever happened to me, it likely happened there, when I hit my head."

"Fine." He offered her his free arm. Emma took it, clinging to his coat sleeve with a determined grip. "What are you expecting to find?" he asked her.

"Maybe some evidence that I was here. My hair or blood on the rock, or maybe something from my clothes. Mostly I'm just looking for meaning. Not only how I got here, but why." It was a half truth, at least. Emma let J.D. steady her as they picked their way down the slope, digging the sides of their boots into the mud. Ruby nestled happily in the curve of his arm.

Water from the snowmelt gurgled around the base of the huge rock, washing sand and gravel down the gully. How deep had the snow been? Emma wondered. How high on the rock would her head have struck?

"There!" J.D. was looking at a sharp outcrop on the rock, a little higher than eye level. Following his gaze, Emma saw a russet stain on the coarse granite edge. "There's no way to be sure, but that could be your blood," he said. "When I cleaned that bump on your head, it was still oozing."

Emma stared up at the faint streak. This had to be the magical spot where she'd flown back through time. But where was the magic? She felt nothing but the cool breeze, heard nothing but the twitter of birds and the bubbling sound of water. J.D.'s arm was solid and real beneath her hand.

If anything had happened, she wasn't aware of it.

"Satisfied?" J.D. asked.

Emma nodded reluctantly. "Let's go back home."

Lifting her skirts, Emma followed J.D. up the slope. This climb was easier than the one she remembered, with no sliding snow and no baby bulge under her coat.

Maybe her idea had worked, and she just didn't know it yet. In this wild setting, where nothing changed, there'd be no way to tell. But what if they came up to the road and found her abandoned car—or maybe saw a plane overhead or heard the roar of a snowmobile? What if they returned to the cabin to find it a tumbledown ruin?

Emma's pulse quickened as they climbed higher. What if she'd really done it? What if they were trudging up slope the 21st Century?

They had nearly reached the road when a buckboard pulled by two muddy horses came jangling around the bend. J.D. hailed the driver, a stout, ruddy man in a ragged coat and a shapeless felt hat. No doubt about it. It was still 1872.

But all was not lost. Glancing into the back of the buckboard, Emma saw that it was piled with sacks of—oh, heavenly day— potatoes!

"How much for a sack?" J.D. asked the man.

"They ain't cheap. Brung 'em all the way up from South Pass City, on this butt-breaker of a road. "Two dollars!"

"You've got a deal." J.D. handed Ruby to Emma and fished the bills out of his pocket. "I'm betting Mame will buy the rest off you."

"That's what I figure. Take your pick, Marshal."

"Not any more. I'm finished with the marshal business." J.D. hefted the topmost bag onto his shoulder. Emma walked beside him as the buckboard pulled away. Hiding her disappointment, she forced herself to think of good things—baked potatoes, fried potatoes, mashed potatoes, stewed potatoes in venison gravy.

Maybe she could even show Mame how to make French fries.

The next morning J.D. went hunting again. He was a crack shot and seemed to enjoy tramping the high meadows in search of game. But Emma could guess the real reason he spent so much time afield. He wanted to make sure she'd have enough to eat when he was gone.

While J.D. was in the cabin, Emma had done her best to keep a cheerful face. But now, as she peeled potatoes for stew, her nerves gave way. The knife clattered to the floor as she began to shake like a drug addict in the throes of withdrawal.

Staggering to the rocker, she sank into it. She'd exhausted her brain looking for a way to save him. She'd begged, cajoled, pleaded and threatened. But J.D. would not budge. He was determined to meet his fate like a man.

Emma was running out of options. If nothing interfered, she would be there, at the piano, playing "Beautiful Dreamer" while the tragedy unwound. And she would be there to cradle J.D. in her arms while his life bled away—a saloon girl in a bloodstained satin gown. One more question answered.

Quivering, Emma buried her face in her hands. Sobs racked her body. She had never felt so helpless in her life.

Ruby's hungry cry roused her. Emma rose, gathered up her howling baby and carried back to the chair. Milk drizzled down the front of her dress as she unbuttoned her bodice. The tiny mouth rooted for the nipple and found it. Little by little, the sucking began to calm Emma's nerves. She needed to stay strong for Ruby, she reminded herself. Whatever happened, she had to be there for her little girl.

She was still nursing when she heard the snort of a horse outside.

She was fumbling for a blanket to cover herself when a familiar voice sang out from the porch.

"Yoo-hoo! Emma, are you there?"

Emma felt a surge of relief at the sound of Mame's voice. If ever she'd needed a friend, it was now.

Without waiting for a reply, Mame opened the door and stepped across the threshold. "I hadn't planned on a visit, but it was such a beautiful day, I couldn't resist—" She broke off at the sight of Emma's face. "My stars and garters, what's happened? Don't tell me J.D.'s been fool enough to—"

"No, of course not. J.D. would never hurt me."

"I didn't think so!" Mame sniffed. "The man worships you, and he'd walk through fire for that little baby! Where is he?"

"Hunting." Emma shifted Ruby to the other breast. "I'm glad you've come, Mame. I'm worried sick, and I've got no one else to talk to."

"Not even J.D.?" Mame took a seat on the hearth and began stroking the cat.

Emma shook her head. "He won't listen. And it's him I'm worried about."

"Won't listen, you say? Hmph! That sounds like J.D." Mame rose. "Let me put some tea on. Then you can talk and I'll listen."

"I hope you've got lots of time," Emma said. "It's a long story. I can guarantee you won't believe it all."

"What I'd believe might surprise you." Mame measured tea into the pot and added hot water from the big iron kettle on the fire. With the tea brewing, she settled her ample hips back onto the hearth. "All right, honey, I'm all ears."

Emma sighed, wondering where and how to begin. "How much has J.D. told you about me?"

Mame's kohl-lined eyes narrowed. "Not much. Just that you showed up in a blizzard, in the middle of the night, wearing some strange foreign-looking garb and talking out of your head. Also that you've become a good mother and a good cook, both of which I already knew. He hasn't told me he loves you, but I'm pretty sure he does. I think the man would do just about anything for you and that little angel of yours."

"Oh, Mame, if you only knew!" Emma's tears welled. She blinked them away.

"What is it, dear?"

"J.D. is going to die."

"What are you saying?" The absinthe eyes widened.

"He's going to be shot Saturday night, at the Laughing Lady. I've told him everything and begged him to stay home. But he doesn't care! He says that if his time's up, he wants to face it and die like a man."

Mame's fingers poked a straying lock of gray hair back under her wig. "So that's why you asked me about shutting down for a night. You already knew. Why didn't' you confide in me before this?"

"Would you have believed me?" Emma closed the front of her dress, lifted Ruby to her shoulder and patted away a gassy belch. "I need to tell you the whole story. Maybe then you'll understand."

Mame held out her arms. "Give me that little cherub. I'll hold her while you talk. Come to Auntie, darlin'."

Passing Ruby to her friend, Emma rose and lifted the small brass mantel clock. Under its base she kept the penny that J.D. had found in the lining of her parka. "Before I say any more, I want you to see this," she said. "J.D. found it a few days ago, inside the coat I was wearing the night I came here. For him, it was proof enough that my story was true." She held it out, then remembered Mame's eyesight. "Wait—I believe there's a magnifying glass on J.D.'s bookshelf."

She found the glass and handed it to Mame, along with the penny. Cradling Ruby in her lap, Mame took the coin and peered at it through the lens. Emma watched her face, expecting to see shock and disbelief, even horror creep over her painted features.

Mame laid the glass on the hearth and handed the penny back to Emma. "Be careful who you show this to, dear," she said. "People tend to fear what they don't understand. Some might suspect you of witchcraft."

Emma stared at her. "You saw it? The date on the penny?"

Mame's rouged mouth twitched at the corners. "I've lived a long time, dear. Long enough to know that some things can't be explained by reason. Your being here seems to be one of them."

"Then you believe me? You won't think I'm crazy when I tell you I came here from the 21ˢᵗ Century?"

"A woman in my profession hears all kinds of stories. Tell me yours, and I'll judge for myself."

Ruby had nodded off. Emma eased her daughter out of Mame's arms, put her to bed and poured two cups of tea. Then she took her seat, and with an urgency born of fear, poured out the saga of all that had happened to her.

Mame listened, taking sips of tea and asking only a few questions. "You say you've read newspaper accounts of J.D.'s murder?"

"Several of them and they all say the same thing. It happened— it *will* happen—this Saturday night at 8:46, with the piano playing "Beautiful Dreamer.""

"And you've seen the photograph of J.D. in his casket. You're certain it's not a mistake. I'm asking because nobody here in Glory Gulch has a camera, let alone knows how to use one."

"The photographer will be here when the time comes. Smith is his name. And it's no mistake. In the picture, J.D. is wearing the same suit I found in that chest. You can even see the little scar on his thumb."

"And the gambler?"

"His name is Virgil Pomeroy. And he'll get away after the shooting. As far as I know, he disappeared and was never caught."

"Pomeroy." Mame's fingertip toyed with the fake beauty mole on her cheek. "I know that little weasel. He's been here before. Usually shows up just in time to fleece the miners out of the gold they've dug over the winter."

Emma swallowed the hardness in her throat. Telling her story had left her drained. She took a sip of hot tea.

"Do you think it's possible to change recorded history before it's written, Mame?"

"I'm not sure what you mean, dear."

"Say, what if someone like me, who'd already read the history books, had been at Ford's Theater the night Abraham Lincoln was to be shot? What if they'd tried to prevent the crime, maybe set the building on fire or locked John Wilkes Booth in his dressing room? Could it have worked? And if it had, would it have changed historical record—every photograph, every word in every copy of every book that already existed in the future?"

Mame's strange green eyes were pensive. "That's a question for philosophers, dear. My best guess is that might be possible if time is simply linear. But I'm not at all sure it is. The fact that you're here suggests that it isn't. The future already exists. You're living proof of it. And if it already exists, then it can't be changed."

"So, to continue with the Lincoln analogy, the assassination couldn't have been stopped. Any fire would have been put out. Or Booth would have escaped from his dressing room. The historical record would be the same."

"I'm afraid you may be right."

"And if I am, there's no way to keep Pomeroy from shooting J.D." Emma felt as if she were sinking into gray water, pulled down by some heavy weight. "It's going to happen, and there's nothing we can do. We can't change recorded history, even when it only exists in the future."

"Recorded history." Mame murmured the words. She seemed to be lost somewhere inside herself. Suddenly her eyes opened wide. "Emma—"

"Yes!" The epiphany struck them both at the same instant. It was Emma who voiced it. "History isn't necessarily what happens. It's what gets *recorded*! People remember what they see and hear, then tell it to others or write it down! It's all a matter of perception!"

Emma seized her friend's hands, not caring that she startled the cat and spilled the tea. "Mame, we wouldn't have to change that part! All we'd have to change is—"

"I know! The perception of reality wouldn't have to change. Only the reality itself! In a word, honey, we stage it!"

"Can we really do that?" Fear washed over Emma, dissolving the elation she'd felt a seconds before. She thought of the bloodstain on the floor. How could they fake that?

"It won't be easy, Mame said. "I think I know a way, but it would demand luck and split-second timing."

"What about J.D.? He's so determined to go through with this. I can't imagine he'll cooperate."

"He won't have to cooperate. He won't even have to know until it's over. He'll be more convincing, in fact, if he *doesn't* know."

*And if it doesn't work, it won't matter because he'll be dead.* Emma left the thought unspoken. She had to believe Mame's plan would succeed, even if they were grasping at straws.

"Take me step by step through the shooting," Mame said. "I need to know exactly how it's supposed to happen."

So Emma recited the events as she'd read them. The card game, where everyone would be sitting, the time, the music, the two shots and the saloon girl, presumably Emma herself, who would cradle J.D. in her arms, sobbing over him as he died.

"Tell me about the shots." Mame was relentless.

"Two of them, fired in rapid succession. The first shot will wound him in the shoulder. The second shot, the fatal one, in the heart. He'll fall over backward and die on the floor." It was all Emma could do to keep her voice from shaking.

And the gun? What kind of pistol will Pomeroy have?

"A double barreled .22 Wesson derringer. I've seen the actual gun in a museum. Pomeroy dropped it on the floor as he ran out."

"Fine little weapon," Mame said. "I used to carry one myself, tucked into my garter, when I worked rougher places than Glory Gulch. I'd load it with blanks so I could fire it to break up fights. With my eyesight, I wasn't much of a shot, and I didn't want to do any damage—or, heaven forbid, shoot myself in the leg." Mame gathered the cups and stacked them on the hearth. "Now, dear, let me tell you what I'm thinking."

Emma stood on the porch, watching as Mame headed back down the trail. The plan they'd devised was so audacious and so risky that the very thought of it turned her knees to jelly. Its success would depend on exquisite luck and timing. Any miscalculation, or unforeseen twist, could be fatal.

The first part of the plan would depend on Mame's cunning. The second, more dangerous part would depend on her own agility and sense of timing. And the entire plan hinged on events unfolding exactly as they'd been recorded. If Mame's subterfuge was discovered, if some bystander interfered, or if J.D. decided to take matters into his own hands, anything could happen.

Could they cheat fate and save J.D.'s life? Or were they simply acting out what fate had had in mind all along? It was a paradox worthy of Einstein, who would be born seven years from now on the other side of the world.

Emma retied her loose apron strings and went back into the house. The cat jumped onto the counter, meowing to be fed. Emma gave it a few scraps of stew meat and stood scratching its bony back while it ate.

Time spent brooding was time wasted, she reminded herself. The past was jumbled, the future uncertain. But whatever happened, she'd be a fool not to savor each remaining moment of her life with J.D. She would fill her senses with him—the way he swore under his breath, the smell of his damp hair, the tickle of his moustache against her skin, the way his big hand clasped the back of her head when he kissed her. She would memorize every inch of his body— the long, pale legs and narrow feet, the ugly wound in his side, the V of dark hair across his chest, tapering to a line down his flat belly. She would make love to him and remember the way his body fit deep inside hers, the tenderness of his hands and mouth, the way his breath caught when he spilled his seed, his vulnerability when he curled beside her in sleep.

If she had to lose him, Emma's one wish would be to discover she was carrying J.D.'s child. But because she was nursing, that was unlikely to happen. She would have to content herself with loving him until their time ran out.

Whenever that might be.

# CHAPTER SIXTEEN

J.D. McNulty didn't want to die. He acknowledged that weakness as he stood alone on the cabin porch, watching sunrise brush the sky with streaks of rose, mauve and gold. If the evening went as predicted, this was the last sunrise he would ever see.

J.D. had never embraced formal religion. He liked to think he had a soul and that it would go someplace after he died. But he couldn't claim to know it as a fact. He only knew that if any awareness remained to him, there were many things he'd miss about this tired old earth—not only sunrises but sunsets and moonrises and soft winter snowfall. He would miss the flash of trout in a mountain stream and the taste of their delicate pink flesh, freshly caught and cooked over an open fire. He would miss the quiet strength of a horse between his knees and the wind in his hair when he rode at a gallop across the open plain.

He would miss the burn of good whiskey down a dry throat. And he would miss—oh, Lord, how he would miss—the sweet, ripe, loving woman who shared his bed.

As if unable to stand being parted from her, he turned his back on the dawn and went into the cabin. Emma lay curled in the rumpled bed, fast asleep. She'd had an exhausting night. First they'd worn each other out making bittersweet love. Then, as they were drifting off, the baby had awakened and refused to go back down. Emma had sat up for what seemed like hours, rocking her by the fire. J.D. had offered to spell her, but she'd insisted on staying up until Ruby cried herself to sleep.

Emma's face was childlike in slumber, so soft and vulnerable that just looking at her made his throat ache. J.D. had known his share of ladies, but never one like this woman who'd come to him from another time. Her intelligence challenged him at every turn. Her passion set him on fire. Her tenderness roused dreams of a warm, loving home, filled with the laughter of children—a home he would never have. But that couldn't be helped. He only knew that, having loved her, he would go to his grave a better man.

There were times, like now, when he'd give anything to have more time with her. A full lifetime sounded about right. But to run from the inevitable would be a coward's way out. And he wasn't prepared to add cowardice to his long list of sins. When the time came he would spit in the eye of death and meet his fate with dignity. And that, J.D. told himself, was that.

Emma had seemed resigned to his decision. But J.D. could tell it was eating on her. Ruby, he suspected, could feel the tension as well. That's why she'd taken so long to settle down last night. But at least she was sleeping this morning.

J.D. leaned over the cartridge box. Emma's daughter was lying on her back, her eyes closed, her thumb in her pretty rosebud mouth. At six weeks, she was growing fast. Her little body was thriving on Emma's milk. Soon she'd be too big for her makeshift bed.

Ruby had grown into his heart as well, J.D. admitted. He wouldn't live long enough to be a father to her. He wouldn't be here to see her first steps or hear her first words. But there was something he could do today, before time ran out.

Walking softly, he turned and left the cabin again. The cat flicked its bobtail, jumped down from the mantel and scampered after him.

Emma awoke to the sound of hammering. Bright sunlight streamed through the windowpanes. The clock on the mantel informed her that it was twenty minutes after eight. Still groggy, she sat bolt upright. A glance into the cartridge box assured her that Ruby was sleeping peacefully. But what a night it had been. Her head ached and her eyes felt as if she'd stayed up all night studying for a history exam.

This wasn't the way she'd planned things. She had hoped to wake up early, while J.D. was still in bed. She'd imagined lying next to him, warm and drowsy, snuggling against his body, nipping and nuzzling him to arousal. And then...

But what was the use? She felt like road kill and probably looked worse. And J.D. hadn't hung around long enough for a morning cuddle. He was already up, dressed and busy on some project outside.

She tried to imagine how he must feel, believing that he was going to die tonight. Emma had been tempted to tell him that she and Mame had a plan—but Mame was right. J.D.'s performance would be more convincing if he didn't know. And if their plan didn't work, giving him false hope would be cruel.

The hammering had stopped. Now it began again. J.D. would be restless today. It made sense that he would find some task to keep his hands busy. But what was he working on?

Then it hit her.

J.D. was building his own coffin.

A tide of panic rose in Emma as she swung her feet to the floor. She dressed hastily, pulling on her chemise and drawers. Even the corset was manageable now that she'd lost her baby weight. But her fingers fumbled as she buttoned the front of her dress. The thought of what J.D. was doing out there behind the cabin brought reality home with the force of a wrecking ball. Until now she'd been playing at make-believe, telling herself that all would end happily. But even with Mame's plan in place, the odds were against it. Death was real and final. And no matter how she might try to save him, if one thing went wrong, J.D. would die tonight.

Pouring some water in the basin, she splashed her face, rinsed her mouth and finger-combed her hair. The mirror showed tired shadows beneath bloodshot eyes. But that couldn't be helped. Emma checked on the sleeping Ruby. Then she went out the door and hurried around the cabin.

She found J.D. in the clearing between the cabin and the smokehouse. He'd improvised a workbench by laying a slab of lumber between two stumps. Wood scraps were scattered around him as if he'd been searching for the right pieces.

He glanced up with an easy smile. "Good morning," he said. "I was hoping you'd get some rest."

"I did, and I'm fine. J.D., what are you doing?"

"What does it look like I'm doing?" Tools and scraps of wood were scattered over the makeshift workbench. J.D. was hammering a nail into what looked like a wooden box. The box was about three feet long, far too small to be a coffin. Emma stared at it, dumbfounded.

"I'm afraid I'm no great shakes as a carpenter," he apologized.

"This part was easy enough. But I'm still trying to figure out the rockers."

"Rockers? You're making...a cradle?"

"Trying to. What did you think it was?" He stared at her in sudden comprehension. "Oh, no, Emma," he groaned. "No, girl, I'm not building my own box. Just trying to make myself useful."

J.D. opened his arms, catching her as she stumbled into them. He held her fiercely tight, molding her against his body. Emma closed her eyes, wishing she could sink into his flesh and be part of him. How could she live without this man?

"I keep hoping you're wrong," he muttered against her hair. "Lord knows, I'd rather discover you were crazy as a hoot owl than have you be right about this."

Emma's arms tightened around him. "I keep hoping the same thing. But we have to assume it's going to happen."

"And if it doesn't?"

"Then we go on from there, to whatever comes next."

"Emma." He lifted her chin and kissed her mouth. "Oh, damn it, Emma..."

He kissed her hungrily, again and again, like a condemned prisoner devouring his last meal. Emma clung to him, torn between the need to offer him a thread of hope and knowing it would be the cruelest thing she could do.

The sound of an approaching horse broke them apart. They hurried around the cabin to see a rider coming around the last bend in the trail. Emma recognized the youth who accompanied them home on Saturday nights to take J.D.'s horse back to the stable.

He hailed Emma as she came within hearing. "Message from Miss Mame," he said, drawing a sealed envelope out of his jacket. "She says I'm to give it straight to you, ma'am. And I since I was coming anyway, I figured I might as well bring you the horse."

"That's right thoughtful of you." J.D. waited for the youth to dismount. Then he took the horse's lead and looped it around an aspen trunk. Emma accepted the envelope and slipped it into the pocket of her apron. She burned to know what Mame had written but couldn't risk having J.D. read it over her shoulder.

J.D. gave the lad some coins for his trouble and stood watching as he set off whistling down the trail. "Aren't you going to open Mame's letter?" he asked Emma.

"In a bit. It's just a note about tonight's program." Emma glanced back toward the house. "I think I hear Ruby. I'll start breakfast after I feed her if you want to go on working."

"Fine. Call me when it's ready." He strode around the house. Moments later, Emma heard the sound of a saw. Moving into the shadow of the porch, she tore open the envelope that enclosed Mame's message. Her fingers shook as she unfolded the single sheet of paper. She had to steady her hand to keep the words from blurring before her eyes.

Photographer A. Smith arrived by wagon last night, bringing V. Pomeroy as a passenger. Gave them rooms and offered free hot baths. Mission accomplished. The rest is up to you. Good luck, dear.

~ M.

The page fluttered from Emma's fingers. A chill passed through her body as she picked it up and crumpled it in her fist. The stage was set, the players were in the wings, and the drama was about to begin.

They rode down the trail through the gathering twilight, between ghost-white clumps of aspen and dark green thickets of pine. J.D. guided the horse, with Emma clinging to his back and Ruby nestled between them. Where her hand wrapped his chest, Emma could feel the steady beat of his heart. She could feel the life that flowed through him with each breath, and she knew one thing. Whatever happened, she could not let this man die.

They had spent a quiet day. J.D. had finished the new cradle that afternoon. After some deliberation, he'd fashioned the rockers by shaping two half-circles of pinewood and nailing them to the bottom of the box. His creation lacked the grace of an heirloom cradle. But it was big enough to last Ruby through her first birthday, and it rocked nicely on the floor.

From the depths of the shed he'd unearthed a can of paint and a moldering brush. There'd been just enough to give the cradle a coat of bright candy apple red. "Red for Ruby," he'd said, and they had laughed together.

Even now, he seemed calm and unafraid. But then, as a soldier and lawman, J.D. had faced death countless times. It wouldn't be like him to show fear. Heaven knows, she had enough fear for them both.

He cleared his throat as they came out onto the overlook. The town lay below them along the bottom of the gulch. Lights glimmered through the dusk. "About the coffin," he said. "There's a man in town named Peterson who's got a shed full of cut lumber. For ten dollars he can throw a pine box together in about half an hour. Mame knows where to find him. He may want a couple of dollars more for the extra length..."

"Don't." Emma's arms tightened around him. "Maybe it won't happen. Maybe it's all some ghastly mistake." She was lying now. She knew there could be no mistake. "Maybe, a few hours from now, we'll be riding home laughing at ourselves for being so silly."

That was another lie. Emma knew the danger and the plan. Whether it worked or not, one thing was certain. After tonight, J.D. would never ride this mountain trail again.

J.D. sat in his usual spot, with his face toward the door and his back to the piano. Through the narrowed slits of his eyelids, he studied the four men at his table. Two of them were miners from town, honest men he'd played poker with a few times before. Smith, the photographer, seemed a decent fellow, too. Balding and angular as a scarecrow, he was taking advantage of the thaw to photograph life in the mining camps. Eventually he hoped to sell his work to a publisher.

The gambler, Virgil Pomeroy, was no stranger. Four years ago J.D. had kicked him out of Cheyenne for cheating some railroad workers at faro. No doubt the little rat-eyed shyster remembered him. He looked like the sort who'd carry a grudge. J.D. could make out the slight bulge of the derringer beneath his black gambler's coat. Maybe Pomeroy was already thinking about using it.

Pomeroy thumbed his pencil-line moustache and studied the fan of cards in his hand. He'd been winning and losing off and on all night. Now he was probably waiting for the right cards and a heavy bet before he used the holdout—a device that held a secret stash of cards—which he almost certainly wore up his sleeve.

J.D.'s own luck had been average for the night. He played conservatively, keeping his bets low. It was the challenge of the game that drew him, not the money. The two miners, on the other hand, had been through a long, hard winter. They'd be pulling out in the spring and were anxious to add anything they could to their meager stash. For an unscrupulous little weasel like Pomeroy, they were ripe for the plucking.

A ripple of applause interrupted J.D.'s thoughts. He glanced at his pocket watch. It was 8:00, and Emma had just entered the room.

She looked ravishing in her satin dress, with her hair twisted and pinned atop her queenly head. But even from here J.D. could see the shadows under her eyes. His determination to die like a man was putting her through hell, he knew. Most women would have fallen to weeping fits and fainting spells by now. But not his Emma. She was as strong as she was beautiful.

He glanced around for Ruby, who was usually left with Angel. Neither of them was in the saloon. But it made sense that Emma would keep her baby in some back room tonight, out of harm's way.

As she took her seat, Smith, the photographer, swung around to look at her. "We could break to hear her play," he suggested.

Pomeroy shook his head. "I came here for a poker game, not a damned piano concert," he snarled. "Now play or fold."

"I'll fold, then," said Smith. "She's a right fetching lady, and I wasn't doing that well anyway. Enjoy your game, gentlemen." He turned his chair around and settled down to watch the show.

"How about you, McNulty?" Pomeroy eyed the pokes of gold dust the two miners had laid on the table. "I hear tell she's your woman. You going to fold, too?"

J.D. shook his head. "Somebody's got to keep you honest, Pomeroy."

The gambler's lip curled. J.D. could see where this was leading, and for a moment he was tempted to get up and walk out. But he knew better. Fate would not be cheated, especially by cowardice.

Would there be heaven, hell or oblivion in that unknown place where he'd sent so many others? Would Maggie be waiting for him with open arms and forgiveness? Would the young Johnny Reb who'd died on his bayonet shake his hand and say he understood?

Would he see the outlaws he'd shot down or led to the gallows? Or would he simply fall into darkness? J.D. didn't look forward to dying. But at least his curiosity would be satisfied.

Emma had begun to play the piano. The first few measures were choppy, reflecting the strain she was under. Then, as she pulled herself together, she began to play more naturally. The first song was "Buffalo Gals," a favorite of the locals. Tonight some of the people sang along with the music and cheered when it ended. Emma waited for the applause to fade, then launched into "Oh, Susannah."

With Smith out of the game and J.D. seemingly distracted by Emma's performance, Pomeroy began to reel in the miners like hapless fish. Bolstered by their early luck, the miners had begun placing riskier bets. J.D. could imagine the wheels turning in Pomeroy's greedy little mind as he waited for the perfect moment to use the holdout and slip that extra card out of his sleeve. He kept his eyes on the little man's hands, ignoring the temptation to check his watch.

When the time came for all hell to break loose, he'd be the first to know.

Emma glanced at the pocket watch Mame had left open on the piano. With minutes to go, her pulse was racing like a runaway train. Sweat poured off her body, soaking through her chemise and corset to stain the back of her gown. Her legs felt numb beneath her. She moved her feet off the piano pedals, shifting her legs to make sure they would work when the time came.

She was playing "The Man On the Flying Trapeze," a song which tended to put people in a relaxed and jolly mood. But with her fingers stabbing at the keys, there was nothing relaxed about her performance.

Out of the corner of her eye, she could see J.D. He was leaning backward in the wooden chair, his eyes on the man across the table. Emma strained to hear their voices above the music. So much depended on what was being said. But she could scarcely catch a word. She might not be able to anticipate her move. She could only do her best to be ready.

She ended the rollicking song with a flourish and glanced at the watch. The minute hand had crept to within a hair's breadth of the nine. It was time.

Forcing the breath through her constricted throat, Emma placed her fingers on the chipped keys and began to play "Beautiful Dreamer."

The wistful old song had become another favorite. A hush crept over the listeners as the notes drifted through the saloon. But the players at J.D.'s table continued their game, ignoring the music.

Nerves snapping with tension, Emma fumbled for the keys. She'd reached the end of the first stanza when the crescendo of arguing voices reached her ears—J.D.'s calm accusation, Pomeroy's rabid denial, then a gasp from the watchers and a screaming curse.

*Now!*

The derringer popped once. Emma flew off the piano bench.

J.D. felt the bullet slam into his shoulder, felt the galvanizing shock to his body and the sudden spurt of blood. As the second shot rang out, Emma hurtled into him, knocking him backward to the floor. The report echoed in his ears, but he wasn't aware that he'd been hit a second time. He was bleeding from the shoulder wound, but otherwise very much alive.

Lord almighty, had Emma taken the second bullet for him?

He groaned and struggled to sit up, but she lay squarely on top of him, pinning him down with her solid weight. Damn it, this wasn't part of the plan. Emma wasn't supposed to die in his place.

"No," he muttered. "No, Emma!"

"Shut up and close your eyes!" she hissed in his ear. "You're supposed to be dead!"

Clutching him in her arms, she began to wail like an Irish banshee. "Oh, no! You can't die, J.D.! Come back to me! You can't die, my love...Nooooooo..." Hellfire, the woman had lungs like a whale. He'd never heard a female make so much noise.

There was a scrambling sound and the crash of a chair as Pomeroy made a dash for the door. "Git the bastard!" somebody shouted, and most of the crowd stampeded after him. J.D. could only hope the little polecat would get away before they strung him up for a murder he hadn't committed.

"Nooo..." Emma continued to weep and moan, defying the

bystander who was attempting to help her up. "Don't touch me! I won't leave him!"

"He's dead, honey." Mame's voice spoke from somewhere behind J.D.'s head. "There's nothing you can do. Come on. Let me get you a drink."

"No!" Emma clung to him stubbornly. J.D. lay still, his eyes closed, his mind churning like a steam engine. They'd carried out the whole scheme behind his back—these two amazing women. Mame could've gotten hold of Pomeroy's gun while he was bathing or sleeping. All she'd had to do was substitute a blank for the second bullet—not the first bullet because the shoulder wound had to be real. Emma had done the rest, covering him with her body, soaking her gown with his blood and hiding the fact that he hadn't been shot a second time.

There was no doctor in this remote mining camp, and no one qualified to act as coroner. J.D. McNulty was dead to history. And the man his death had left behind was free to start a new life.

J.D. couldn't help it. Laughter welled up in his body until he shook with it. He had to bite his cheeks to hold it in. His shoulder hurt like blazes. The wound was going to need some attention before it bled too much. But damnation, it was good to be alive!

Emma was plastered on top of him, her right ear close to his mouth. J.D. couldn't resist whispering. "Miss Emma Carlyle, if you'll do me the honor, I hope you won't mind being married to a dead man!"

She made a little choking sound. When she laid her cheek against his, J.D. felt the wetness of tears.

"Clear out everybody! We're closed for the night!" Mame was shooing the last of the spectators out the door. "Tell Peterson we'll need an extra long pine box, delivered here first thing tomorrow. And tell him to do his best work. It's for one of the greatest men in the history of Wyoming Territory—Marshal J.D. McNulty!"

The next day, at 11:00 a.m. Mr. Asa Smith set up his camera, carried it into a back room of the Laughing Lady, and took the photograph that would appear in generations of books and articles on Wyoming history.

Emma stood beside the casket where a powdered and pale J.D.

lay in his black suit, his hair carefully combed, his hands crossed on his chest. She'd arranged them in that position, exactly as she remembered.

Refusing to be photographed herself, she hovered protectively over J.D. until Smith was ready. Then she allowed him to take just one picture. That, she declared, would be all he'd need.

When the photographer was finished, she turned him over to Mame, who ushered him into the saloon for a free drink. Only after the door was safely locked behind them did J.D. sit up.

"Hellfire," he muttered, rubbing the powder off his nose. "I thought that fool would never get done fidgeting. I damn near sneezed!"

Late that night, lit by a waxing moon, a loaded buckboard stood in the alleyway next to the Laughing Lady. The driver sat hunched over the reins. His clean-shaven face was overshadowed by a low-brimmed hat. Spectacles masked his striking blue eyes. The woman beside him was wrapped in a thick woolen shawl. In its folds, she cradled a sleeping baby.

Only Mame was there to see them off. Emma gripped her hand as they said goodbye. "We can't thank you enough, Mame. We owe you more than we can ever repay."

"You can repay me by being happy," Mame said. "Just knowing you're together will be enough."

J.D. was concerned with more practical matters. "You'll see to the coffin?"

"I already have. Mr. Smith will haul it to South Pass City on his wagon tomorrow. He'll have the photograph he took. That should be enough to convince anyone that it's you inside, not 185 pounds of bagged mine tailings."

"And you'll keep the cat?" Emma asked anxiously.

"Of course, dear. We're two of a kind, that old cat and I. We'll get along fine."

J.D. made a last minute check of the buckboard and its contents. Their secret getaway had taken some arranging. Emma had made a hasty visit to the cabin to collect the bags of gold and a few essentials, including Ruby's bed and J.D.'s wedding photograph. Sadly, J.D.'s precious books had to be left behind, as did most of the furniture, tools and kitchen supplies, but those things could be replaced.

The buckboard and team would be sold in Green River for train fare to California. Mame had surprised them by repaying the cash J.D. had lent her to purchase the Laughing Lady. Their lives might not be easy at first, but at least they'd have enough money for a new start.

J.D. pulled the buckboard out of the alley and into the rutted street. Mame walked alongside, staying close to Emma and the baby.

"I wish we could stay in touch," Emma said. "If we could write—"

"No dear." Mame shook her curls. Her eyes glimmered in the darkness. "You're going off on your own, and so am I. We won't know how to get in touch. Maybe it's for the best."

"We'll never forget you!" Emma reached out and clasped her hand as the buckboard began to move.

"And I'll never forget you. Be happy, Emma! Take care of that big lummox and that sweet little baby!"

Their fingers parted as the wheels picked up speed. Moments later, J.D. swung the buckboard onto the main road. Twisting in her seat, Emma looked back at Glory Gulch for the last time.

Where Mame had stood watching them, only moonlight remained.

# *EPILOGUE*

Tilly Farson glanced up from the counter as the door jingled open. The girl who strode into the bookstore was tall and slender with crisp, dark curls. Dressed in jeans and a canvas coat, she was lugging a heavy briefcase with a laptop stuffed into one compartment. A college student, Tilly decided, most likely on spring break.

"Good morning," Tilly said with a smile. "It seems you're my first customer of the day. What can I do for you?"

The girl's striking blue eyes stared at the poster-sized photo behind the cash register. "Wow! Something tells me I've come to the right place. That's J.D. McNulty isn't it? I'm writing my senior paper about him. My professor says you're an authority."

Tilly adjusted her thick spectacles on her nose. "That's not quite true. Nobody can claim to be an authority on a man like J.D. But if you have questions, I'll do my best to answer them. Sit down, dear. I'll get you some cocoa and some oatmeal cookies. Then we'll talk."

"That sounds heavenly." The girl sank into one of the matching wingback chairs. "My name's Katy, by the way. Katy Cox."

"Pleased to meet you, Katy." Tilly poured hot cocoa into two mugs and arranged the cookies on a saucer before she took her own seat. "Now, how can I help?"

"First off, maybe you can solve a mystery for me. " Katy blew on her cocoa and took a tentative sip. "My mother's family claims to have descended from J.D. If that's true, he'd be my great, great grandfather. That's why I chose him as my topic. But I've run into a problem."

Tilly suppressed the urge to comment. Let the girl talk.

"I've spent hours doing research on J.D. And every single account I can find says that he was murdered, shot dead by a gambler in 1872, and that he died without ever having children. How is that possible?"

"Maybe it isn't," Tilly suggested gently.

"It can't be. My grandmother told me that J.D. McNulty was her grandfather, and that he passed away in 1897. She actually knew him. Here—" She rummaged in her briefcase and came up with a large sepia photograph protected by a plastic sleeve. "My grandmother gave this to me before she died. It's a portrait of her mother's family. Look at it!"

Tilly gazed at the photograph through her thick lenses. It was a traditional family scene, taken at Christmas time in front of a decorated tree. The man was dark and rangy, with piercing eyes— unmistakably J.D. The handsome woman standing by his chair was blond and regal and so very familiar. Tilly's throat tightened.

"He went by the name J.D. Carlyle," Katy said. "But the family knew his real name was McNulty. And his wife's name was Emma. That's all we know about her. No one's ever found any trace of her family."

"And the children?" Tilly studied the three pretty school-aged girls clustered around their parents. So these were J.D. and Emma's offspring. Darling Ruby and two little sisters who looked like their father.

"The blond girl was J.D.'s stepdaughter," Katy said. "The family called her Aunt Ruby. She lived into her nineties; never married, but had a wonderful career as a Hollywood script writer. After she retired she traveled all over the world. I only wish I'd been born soon enough to know her."

"And the other girls?"

"The younger girl is my great grandmother. Her sister married and moved back East. The rest of the family stayed in California."

Tilly returned the photograph. "Well, I'll be," she murmured. "After all these years..."

"So do you think J.D. could really be my great, great grandfather?" Katy asked.

"The photo looks very convincing," Tilly hedged. "But you'll need to draw your own conclusions. In any case, you should finish your research paper, dear. I have something that may help you."

Rising, she walked behind the counter, opened a drawer and took out a battered canvas briefcase crammed with notes. "This is very precious," she said, placing it in Katy's lap. "But the person who left it here isn't coming back. Somehow I think she'd want you to have it."

"Really?" Katy pawed through the notes, exclaiming over each new discovery. "This is amazing! It should give me everything I need. And I'll see that it stays in my family. I know my mother will want to see it. Thank you so much!"

"Not at all. It's as if that briefcase has finally found its way home. Come back anytime. I'd love to have a copy of that photograph, and your paper, too."

"Certainly!" Katy stood, hefting the briefcase under one arm. "I won't take any more of your time. But thank you again! Thank you so much!"

Another moment and she was out the door. Tilly stood in the stillness the girl had left behind. J.D. and Emma's great, great granddaughter. Even after all these years, life was full of wonderful surprises.

Her lenses had begun to mist over. Lifting the spectacles off her nose, Tilly polished them on her sweater. The eyes behind them were a remarkable shade of green—as green as absinthe.

"This calls for a celebration," she said aloud. "How about it, old boy? A plate of tuna for you, and a shot of good brandy for me!"

Something stirred on a high shelf. A battle-scarred yellow cat with one eye and a bobbed tail jumped to the floor. Purring, it rubbed its scruffy body against Tilly's legs. Then it raced ahead of her into the kitchen.

# *ABOUT THE AUTHOR*

ELIZABETH LANE's travels in Latin America, Europe, and China manifest themselves in the exotic locales seen in her writing, but she also finds her home state of Utah and other areas of the American West to be fascinating sources for historical romance.

The author of more than thirty-five novels, Lane loves such diverse activities as hiking and playing the piano, not to mention her latest hobby—belly dancing. She blogs regularly on Petticoats and Pistols (www.petticoatsandpistols.com) and Unusual Historicals (www.unusualhistoricals.blogspot.com). You can learn more about her and her books at www.elizabethlaneauthor.com.

www.ingramcontent.com/pod-product-compliance
Lightning Source LLC
Chambersburg PA
CBHW020840260626
47169CB00003B/1072